KOTARO ISAKA

Kotaro Isaka is a bestselling and multi-award-winning writer who is published around the world. He has won the Shincho Mystery Club Award, Mystery Writers of Japan Award, Japan Booksellers' Award and the Yamamoto Shugoro Prize and fourteen of his books have been adapted for film or TV. He is the author of the international bestseller *Bullet Train*, which was made into a major film starring Brad Pitt and Sandra Bullock in 2022.

SAM MALISSA

Sam Malissa holds a PhD in Japanese Literature from Yale University. He has translated fiction by Toshiki Okada, Shun Medoruma and Hideo Furukawa, among others.

ALSO BY KOTARO ISAKA

Bullet Train
Three Assassins

Kotaro Isaka

THE
MANTIS

Translated from the Japanese
by Sam Malissa

VINTAGE

3 5 7 9 10 8 6 4

Vintage is part of the Penguin Random House group of companies whose
addresses can be found at global.penguinrandomhouse.com

First published in Vintage in 2024
First published in hardback by Harvill Secker in 2023
First published in Japan with the title *Ax* in 2017

Copyright © Kotaro Isaka / CTB Inc.
English translation rights arranged through CTB Inc.
Translation from the Japanese language by Sam Malissa

Kotaro Isaka has asserted his right to be identified as the author of this
Work in accordance with the Copyright, Designs and Patents Act 1988

penguin.co.uk/vintage

Typeset in 10.14/14.85pt Scala by Jouve (UK), Milton Keynes
Printed and bound in Great Britain by Clays Ltd, Elcograf S.p.A.

The authorised representative in the EEA is Penguin Random House Ireland,
Morrison Chambers, 32 Nassau Street, Dublin D02 YH68

A CIP catalogue record for this book is available from the British Library

ISBN 9781529920666

THE MANTIS

AX

KABUTO SLIDES THE KEY INTO the front door lock. So slowly, but it still makes a loud ratcheting noise, which irritates him to no end. *When are they going to invent a silent lock?* Concentrating all his focus on his hand, he gingerly turns the key. The click of the unlock makes his stomach clench. He opens the door. The house is dark. Silent.

He slips off his shoes. Pads noiselessly down the hall. The lights are off in the living room. Everyone in the house seems to be asleep. Everyone of course being just two people.

Holding his breath and being careful about every movement, he goes up to the second floor. Enters the room to the right. Flips on the light, then listens. He exhales, feeling a moment of release.

'Hey, Kabuto, you're a married man, you're probably headed home now. You'll have to sneak a late-night instant ramen.'

A man in the same line of work had once said this to him. A strange man, obsessed with the children's TV show *Thomas & Friends,* who went by the moniker Lemon. He was fairly wild, and often seemed to speak and act nonsensically, but he was good at his job. They had both been contracted by separate clients to take out the same target, so they had teamed up. After the dust settled, Lemon had asked, 'Who knows the name of the person in charge of facilities on Sodor Island,' quizzing the group on Thomas trivia like it was special knowledge. When no one wanted to play along, he switched to asking Kabuto about himself.

'Does your family know you do this kind of work, Kabuto?' This question came from Lemon's partner, Tangerine. They were the same height and looked a fair amount alike, but their personalities were diametrically opposed, which might have been why they were such an effective team. It was evidently rare for them to encounter someone in their field who had a wife and child, because they were eagerly asking him all sorts of questions.

'Of course they don't know,' Kabuto answered right away. 'If they knew I was doing the kind of rough stuff that we do, they'd be pretty disillusioned. They think I work for an office supplies manufacturer.'

'That's your cover?'

'Yeah, well.' The truth is that Kabuto actually does work for an office supplies company. When his son was born, in his mid-twenties, he took the job, and has stuck with it until now, in his mid-forties. He's one of the old campaigners of the sales team.

'Kinda lame though, huh, the man of the house goes out and risks his life to provide for the family and then has to come home and have instant ramen for dinner,' Lemon said, clearly poking fun at him.

'Don't be stupid,' Kabuto growled. 'There's no way I would eat instant ramen.'

His tone was so forceful that Lemon instinctively took a step back and took a fighting stance. 'Hey now, no need to get angry.'

'No, you misunderstood me,' Kabuto said, softening his voice. 'What I mean is that instant ramen is too loud.'

'What do you mean, too loud?'

'The plastic packaging makes noise. Pulling open the lid on the cup makes noise. Pouring in the water makes noise. It's all too noisy to eat late at night.'

'No one would notice any of that.'

'My wife would,' Kabuto said. 'I once woke her up with my instant ramen noise. She takes her job seriously and is out the door early every morning. She's got a long commute. If I wake her up late at night, it's bad.'

'Come on. How bad could it be?'

'If I told you the atmosphere is heavy on a morning after I wake her up, it would be a major understatement. She sighs so much it sucks all the air out of the room. It's not just a metaphor, I actually have a hard time breathing. *You were so loud, I couldn't sleep* – when she says that, the way my stomach tenses up . . . I wouldn't expect you to understand.'

'Gimme a break, Kabuto. I can't imagine you ever being nervous about anything.'

'Sure. I don't get nervous on a job. I just do what I have to do.'

'But it's different with your old lady, huh?'

Kabuto nodded. *Way different.*

'Okay, so, what do you do? If instant ramen's no good. I guess you'd have the same problem with a granola bar wrapper making noise.' Tangerine gazed inquisitively at Kabuto with his melancholic eyes. 'What do you do if you're hungry?'

'You might think a banana or onigiri would work,' Kabuto said gravely.

The pair nodded, impressed. 'Good thinking.'

But Kabuto immediately shot back, 'Anyone who thinks that is just naïve.'

'Naïve, huh?'

'Yeah, why naïve? Banana and onigiri don't make any noise . . .'

'Think about it this way – sometimes my wife waits up for me, even though I get back late. Sometimes she's made dinner for me. A midnight meal.'

'Oh yeah?'

'On average three times a year.'

'Wow, that's a lot.' Tangerine was obviously being sarcastic.

'But I need to be ready to eat in case she's cooked. And when she cooks, she cooks a lot. So I have no room to eat an onigiri or a banana.'

'Yeah. So what?'

'Convenience store onigiri have a short shelf life. By the next day they're already bad. Bananas don't hold very long either.'

'So?'

'So there's only one logical conclusion.'

'Which is?'

'Fish sausage. Preserved fish sausage. Doesn't make any noise, stays good for a long time. Fills you up. It's the best of all options.'

Lemon and Tangerine said nothing.

'Sometimes when I'm in a convenience store late at night I see some guy like me who's clearly on his way home after a long night at work and he's buying an onigiri or a banana; I can't help but feel sorry for him. He still has some things to learn.' Kabuto went on, 'The solution is fish sausage.' The pronouncement had weight and finality.

Lemon stared for a few moments and then started clapping, slowly at first, then picking up speed. He stayed seated, but his energy was that of a standing ovation, and his face showed that he meant it. 'Kabuto, I appreciate your sad tale and the stylish way you told it. I am genuinely impressed.' His hands kept clapping out a high-tempo rhythm.

Next to him Tangerine rolled his eyes and curled his lip. 'The whole industry respects you. Everyone tips a hat to you, and if they could they would tip two hats. There are a lot of people who would be disappointed if they knew you were this frightened of your wife.'

Now Kabuto reflects for a moment. *Come to think of it, I haven't seen those two in a while.* He pictures how proud Lemon looked upon announcing that it was Jenny Packard who oversees facilities on Sodor Island.

4

He reaches into his suit jacket pocket and produces a stick of fish sausage. Quietly peels off the plastic and bites off a mouthful. It soothes the rumble in his gut. His chair creaks and he feels a flash of fear. He holds perfectly still, listening for any sign that his wife's sleep has been disturbed.

By the time Kabuto wakes up in the morning, his wife is just about to leave for the day. 'Sorry, I left some breakfast for you on the table, eat up,' she calls back to him as she opens the front door and hurries out. 'I forgot that I have a meeting.'

'Enjoy,' he says, washing his face. Then he relieves himself and heads down to the dining-room table. He glances at the clock on the wall. Seven thirty.

The house always feels calmer when his wife is out. It's not that he doesn't like her or has a hard time being with her or anything like that. Over their years of marriage he has only grown to love her more, that much he can say with confidence, but it's also true that he is always nervous about keeping her happy. He feels like he's trying not to step on a tiger's tail, only his wife's tail is invisible as it snakes across the floor all through the house, and he never knows when he's about to trip over it.

The television is on. Morning news, then the weather, with a young woman standing in front of a map and detailing the forecast for the week in the Kanto region.

'She looks like Mom, don't you think?' Kabuto says. His son Katsumi is already seated at the table, munching on toast. He has a well-shaped nose and striking black eyes. Still in high school, but already looking like an adult. An attractive mix of strength and vulnerability, even if Kabuto sets aside his parental bias. The boy takes after his mother.

'Like Mom? No way, she looks nothing like Mom. She's in her twenties.'

'Another twenty years though, she'll look like your mom.'

'That's the same as saying, like,' Katsumi points at the teacup on the table, a classic foreign brand, 'in a thousand years this thing'll be an earthenware cup.'

'And would that be a bad thing? Earthenware's more valuable than some teacup. And anyway, we're not talking about ceramics here. I'm telling you, the weather girl looks like Mom.'

'Dad, you're pretty rigid in your thinking.'

'Me? Rigid?'

'Yeah. Once you decide that something's a certain way, it basically becomes the truth to you.'

'Hunh. I wonder.'

'Like that time we were walking and there was a crowd of people in front of a building and we could hear a fire truck siren getting closer and you were like, "Oh I see, that building must be on fire."'

'Yeah, I remember that.'

'But it turned out that they were just having a sale and people were lined up for that.'

The day before the episode in question Kabuto had gotten intel from another professional like himself that there was a group going around committing arson, so that was in his mind when he guessed that the building was on fire. But he couldn't tell his son any of that. And it was true that he had gotten it wrong. 'Was that what it was?'

'Or when the regular delivery girl stopped coming by and you were like, "Aha, she must not have had a driver's license and got caught," and you were all serious about it.'

'There were stories on the news about that kind of thing happening. Delivery drivers with no license.'

'That's what I mean, Dad. You always put two pieces of info together and jump to a conclusion. You're always trying to say that everything's connected. Whenever you say "Oh I see" or "Aha", I know to be skeptical.'

The pronouncement takes Kabuto by surprise, since he

doesn't have any awareness of this himself, but he doesn't push back. He just replies vaguely, 'Maybe so.'

But Katsumi seems to already be on to the next thing. He's staring at the TV again.

'Are you really having an affair?' he mutters.

Kabuto nearly falls out of his seat. His nerves jangle. 'What the hell are you talking about?'

His voice is much louder than he intended.

'Huh? The weather girl. I saw something online the other day that she was having an affair with the producer of her show.'

'*Oh*. Oh, you mean her.'

'What do you mean, I mean her? Who else would I be talking about?'

'Uh. Nobody.' Then Kabuto thinks that this might be misconstrued and he adds, 'I'm not having an affair, you know,' but this only sounds even more fishy.

'Yeah, hot girls are trouble,' Katsumi says unexpectedly. He props his elbow on the table and rests his chin on his hand, frowning and staring at the TV, seeming to talk to himself. But Kabuto can't just let this go unanswered.

'What do you mean?'

'Men are helpless around beautiful women.'

'That's some worldly wisdom for a high schooler.'

'I mean, I learned it in school.'

'Oh yeah? In what subject?'

Katsumi seems to suddenly remember that he's talking to his father and sits up straight with a start. 'Oh, um, not in class. I have a teacher who's been out on maternity leave for the past month and there's this substitute who's pretty hot.'

'Hot is subjective.'

'She's teaching Japanese, but she sucks at it. She can't write kanji, and she couldn't read the characters in Osamu Dazai's name.'

7

'Surprising that she even got the job.'

'Well, when you look like she does, you get a pass.'

'I'm sure that's not how it worked.'

'All the male teachers are always all smiley with her, and the principal is like tripping over himself when she's around.'

'I bet you and your buddies are the same.'

'I mean, I'm not gonna deny it.'

Katsumi falls silent. Kabuto eats his toast and watches TV. After a few moments Katsumi begins again.

'The other day I saw something I shouldn't have.'

Kabuto thinks, *Oh, I guess we're not done talking,* but almost immediately he tenses up. *Saw something he shouldn't have?* His son must have witnessed some part of his night-work. 'What are you talking about?' His voice is hard again.

'After classes were done for the day, when it was starting to get dark out, I spotted her in the AV room.'

'*Oh.* Oh, you mean the hot teacher.'

'And she was with another teacher. A younger guy. He's the homeroom teacher for the next class over, nice guy, really devoted to his job. Mr Yamada. The two of them were in there, getting after it.'

'Hey, good for Mr Yamada. A dramatic development.'

'No, it's not a good thing. Mr Yamada's married.'

'Whaaat?' Kabuto hugs himself and pulls a face. 'Now it's the other kind of dramatic. Watch your step, Mr Yamada.'

'What do you mean?'

'Is this relationship between Mr Yamada and the hot teacher public knowledge?'

'I think we're the only ones who know. We were in the AV room and the two teachers came in so we hid.'

'We? It wasn't just you who saw the teachers in their moment of passion? You and who else?'

It's plain to see that Katsumi had let slip a detail he didn't

8

mean to. Kabuto figures his son was in the AV room with a girl from his class.

'We, um, I mean me,' Katsumi mutters, looking away. 'We means me and you. I just told you, right? So now you know. So we're the only ones who know.'

'Yeah, okay. We can leave it at that.'

'She's like some kind of black magic woman. If she could seduce a dedicated guy like Mr Yamada.'

'Who knows, maybe he made the first move.'

'No, not Mr Yamada. He's like a real honest type. I bet he's got a guilty conscience. He seems to be having a hard time.'

'Having a hard time how?'

'He hasn't been coming in to school. Teacher truancy. The other teachers said he's sick and he needs time to recover but I think he's just refusing to come in.'

'Teacher truancy, huh?'

'Girls are dangerous.'

'Some are, some aren't. There's all kinds of women, and men.'

'Makes me think of praying mantises, how the females eat the males in the middle of sex. Is that really true?'

'Apparently so.'

'It's like the females are just using the males to mate.'

'No, that's not it,' Kabuto says. He had heard about this from another professional in his world. 'Praying mantises have a wide field of vision. They also have trigger reflexes. They mistake the male behind them for an enemy and then attack. It's an accident.'

'It's still scary.'

'Have you ever heard the expression "the ax of the *toro*"?' Kabuto had heard about this too from the same colleague. At the time he didn't know that *toro* was an old word for praying mantis. He guessed that it was something to do with rich cuts of tuna and he got laughed at.

9

'You mean like the tuna?' Katsumi asks.

Kabuto sighs. 'It's a praying mantis. Picture a mantis raising up its blades like little axes. It looks fearsome, but it's still just a tiny insect.'

'So is it like being a sore loser? Like "the howl of the loser dog"?'

'Similar, but not exactly the same. The mantis actually thinks it can win. Even though it's tiny, it's still ready to fight to the death. That's the ax of the *toro*.'

'When Mom gets annoyed with you, you could fight back sometimes, give her a good chop.'

'A chop with my ax?'

'But I guess the expression doesn't say anything about the mantis being able to do any damage, does it?'

'Basically it means fighting back even when there's no hope of winning.'

Katsumi gives his father a sympathetic look, as if he's picturing him standing there with a broken ax.

'But I wouldn't underestimate the mantis blade,' Kabuto says.

'You could still get chopped.'

'Exactly. Anyway, that's surprising to hear your teacher isn't coming in to school.'

'It's actually not that uncommon. I think it's a little tougher to navigate the world nowadays than it was back in your day, Dad.'

'Life's always been tough.'

'Yeah? Like how?' There's a challenge in Katsumi's voice, a testing brassiness. Kabuto can't help but think about how for a son, the father is both ally and rival.

'Well, let's see. It wasn't easy for the people who built the pyramids, when someone told them to haul all those big stones. Three thousand years ago that kind of thing happened all the time. Try making bronze urns or painted earthenware pottery for a living.'

'We're going back to Mesopotamia? Also, you really seem to like earthenware pottery.'

'That's got nothing to do with anything!'

'Oh, hey, Dad – are you coming to the parent-teacher conference?' Katsumi keeps his eyes on the TV as he asks.

'Parent-teacher conference?' Kabuto knits his brow. 'I guess parents are supposed to go to those.'

'I mean I think it's fine if just Mom comes.'

'No, no, of course I'll go too,' Kabuto replies quickly.

'It's all good. It's the middle of a weekday – you have work, right?'

'Do you know what the one thing I want to do most is?'

'No, what?'

'I want to worry about my son's future. Whether it's school, or anything, I want to rack my brains thinking about what path you should and shouldn't take.'

Katsumi cringes. Kabuto pays it no mind.

'I advise you to undertake this surgery.' The man sitting in front of Kabuto wears a white coat and round glasses. His expression is flat, devoid of any feeling. He seems like just another of the medical devices in the exam room. He might have his own x-ray scanners built in.

They're on a middle floor of a building in a corner of town packed with offices, at the doctor's internal medicine practice. A handful of people sit in the waiting room. Given the doctor's skill as a diagnostician and his aptitude in prescribing the right medicine, it would make sense for the waiting room to be more packed. But the doctor's chilly demeanor suffuses the whole practice, which works against him. Still, he manages to keep a sufficient stream of patients coming in.

'I think I'm going to have to pass on this one, doc. This is a risky procedure, isn't it?' Kabuto points at the chart in the doctor's hands.

The doctor nods.

'I told you, no more risky procedures. Because, you know, it's risky. I could die.'

'You are not in an at-risk age group.'

The doctor's own age is tough to place. His blank face has few wrinkles and a good luster. But Kabuto's been getting his contract work through this doctor for twenty years, and the man looks basically the same. He could very well be quite old. His demeanor has always been mild but it was clear from the start that he was well-established in their shadow world.

'Sorry. I won't do it,' Kabuto replies.

'No matter what sort of operation, you always perform it with a level head and a skilled hand. There are not many people who can do that.'

The doctor doesn't deal with flattery. He has no use for it, just like how a navigation app doesn't compliment you for your driving. Kabuto knows that the doctor's praise is legitimate.

'I'm trying to get out of the game as soon as I can.'

'Retirement requires capital.'

He's never going to let me retire. Kabuto knows it deep down. For almost twenty years, all of Kabuto's jobs have come through the doctor. Eliminate this one, dispose of that one. He figured he wasn't the only one of the doctor's professionals; there had to be other special patients like him.

The charts are always full of information about the target. The name and address of the person who is supposed to be operated on, and if those aren't available then other identifying details, along with any special conditions set by the client, all written out in a mix of medical jargon and academic German that most people would be unable to make heads or tails of. There's often a photo of the target, but without looking through a special filter it just appears to be a splotchy x-ray.

The office keeps a set of mixed records: charts for actual patients, and materials for jobs the doctor handles, disguised to look like patient charts. It's a perfect way to conceal information. Since they ostensibly contain medical details, anyone who might be interested would have a hard time accessing them.

There's a senior member of the nursing staff, a woman of similarly indeterminate age, who clearly knows about the doctor's side business. The younger nurses likely don't have a clue. Which is probably why the doctor relies on codewords that sound like medical jargon and documents that look like patient files. 'Surgery' means a hit, and 'risky procedure' means that the target is another professional.

Kabuto has been wanting to retire ever since Katsumi was born, though he didn't broach the subject with the doctor until five years ago. The doctor was neither upset nor pleased by this. He merely pronounced, 'That will require capital,' as if he were reciting a statute from the legal code. Kabuto wasn't sure what this capital was supposed to be for, or where it would come from, but it was clear enough that he couldn't even afford to buy the kind of prefab house he wanted for his family, and so he found himself in the nonsensical predicament of needing to do more of the job he wanted to quit in order to earn enough money to stop doing it.

'As I'm sure you understand, assisting with a risky surgical procedure garners a much higher fee. And you yourself have often said that if you must perform a surgery, you prefer it to be one that carries no guilt.'

'True. I didn't always feel that way, but true.'

When Katsumi was a little boy, Kabuto used to read him old Japanese folk tales.

On some level he believes that this influenced his own way of thinking.

The kindly old man would be rewarded for his effort, and the wicked old man would meet some awful fate. Good triumphs in the end. Reading tales like that, Kabuto started feeling that he

13

shouldn't be killing innocent people. He even thought about the fact that his victims had parents, who probably read them the same folk stories when they were little.

He's aware that there's a gulf between idealism and reality, but to the extent possible he's tried to avoid killing people who have done nothing wrong.

'Given your preference, it makes even more sense for you to undertake this high-risk surgery.'

The doctor has a point. When the target is someone who makes a living in the criminal underworld, it reduces Kabuto's sense of wrongdoing. It's just one wicked old man getting rid of another.

'Yeah. Well. If any other promising operations come up, let me know.'

'Certainly. Though I will say that in a short while it will become more difficult to do any of these sorts of procedures.'

'Really? Why?'

The doctor proceeds to explain the situation as if he is going over symptoms and treatment plans, mixing in codewords and scribbling symbols on a sheet of paper.

He relates that there is a certain group operating in their ward of the city, planning a major disturbance, most likely a bombing or series of bombings. In the meantime they're holed up somewhere. If they carry out their plan, the Metropolitan Police will lock things down for a while.

'And I suppose that would put a freeze on our work,' Kabuto says quietly.

'Precisely,' the doctor says with a nod.

'Well in that case, why don't you just set me up with a job to take out this gang and their explosives,' Kabuto says, intending it as a joke.

But the doctor doesn't crack the slightest smile. 'Do you have enough medicine?'

By which he means ammunition.

'I could use some more.' It never hurts to stock up. There are several places where a professional can get guns and ammo, stores that have legit businesses as fronts – there's a fishing supplies shop, and a video rental spot – but it saves him time to get it directly from the doctor.

The doctor writes out a prescription.

Kabuto takes it to the pharmacy next door, where he receives a card. The card has the combination to a coin locker nearby. By the following day the locker will be stocked with the ammunition he requested.

On his way home from the station, Kabuto passes by Katsumi's school. It's not his normal route. He must have still been thinking about the other morning when Katsumi asked him if he was planning to attend parent–teacher conferences.

'Do you even worry about our son at all?' His wife had confronted him with this question some four years earlier.

They were in the living room watching TV one night and the news was running an exposé about the school lunch system, when Kabuto casually floated the question – and floating really is the best way to describe it, it was so lightly posed – 'Does Katsumi's school do lunches?' There was nothing at all behind the question. It was just a bid to start up the back and forth of words between himself and his partner, like tossing a ball in a game of conversational catch. It is true though that somewhere in his head he had the notion that Katsumi's school didn't serve lunch and that everyone brought their own. But given the program they were watching, it seemed like a harmless topic to bring up. A perfectly reasonable ball to toss to his wife.

But she returned his gentle throw with a full-force fastball. Then he knew he was in for it. He thought they were just playing catch, but she had her bat at the ready and when he lobbed an easy pitch she swung at it: *Don't you know whether your son's school serves lunch or not? Don't you see me making his bento every morning?!* Her words came rapid fire, quickly expanding to other topics: *You wake up so late every day,* and *Must be nice to work for such a laid-back company.*

When this happened, Kabuto switched off. If he argued it would only prolong the episode. He just tried to halt the cogs in his mind from turning and agree with her. 'I guess I could pay more attention when it comes to our son.' Acknowledge his faults, repent for his wrongdoings, and promise to improve. That was the smoothest way to solve it. 'I do my best to help him, and help you with him, but when I hear what you're saying, I can really see how what I was doing wasn't enough. Thank you for helping me see that.' It was important to move from self-deprecation to appreciation.

Memories of that episode swirl into his thoughts about the upcoming parent-teacher conference, making him feel like it's a good idea to go by his son's school and at least scope it out.

Walking on the street along the edge of the property, he takes in the expansive grounds. An old-looking school building and a huge, packed dirt field. Among the closely crowded homes in the neighborhood, this much open space feels almost excessive. Apparently the former property owner declared after the war that he wanted to dedicate all his land for the education of children, but Kabuto doesn't know if that's a true story or not. It could very well be that if the number of students dwindled enough they would waste no time in demolishing the school and build fancy new housing in its place.

Marveling at how much prime land the school is sitting on, Kabuto comes to a stop, taking it all in.

Groups of students are running around: the soccer team, the track and field team. *Come to think of it, what extracurriculars does Katsumi do?* He can't remember. And he definitely can't ask his wife.

As these thoughts float around his head, he notices through the fence a woman standing in the massive schoolyard, near the track. Looking sharp in a black suit, definitely a woman and not a teenage girl. Probably in her late twenties.

Right away he guesses that it's the one Katsumi mentioned, the good-looking substitute for the teacher on maternity leave.

She's bent over and feeling around on the ground, looking serious, like she dropped something or there's something valuable buried there. Then she looks up and sees Kabuto watching her. She seems startled.

He feels like he should leave, but that would seem odd, so he bobs a bow at her. She awkwardly dips her head in response. *She probably thinks I'm some creep watching the kids.*

He wants to shout, *My son goes here,* but he's too far away, he would need to holler at the top of his lungs.

But then the good-looking teacher smiles at him. He has no idea why.

Kabuto looks left and right. Making sure his wife isn't there to see what just happened.

'You know how there are some houses on the next block that don't follow the trash disposal rules at all?'

It's night, Katsumi is upstairs sleeping, and Kabuto is in the living room eating cake. His wife bought some on her way home from work. There was a new cake shop she wanted to try, so she bought a slice of each of the six varieties they had left in the display case at the end of the day. 'Katsumi said he didn't want any, so you and I can try them,' she said happily. Kabuto has never really liked sweet stuff though. He's been telling her that since before they were even married, but somehow she never seems to believe him. 'What, are you saying you hate sweet things? That you'd rather die than eat sweets?' Whenever she says that he has to concede that no, his feelings about sweets don't quite rise to the level of hate, and of course he wouldn't rather die. Which then ends up with her forcing him to eat more sugary treats. Which then sets the precedent, because next time she says, 'You ate it last time, why can't you eat it now?'

Splitting six pieces between two people shouldn't have been that bad. But his wife declared that she would have a single bite of each one, just to sample the flavor, and he could eat the rest. At face value this seemed generous, a woman holding herself back so her husband could enjoy even more, which made it even harder for him to protest.

So they're sitting at the table and she's taking tiny nibbles when she brings up these houses that don't follow the protocol for getting rid of their garbage.

'Oh yeah, I think I know those houses!' Kabuto responds with hearty interest.

'Right? There's that group of six prefab houses?'

'Right, right.'

'And two of those just do not know how to behave.'

'So what's happening with them?'

Of course, Kabuto has no memory of any of this. She must have told him about it one morning a while back, and he was probably exhausted from working late the night before, in no state to absorb neighborhood gossip. It happens a lot. But even when he's tired, he must pay attention to her. One time she told him that if he didn't want to listen to her, it was fine, she didn't mind, he didn't have to listen. After that he made sure to always respond eagerly, no matter how tired he might be. Expansive gestures and breathless interjections – *Oh really? Wow, you don't say!* Making a show of hanging on her every word. Sometimes he worries that he might be overdoing it, but his wife either hasn't noticed his exaggerated reactions or doesn't mind them because she's never voiced any complaints.

'Well, recently there hasn't been any trash put out on

non-collection days, so everyone thought that maybe these houses finally started following the rules. But it turns out they moved away.'

'Really? So they're gone, huh?' The way he says it makes him sound both surprised and impressed at this mundane bit of news. There's nothing particularly special about a family moving. He just has a deeply ingrained habit of answering with great enthusiasm.

'The houses were pretty new too. What's weird is that *both* of them moved away.'

'They both moved?' That actually is a bit odd. 'I wonder if there was something that made them both want to move away.'

'Don't tell me you think there's something bad going on in the neighborhood, I don't want something else to worry about.' She pouts.

'Maybe there was friction with the neighbors. Noise disturbance, something like that.'

'*Oh*,' her eyes widen and she claps her hands together. 'There's something else I wanted to tell you!'

'Is it about the rest of this cake?' He looks at how much is left on the plate and groans. His stomach is full and his bloodstream feels like it's turned into frosting.

But she doesn't appear to have registered his question. Almost like she's got a filter to block out any of her husband's complaints or demands. She doesn't react at all. He ventures a test: 'Or did you want to talk about the frequency that we make use of our marital bed?' he says quickly. 'Because I'd be fine to increase that.'

For better or for worse, she doesn't acknowledge that. 'I heard something kind of juicy about one of the high school teachers.'

'Juicy?'

'It's just a rumor, but one of Katsumi's teachers—'

'Is missing in action?'

'Oh!' She looks at him. Clearly she wasn't expecting that response.

'Mr Yamada, right?'

'How do you know about that?'

'Well,' and here Kabuto makes sure his voice is brimming with feeling, 'it's about our son's school. I try to have my antenna up at least a little.'

A blush of appreciation shows on her face, like maybe she's realized that she had underestimated him. 'So apparently Mr Yamada hasn't been home either. Even though he has a wife and kids.'

'Hm. I wonder what that's about.'

'Maybe he couldn't handle his work and was too ashamed to go back home.'

The woman Kabuto spotted that afternoon in the schoolyard pops into his mind. 'Or maybe he's shacked up with that good-looking substitute teacher.'

His wife's voice stabs at him: 'What good-looking substitute teacher?'

He has the sudden feeling that he's been seized by the collar.

'It was, uh, I mean, that's what Katsumi said. That Mr Yamada seemed awful friendly with a pretty new teacher. But, you know, of course, beauty is subjective.'

'Mr Yamada is a married man.'

Kabuto exhales deeply at that, shaking his head with apparent disbelief. 'I know. How could a married man ever get close to another woman? It's always struck me as far-fetched, like an urban legend or something.'

'But I didn't hear anything about that from anyone else. All I heard was that Mr Yamada was having a hard time at work.'

'I wonder.' Kabuto keeps his answer vague. He's all too aware that if they delve much deeper in this direction he'll end up on the receiving end of his wife's attack systems.

'Ah, I was meaning to ask you,' she says, her voice pitching upward. 'What are you doing the Friday after next?'

'What's happening that Friday?'

'It's Katsumi's parent-teacher conference, and if you're available I want you to come.'

He nods vigorously and answers immediately. 'Of course I was planning to go.'

'Well well.' She seems pleasantly surprised. 'But you'll probably have some work emergency and you won't be able to come.'

'I'm not proud to say it but I'm not all that busy at work. I could use a little fire drill now and again.'

'Come on, there have been so many times when we had a family thing but at the last minute something came up and you couldn't be there.'

'And I always felt really bad about it. I don't even like to think about those times.' He tries to strike a solemn, repentant tone, but the truth is he can't even remember the episodes. Most likely it never had anything to do with his office job, and instead it was his other job that made him miss out on family plans. 'Don't worry,' he says, nodding reassuringly. 'There won't be any emergencies.'

'This is an emergency operation,' the doctor says firmly, sitting across from Kabuto in the exam room. 'The Friday after next will be our only opportunity.'

His voice is completely devoid of warmth, as if it were computer-generated. But this computer has no cancel option – the notification window only has a button for *accept*. The only way to avoid answering is to force the computer to shut down.

'I don't care if it's an emergency, that day is off the table.' Kabuto holds his hands out in front of him, as if to ward off the threat emanating from the computer. 'I'm busy. Think about it. I have an office job. During the workday, that's where I need to be.'

He has no intention of saying anything about his son's parent-teacher conference.

He's been working with the doctor for a long time. Since

before he was married, when he first got involved in the business, he's been getting jobs from the doctor. In all that time, he's done his utmost to tell the doctor as little about his personal life as he can. As far as the doctor is concerned, he has no name other than his professional alias, Kabuto. Of course, the doctor could easily find out more if he wanted to. Kabuto has vaguely touched on the fact that he has a family, but there was no need to get any more specific than that.

'And you cannot take a day off of work?'

'Not that day,' he insists. 'I'm sure we could do the operation a different day.'

The doctor looks at the chart in his hands. Kabuto still has no idea who the target is.

'A different day is impossible. This particular surgery represents a valuable opportunity. Letting it slip by would be a terrible waste.'

'What do you mean, a valuable opportunity?'

'The surgery fee is quite high.' The doctor shows the chart he's holding to Kabuto, a gesture that would look to anyone else like he was sharing the results of bloodwork.

That is a lot of money, Kabuto has to admit to himself. 'But didn't you say that there's some kind of looming bomb threat that'll result in tighter police surveillance? Is that all cleared up?'

'This is precisely that,' the doctor says immediately.

'Precisely what?'

'As you recently said. Your preferences when it comes to your work.'

Ah. When he joked about wanting to take on the explosives gang. 'Oh, that.'

The doctor nods.

'Well. It's true that I'd feel a little better about a job like that.' If the target is high-risk, that is, another professional, and if he can prevent a bombing, he won't have as heavy a weight on his conscience.

The doctor is right. It's not often that everything lines up so neatly like this. It would be a shame to let it slip past.

'I'll do the surgery.'

'A wise decision,' the doctor says, then proceeds to give him the details. Kabuto can't exactly walk out of there with printouts, so he memorizes the information that the doctor shows him on his computer.

There's a photo of the target. A headshot of a man, somewhat frail-looking. 'Well, this should be easy,' Kabuto mutters.

'Yes, based on the man's face, he is not the most formidable physical specimen.'

The man specializes in fabricating portable explosives, like some kind of bomb craftsman. He's been living overseas for several months. Now his accomplices have called him back to Japan.

If Kabuto waits at the arrivals terminal at the airport when the man's flight comes in, it should be easy enough to intercept him. On the other hand, if Kabuto misses the target at the airport, it will become much more difficult to find where he's hiding out.

'And that is why it must be that day. This is a critical operation.'

Kabuto asks about the other members of the target's group and the doctor answers that they likely have various specialties. If their plan is to occupy a given area, they will need someone to do reconnaissance, someone to secure an escape route, and depending on their means of escape, a skilled driver or pilot.

'Like in the old sports manga where they'd put together a team of students who all had their own special talents, huh?'

'Yes, not dissimilar to a sports team.'

Kabuto's shoulders slump a little. 'It would be great if this guy's flight gets canceled for bad weather or something. Even if it was one day later, that'd be huge.' *Then I could go to Katsumi's parent-teacher conference.*

The doctor says nothing, just stares at Kabuto, his face blank.

*

23

That night, Kabuto is sitting in his living room watching TV, but he's barely paying attention to what's on the screen.

Timing, timing, he thinks, like a mantra in his head. *It's all about the timing.* He takes several deep breaths, careful not to let his wife or son notice.

After a bit, Katsumi puts his phone away and murmurs something that must be goodnight, though Kabuto has to strain to make out any actual consonants or even vowels. As Katsumi heads upstairs, his mother calls after him, 'Goodnight!' Kabuto listens carefully, trying to gauge her mood from the tone of her voice.

Her reactions to the things he tells her vary depending on her mood. Especially when he's telling her things she's not likely to be happy about.

When she's in a good mood, like when she's got a great new haircut or someone thinks that she's younger than she actually is, he's not so worried. On the other hand, if she's in a bad mood, her response can make him feel like he's in a silent blizzard, noiselessly freezing the entire house.

Gauging the tone of her voice and the look on her face, Kabuto decides that he's going to tell her. First he goes to the bathroom to pee. Then he begins: 'I hate to have to tell you this, but . . .' He never feels this nervous when he's about to attack some punk and strangle them to death. It makes him wonder how he can be so calm when taking someone's life. *It's bizarre that I'm more on edge in my own home,* he reflects somberly.

'What is it?' she asks. Now he can't tell if she's in a good mood or a bad one. *No turning back now. I have to tell her sooner or later.*

'Something came up at work on the day of Katsumi's parent-teacher conference. Something I can't get out of.' He tries not to make too big a deal out of it, neither groveling nor sounding flippant, trying to walk the line between apology and nonchalance.

Good fortune or bad, he wonders. He wants to squeeze his eyes shut. He waits for his wife's response, his heart hammering.

'You're kidding, right?' She's surprised, and there's a notable barb in her voice. 'What happened to taking the day off?'

Believe me, I tried, he wants to retort. 'But listen,' he says instead, with a reassured air. 'The conference is from two, right? I'll do my best to finish up at work quickly and I'll get over there as fast as I can.'

The bomb craftsman's flight gets in at twelve, so if Kabuto times the trains right he should be able to make it on time.

'Yeah, yeah,' she says dismissively. He can tell what she's thinking: *Don't make any promises you can't keep.*

'I'm doing this for my family.'

'You have a family?'

Kabuto realizes with a shock that he blurted out an unnecessary personal detail. 'That's got nothing to do with you,' he mutters, wrenching the man's arm upward.

They're in a field, not far from the airport. Brown grass spreads around them, surrounded by a fence of trees. They're locked in struggle among the weeds.

Kabuto is wearing an airport janitor's uniform.

'Damn, you're sturdier than I thought you'd be,' he gripes. The headshot he had seen at the doctor's was of a man with a slight, weak-looking face, but the body under the face turned out to be thickly muscled. *I got sold a bill of goods.* 'And how come your plane was late?'

'Talk to the pilot. Or the air current.'

If he can wrap this up quickly, he'll be able to make it to Katsumi's school on time. That's what he was hoping for anyway, but the plane arrived twenty minutes behind schedule. Kabuto waited in the arrivals terminal until he spotted his target, the bomb craftsman, strolling out at a leisurely pace, which only annoyed Kabuto more.

Disguised in the uniform, he followed his man down the

escalator, keeping a bit of distance. Tailed him toward the taxi stand. At that point he caught up and called out to him: 'Excuse me, sir!' The man stopped and turned around to see what looked like a janitor approaching. 'You dropped this.' Kabuto held out something small, flat and plastic that looked like a protractor. The man had never seen it before, but he reflexively took it.

At the exact moment that Kabuto handed it over he pushed a button on the remote in his pocket.

The man's body spasmed and Kabuto caught him as he fell. The device had delivered a strong electric shock. But even if the scene showed up on a security camera, it would just look like someone having a sudden collapse and a janitor helping to support them.

Kabuto carried the man over to a fake taxi he had parked nearby, loaded him into the car, and drove away. When they reached the trees at the edge of the field, he hauled the bomb craftsman out of the car and slapped his face a few times.

Once the man was awake, Kabuto challenged him: 'Come on.'

At first his opponent was still in a daze, but after a few moments he realized what was happening. His eyes sharpened and he came at Kabuto.

They locked up, then broke, then locked up again. It was more grappling than throwing proper punches and kicks. All the while Kabuto steadily dealt damage with vicious close-range blows to the collarbone, solar plexus, throat, fingers, trying to wear his target down.

The man wasn't as fast as Kabuto had worried he might be. He was able to control the fight: attack here and he moves this way, strike there and his joint bends that way. *If only my wife were so easy to handle.*

'I'm doing this for my family.'

Before long the man grunts, 'Why?' He takes a swing at Kabuto, who dips his head back to evade.

'It's just a job.'

'No—' The man rushes him and Kabuto sidesteps like a bull-fighter. The man whips back around. 'Why didn't you finish me off after you shocked me?'

'Oh,' Kabuto says, controlling his breathing and keeping his eyes on his target. 'I don't like taking out someone who can't fight back. Prefer a fair fight.'

'There's no such thing as fair.' The bomb craftsman furrows his thick brows.

Be fair. Kabuto is always trying to teach that to his son. He's never been all that interested in loftier lessons like *do the right thing*, or *do your very best*, or *don't be afraid to fail*. But he feels strongly about this one thing: As much as you can, be fair. That's all. Whether you're attacking someone or protecting someone, try to be fair about it.

'Dad, that's like, pretty vague.' Recently Katsumi had started saying this about his father's teaching, if it could even be called a teaching. 'It doesn't give me any kind of concrete direction on what to do.'

'Well, concrete, I mean, it depends on the situation. Say you're making fun of someone.'

'Making fun of someone? What am I, in elementary school?'

'It's just an example. So, you should never make fun of someone's name, or their face or body.'

'Why not?'

'Because those aren't things they can change. If you go after someone over something they can't do anything about, that's hardly fair. Right?'

'Okay, so what can you make fun of someone about?'

'Let's see.' Kabuto thought about it for a moment. 'Their snacking habits. That's something they have complete control over. You can say, "Ha ha, you just can't stop snacking at night, can you?" Or something like that.'

'Right. Sick burn, Dad.' Katsumi rolled his eyes. 'So what should I do if someone says to me that my dad is a lame corporate nobody?'

'Someone said that to you?'

'It's just an example.'

'Well, if they did, don't worry about it.'

'Don't worry about it?'

'If someone says that to you, do they score any points? If your dad is a corporate nobody, does that mean this other guy did anything special? Nope. He's just pointing out a fact. It might not even be true. But even if it is, it's just saying words. Anyone can do that. But they don't, because they have common sense. So this guy who says this, all he's doing is abandoning his common sense and letting his emotions take over so that he's just stating facts that won't change, whether he says anything about them or not. Like I said, not scoring any points on you. And then you can just say the same kind of thing back to him. Your ancestors were apes, something like that. That's a fact too.'

'And that's your idea of fairness?'

'Yep. And if there's something that you feel fine doing but you don't like when someone does it to you, that's unfair.'

'Fine for me to do but not fine for someone else. Okay, how about when you come home late and Mom gets mad because she says your footsteps are too loud and she can't sleep. But when you have a day off, she runs the vacuum cleaner while you're trying to sleep. So that's unfair, right?'

When he heard his son say that, Kabuto's eyes almost welled up. He felt the deep emotional impact of finding someone who truly understood his plight. But he couldn't suddenly throw his arms around his boy. If he expressed out loud his appreciation for his son's empathy, there was a non-zero chance that his wife would find out. It's not like he thought his son was a double agent, working both of his parents. But you could never be too careful.

Kabuto has the man from behind, crushing his neck in the crook of his elbow. Finally the man stops breathing.

He buries the body among the trees. The doctor told him that it was fine for the surgery to leave scars, which means that he doesn't need to be overly careful about covering up the hit. The bomb craftsman likely carefully concealed his own identity, so even if his body is found it won't be easy for anyone to determine who he was.

Before he covers the body with dirt, he removes a phone from the man's jacket pocket. There are cases he has heard about where a buried phone ringing led to the discovery of a corpse. The phone has a strap with a little charm shaped like a stick of dynamite. *This guy really liked explosives,* he thinks, chuckling.

He glances at his watch, then takes off the janitor uniform and changes into a suit. Gets in the taxi, drives back to the airport. He'll ride the train from there. Should be quicker.

By the time he arrives at the front gate of the school, his watch shows ten minutes past two. *Made it,* he thinks, although he knows that from his wife's perspective he most certainly has not made it. He enters the school grounds, wondering whether it would look weird for him to sprint to the classroom. Then he realizes that he has no idea which class number Katsumi is in, and his spine turns to ice from one thought: *She's going to yell at me!*

He pulls his shoes off in the school building entrance and looks around for guest slippers but doesn't see any, until he spots a nearly-fallen-apart pair by the far end of the shoebox. He shoves his feet into them and takes the stairs two at a time. He guesses based on nothing that the higher class years are on the higher floors, so third-year students should be on floor three. When he emerges into the third-floor hall he looks up and down its length but there's no sign of anyone around. No adults, no students. He checks his watch again. The hush feels like school is closed. The kids must get sent home during parent-teacher conferences.

I could still make it. He pictures his wife's rage gauge, edging into red.

Walking down the hall, he spots a room with a placard that reads *Audiovisual Room.* The door is ajar. *This must be where that good-looking substitute teacher has her trysts,* he thinks, recalling what he heard from Katsumi. He peeks inside and has a little shock: there she is. The good-looking substitute.

'Can I help you?' She steps closer to the door.

'Oh, uh, I'm Katsumi's dad.' His answer is awkward, almost guilty, even though he knows he's done nothing wrong. She doesn't appear to recognize his son's first name, so he gives his full name. 'I'm here for the parent-teacher conference.'

'Aha, well, you're in the wrong place.' She points down the hallway and directs him to turn right at the end. 'It's in the next building.'

Kabuto watches her pale, delicate finger as it passes in front of him. It moves like the head of a white snake, elegant and hypnotic.

Then two things happen at once.

His phone rings. He pulls it out of his pocket and sees that it's his wife calling, so he answers and presses it up to his ear.

As he takes his phone out of his pocket, another phone comes out with it and clatters to the floor. It takes him a moment to process that it's the phone he took off the man he dispatched near the airport. The dynamite charm swings about as the phone spins on the ground. The good-looking teacher gently picks it up and holds it out toward Kabuto. 'This phone—'

He waves at her to wait a moment as his wife's voice sounds in his ear.

'Where are you? I guess you're not going to make it after all.'

'No, no, I'm here.'

'This phone,' the teacher tries again. 'Where did you get this?'

'Hang on a second, I don't have—' But before he can finish speaking his wife cuts him off.

'You don't have what?' Her voice is tight.

'No, I didn't mean that—'

'Where did you get this phone?' The substitute flips it open as if it's hers and taps a few buttons. Kabuto wants to scold her for messing with someone else's phone, although it's not like it belongs to him either. 'Wait, this is . . .'

He looks up at her. Her eyes are hard and the smile she was wearing is gone.

'Is that a woman's voice?' his wife asks. 'Who are you with?'

'No, it's nothing like that.' Kabuto's head feels hot. Fires are breaking out all around him and he doesn't know which way to go first. If he doesn't put them out then they'll spread. *Calm down. Think. One thing at a time.* But his wife's accusing tone and his vague guilt about being near this beautiful teacher are shaking his equilibrium. Before he knows what he's doing, his hand shoots out and clamps over the teacher's mouth. 'Can you please keep quiet for a moment?'

'What do you mean, keep quiet?' his wife shrieks through the phone.

'Nothing!' he says, looking at the woman in front of him. She's glaring down at the hand held over her mouth. There's dried blood on his knuckles and wrist that must have come from the bomb craftsman's nose and mouth.

Wait— The moment he thinks it he drops the phone, because the good-looking teacher has punched him in the face.

What— He sees the phone fall. *Hey*— He almost shouts out loud, but then his arm is twisted behind his back.

Kabuto has no time to process what's going on. He jerks his body around and wrenches his arm free. The good-looking teacher isn't pretending to be a teacher anymore. Her foot arcs through the air toward him. He dodges, then ducks into the AV room. It wouldn't be good if someone spotted them in the hallway.

She lunges after him. He tries to make a move like he normally would but he's forgotten that he's wearing junky old guest slippers and he slips and falls over backwards. She pounces on top of him. '*Where* did you get that *phone*?'

'I—' But before he answers he realizes that his phone is on the ground nearby. If the call is still going on then his wife will hear. He's on his back with the woman straddling him. He tries to shake her off but she seems to know the right technique to pin him down because he can barely move. It finally dawns on Kabuto that this is no ordinary woman.

He struggles back and forth, working his shoulders. She must think he's trying to attack her and she pins him even more firmly. He's breathing hard.

The situation is so ridiculous he almost clicks his tongue. Here he is, alone with another woman, both of them panting and grunting, and his wife could be hearing everything. No doubt she would assume that he was in flagrante delicto. Explaining to her that he was only fighting with the woman would do little to help the situation.

The woman is about to say something so he strains with all his might and twists free. Now that he knows she's not some teacher but a trained opponent, there's no need to hold back. When Kabuto is really fighting there are not many who can keep up, not even among his fellow professionals.

He gets behind her and wraps his arm around her neck,

aiming to crush her windpipe in the crook of his elbow. He squeezes. She stops moving.

He carries her to the back of the AV room and lays her down among the various equipment. From the looks of it, hardly anyone ever comes back here. Then he collects his phone and sees with a rush of relief that the call with his wife had ended. He steadies his breathing, then calls the number he has memorized. A female voice answers and announces the name of the practice. 'I've had a sudden flare-up, I need to talk to the doctor.'

Kabuto exhales long and low. A sudden flare-up is code for needing the doctor's advice about a job.

When he finally arrives at Katsumi's classroom, his wife and son are stepping out and the next student and their parents are entering.

'Oh hey, Dad,' Katsumi looks up and says. He seems happy to see him, and also a shade embarrassed about it.

What's he so happy about, Kabuto wonders. He dips his head. 'Sorry I didn't make it in time.'

'All good. You had work, right?' Katsumi sounds quite mature, his voice both casual and warm.

'Yeah, yes. Yes I did. I had work.'

'You shouldn't push yourself so hard, Dad.' Katsumi points at his father. 'Your suit is a mess.'

Kabuto looks down at himself with a start. His tie is twisted, his collar is askew, there's dust all over his jacket. He hastily straightens himself out.

'Well, you clearly made an effort to get here.' Only when he hears his wife say this does Kabuto feel safe looking at her. He was sure that her face would show dissatisfaction, or maybe two different kinds of dissatisfaction, or maybe even three, as she stared at him in icy silence. But, miraculously, she speaks kindly,

33

and her expression is soft. 'The meeting with his teacher went pretty well, too.'

Her manner is so gentle that it puts him on guard. 'Oh! Well, that's – that's great!'

'Mom's in a good mood because my teacher thought she was in her early thirties.'

'Aha.'

'He thought I look ten years younger than I am!'

'I see.' Now Kabuto understands why her mood is so forgiving. But before he can stop himself he points out, 'A woman in her early thirties with a son in the third year of high school doesn't add up.'

Her eyes flash with sudden threat. *The tongue is the root of evil* – the old expression blares in his mind as he curses himself for his lack of verbal restraint. Kabuto immediately sputters, 'Of course, you look so good that he probably wasn't even thinking about whether or not the math works.' He's not sure if that will help, but it's worth a shot.

'My homeroom teacher is a math teacher,' Katsumi points out.

'That's how good your mom looks, that it would make a math teacher mess up his calculations.'

'Who knows,' says Kabuto's wife, looking quietly pleased.

It's okay, it's all okay, it all worked out fine, he says to himself soothingly.

Then his thoughts turn back to the substitute teacher.

Back in the AV room, when he got the doctor on the phone, he said, 'After I took out the target I was attacked by a woman at a different location. She saw that I had the bomb guy's phone and she came at me, but I'm not sure what it was all about.'

The doctor answered tonelessly, 'It appears to be another tumor of the same sort.'

'You mean she was on the team planning the bomb attacks?' Kabuto sighed.

34

She recognized her accomplice's phone, whether from the charm or the shape and make of the phone itself. Come to think of it, she had been pushing buttons on the phone. Probably checking the call history. Based on Kabuto's reactions and the blood on his hands, she figured out that he was an enemy. Or at least that explanation made sense to him.

From what Katsumi said, the woman had come to the school a month ago. And she was working as a Japanese teacher but couldn't read kanji properly. As a substitute, she was filling in for another teacher who was out.

Kabuto wondered where the regular teacher actually was. The possibilities didn't seem promising.

But why would the woman be looking to infiltrate this school in particular?

The schoolyard. If there's anything special about this school, it's how big the grounds are.

'A heliport?' Kabuto was still on the phone with the doctor but he was talking to himself. 'That has to be it.'

'Has to be . . . what?' The doctor sounded dubious.

'Didn't you say that the explosives gang might be using a helicopter?'

'I did not specifically mention a helicopter, but if they were planning a large-scale occupation operation it would not be surprising that they have one ready in case they needed to escape.'

The last time they met, the doctor had also suggested that an operation like this would require someone to scout out the location. Then he recalled what he had heard from his wife: that the residents of two of the prefab houses had moved away.

Maybe a member of the team was using those houses as a base for reconnaissance and planning. That would explain why they weren't following the local trash collection rules. It wouldn't be surprising for someone like that to ignore the rules. Then maybe their plot reached the operational phase and they abandoned the house.

35

No, all of that was too much of a stretch. If someone was trying to blend in, they would make sure to follow the trash rules.

Kabuto continued to try to piece it together. He thought about the beautiful substitute teacher.

Say they were planning to use the high school as a heliport during their operation. To make that possible, she had set herself up at the school. If that were true, it put a different spin on the story of Mr Yamada, the dedicated teacher who was missing. Maybe they weren't having an affair – maybe instead he had noticed something off about her, like that she was taking measurements at the track, or that she was fiddling with the lighting equipment in the AV room that they would normally use for student performances, something that set off his alarms and made him confront her. And then he disappeared. She had found a way to shut him up.

'I'm not sure what to do with her body,' Kabuto told the doctor.

'My office will handle the disposal of the medical waste,' the doctor replied. 'Later tonight, please bring it to the following location.'

Kabuto would have to break into the school at night, collect the body, and deliver it to where the doctor told him, hoping that no one discovered it in the AV room in the meantime. He wasn't thrilled about it. He would have to come up with some reason to tell his wife why he was going out. Just thinking about it made him feel a little glum, but he didn't have much room to complain. 'If you can get rid of the body, I'll appreciate the help.'

Is it possible the doctor knew about the substitute teacher? As he was about to end the call, the thought occurred to him. Maybe the doctor was aware that one of the conspirators was disguised as a teacher at the school. Maybe the doctor even knew that Kabuto's son was a student there. 'Were you expecting me to deal with her too?' he almost asked. The doctor's completely emotionless delivery always made Kabuto suspect he was up to something.

'Dad, something wrong?'

Kabuto was deep in thought and had fallen a few paces behind. He catches up to them and mumbles an excuse that he was thinking about work, which isn't untrue.

'You sure you weren't thinking about the hot teacher?' Katsumi teases.

Actually, I was, but he can't say that, so instead he says, 'She's not as good-looking as your mother.'

'Wait, what are you talking about?' his wife demands to know. 'Have you already met this woman?'

Kabuto glances down at his pocket as if his phone were vibrating. 'Oh, I've got a call coming in.' He takes it out and hustles ahead down the stairs.

As he goes he hears Katsumi telling his wife that he had compared her to earthenware pottery.

Kabuto walks briskly away from the station. He's just come back from performing another surgery. This one wasn't assigned by the doctor. He was having a drink in a bar and the bartender mentioned that one of the other patrons had a helicopter pilot's license. Kabuto immediately suspected the man of being a member of the group planning the bomb attacks.

No explosions had yet taken place. It might be that they were still coming, or it could be that once the bomb craftsman and the substitute teacher vanished the plan fell apart and was abandoned.

He intimated his hypothesis to the doctor. The doctor responded, 'Often it is only a common cold, but when the patient does some research they become convinced that it is something far more serious.' He spoke quietly. 'Your thinking is a bit rigid.'

'My son tells me the same thing.'

But this wasn't just idle theorizing. Kabuto was personally invested. If this group was planning to use the high school as a base then the explosions would be in the surrounding area and the school itself would be occupied. If he hadn't eliminated the substitute teacher, his own son might have been harmed.

In other words, thanks to Kabuto's efforts, the neighborhood was safe. At the very least he had taken his son out of harm's way. He was proud of himself. *I might be a guy who's always tiptoeing around his wife but on this thing I actually made a difference.*

And he had another thought: *Don't underestimate the mantis blade.*

He looks at his watch. Nearly midnight. His stomach is grumbling as loud as a cicada.

He stops at a convenience store. Walks past the rack of magazines and the rows of juices.

When he gets to the aisle where they keep the sausage, he finds the one he wants and grabs it. Just then another hand reaches in from the side. Kabuto turns to see an unfamiliar man in a suit, ten or so years older than him, taking the same fish sausage with a practiced gesture. There's no hesitation, no wavering in the face of temptation from any of the other items on the shelf, just unclouded resolve to claim the sausage.

The two men look at each other, and then each looks at the sausage in the other's hand.

Kabuto suspects that they're both thinking something along the lines of *great minds think alike*, or maybe *game recognizes game*. At least, he's thinking that. He's full of respect for a fellow adherent of fish sausage, the ultimate late-night food, and he offers silent encouragement to the man: *I'm rooting for you, buddy.*

He takes out his wallet and gets in line.

STING

KABUTO PICTURES THE MAN'S LIFE expiring. A bathroom stall would work. He lays out the scene in his mind: his hands on the man's neck, the man no longer breathing.

He's scouting out the location for his next job.

He's not fully clear why this man is the target. He just got the job from the doctor. The doctor got the contract from the man's wife.

There are some jobs where Kabuto scouts things out ahead of time, and there are some where he doesn't. It's case by case. In this case, he's scouting.

He went to the man's office building and scoped out the scene. Before long he spotted the target: muscular guy, aggressive face. Barking orders at his coworkers. Clearly a man who would terrorize his wife. A man who dominates his household – the furthest thing possible from Kabuto's own existence.

He must be a violent husband, which is why his wife wants him gone. Kabuto has a growing certainty that this man has never once paid attention to the expression on his wife's face to gauge her mood. No way. Which means that he has only himself to blame if he winds up dead. Kabuto lets his imagination run a little.

When he's gotten enough intel he exits the building and takes off the gloves he was wearing. Removes the cap and the glasses. Peels off the adhesive mustache.

Checking his watch, he sees that it's past 3 p.m. He takes out his phone. Several missed calls. From his wife. Calling every ten minutes.

Is she in trouble? Kabuto immediately calls her back, feeling a flash of dread. The wait between each ring is interminable.

He's thinking of a conversation he had with the doctor the other day. 'It seems there is someone looking to perform surgery on you,' the doctor reported in his usual flat manner. And by surgery, he doesn't mean a helpful medical procedure. 'Are you familiar with the Hornet?'

'I assume you're not talking about the insect.'

There's a professional who operates under the alias the Hornet. Uses poison needles to eliminate targets. A while back, the Hornet became infamous for taking out a man who wielded vast power in the underworld. Much of the work the doctor brought to Kabuto was subcontracting for this powerful man, so when he was gone the number of jobs shrank dramatically.

'I heard the Hornet was dead. Killed in that E2 thing.'

There was another episode, more recent, that took place on a particular E2 model of the bullet train, the Tohoku Hayate Shinkansen. On a Hayate that left Tokyo heading northward, a number of professionals clashed and multiple people ended up dead. In the industry it had become known as 'the E2 Incident'. No one seems to know for certain exactly what happened or who was involved, but rumor has it that the Hornet was there and didn't make it out alive.

'The female is deceased but the male is still buzzing,' the doctor said.

Kabuto had also heard the rumors that the Hornet was actually a pair of professionals, a man and a woman working together. He'd never been certain if it was just a story, until now.

'Male hornets aren't supposed to be venomous.'

'I advise you to keep your guard up,' the doctor urged.

At the time he didn't pay all that much attention to it. He couldn't think of any reason anyone would order a hit on him.

But now that he sees these missed calls from his wife and recalls the doctor's warning, his whole body is suddenly gripped by fear. *Someone's after me*, Kabuto tells himself, the thought beginning to tumble into the valley of conclusions, picking up speed as it rolls down the slope. *They're after my family*.

Then he hears a voice on the other end: 'Why didn't you answer?'

'Oh! You're okay.'

'Who said anything about being okay? And *why* didn't you answer my calls? What's the point of carrying your phone if you don't pick up?'

'Sorry, sorry, I'm really sorry. I was – uh, I was –' He fumbles desperately for an excuse but she cuts him off, her voice pitched high.

'There's no time for that! A hornet—'

It's him. Kabuto pictures the professional killer outside his home at that very moment and his spine freezes. 'Stay inside and lock the door. Do *not* leave the house.'

'I'm telling you, leave it alone and call the ward office,' Kabuto's wife says firmly to him as she stands up from the dining-room table. 'I'd rather not have you getting stung.'

Kabuto is gently miffed at her phrasing – *I'd rather not have you getting stung*, instead of *I'd hate for you to get stung* or *I'm worried that you might get stung* – but he lets it go. 'It's just a wasp's nest. It's not giant hornets, or even regular hornets. Getting stung wouldn't be the end of the world.'

'I looked online and wasps are plenty dangerous. Either way, I don't want you dealing with it yourself,' she calls back from the kitchen.

41

'Fine,' he assents. Phrasing aside, it's at least nice that she's thinking about his well-being.

When she said she saw a hornet, he immediately got it in his head that she was talking about the assassin. But when he actually listened to what she had to say it became clear that she had found a nest in the yard. Not thinking, he breathed a sigh of relief into the phone and said, 'Oh *that* kind of hornet. Okay, good.'

'*Good?* Good how? What do you mean, oh *that* kind of hornet? Are you even listening to me?'

Her stinging words brought on the familiar pain in his stomach. 'Good that you aren't hurt, is what I meant.' His explanation wasn't very convincing. 'Anyway, don't touch it. I'll handle it.' With that, he dashed for the subway.

On the way home he stopped at a hardware store and picked up some wasp and hornet spray. When his wife spotted it she forbade him to use it. 'I don't want you handling this yourself.'

'Maybe I should do it,' Katsumi offers between mouthfuls of corn on the cob. The gleaming yellow kernels look sweet and inviting, and Katsumi has been gobbling cobs one after the other. 'Could even bring me good luck.'

'How would this bring you good luck?'

'Like if I get stung, I get into the school I'm going for. You know, the wasp hits its mark and so do I.'

Katsumi is gearing up for his college entrance exams, and has been attending extra lessons at a test prep school throughout his summer break. He hasn't spent much time outdoors at all – compared to most years his skin is pale. His eyes are bloodshot too, from staying up late studying. When Kabuto was in high school, he was already off the path to college or employment, instead walking the back alleys and side streets of life, getting involved in shady business. Because of that, when he watches his son dedicating so much energy to studying he feels an odd combination of pity and envy. Although if he's being honest with himself he'll acknowledge that it's mostly envy. Katsumi won't have to put his life on the line to make his way in the world; he can forge a path by sitting at a desk and solving problems on a test. To Kabuto it's emblematic of how far things have come since his day. These are opportunities available only in certain countries, to certain generations, and only to a limited number of young people at that.

'Leave it be, Katsumi. I don't want you getting stung either,' his mother says, returning from the kitchen.

'It'll be fine. I'll use the spray.'

'Don't even think about it.'

'We'd rather not have you getting stung,' Kabuto offers.

His wife immediately shoots back, 'We'd *rather not* have him getting stung? I'd say it's a bit more serious than that. I'm genuinely worried he might get hurt.'

'I see how it is,' Kabuto murmurs. *A little different than how you phrased it for me, huh?*

'But you know,' she says, adding another batch of freshly boiled corn to the platter, steam wafting off the yellow kernels in a way that somehow strikes Kabuto as ill-omened, 'three days from now we're going camping with the Satos.'

'Yes, of course,' Kabuto agrees calmly, as if he knows exactly what she's talking about. In fact, he has absolutely no recollection of having talked about any plans to go camping. Based on how his wife brought it up, it's something she's already told him. If he were to ask what she was talking about she would voice her frustrations about how he never listens to anything she says. Or maybe she'd say nothing, which would be worse. She would wear her dissatisfaction on her face but stay silent, plunging the whole house into a deep freeze. With the kind of dangerous work Kabuto gets after on a day-to-day basis, at the very least he wants his family time to be peaceful.

43

So rather than asking what camping trip she's talking about, it's best to push down his uncertainties and genially offer some bland comment, like 'Camping should be lots of fun!'

But where's the campsite? Are we going to the mountains? Or to a river?

He searches his memory but comes up with nothing. She probably told him about it when he was just back from work, wrung out and exhausted, about to pass out. And he probably responded with his usual clownish enthusiasm to really show her he was listening. Maybe he said, 'Camping in the mountains is the best!' Or maybe it was, 'The river should be beautiful!' Either way, it would have just been a reflexive response to make it through that particular interaction, and nothing actually lodged in his brain.

Is he even part of the camping plan? He isn't sure about that. After thinking for a moment, he says, 'Hopefully the weather's good.' That seems safe. It's a fair bet that camping involves being outdoors. *Right?*

'I feel a little bad that you'll be stuck at home, though,' his wife says.

'Ah, don't worry about that.' *So I'm not supposed to go.* He feels the satisfaction of having uncovered an important clue. He risks a glance at the kitchen counter for anything else he might be able to use. There's a pile of books and magazines, and one title sticks out: *Four Seasons in the Mountains – a Guide to Plants and Flowers.*

So they're going to the mountains. Otherwise, why else would she have that book? Now that he's thinking about it, he's starting to get the feeling, just the vaguest sense but it's there, that when his wife told him late one night that she was going camping she mentioned something about the mountains. The most indistinct of memories, but it's starting to take shape.

The family conversation unfolds without further incident.

Now we'll just watch some TV, then get in bed, and I'm home free. He feels an urge to add: 'When you're in the mountains, if you find any interesting insects, be sure to tell me about it.' He had made it this far safely, and he was feeling like he wanted to put a bow on his evening of communication with his wife and son. They both know that he's into insects, and whether or not they approve of his hobby, it feels like a reasonable thing for him to request.

'The mountains? What are you talking about, mountains?' As soon as he hears the edge in his wife's voice, he realizes he's stepped in it. His stomach tightens. He should have quit while he was ahead, but he got too eager, like the man in the Chinese parable who painted legs on a snake. His body floods with regret. 'We're camping by the seashore. I must have told you a dozen times. Why would you say we're going to the mountains?' His wife's words thrust at him like a spear. 'When I first told you, you said, "Oh wow, the seashore, that's great for summer camping!" What was that, just an automatic answer? Or was it someone else besides you who I'm remembering said that?'

In situations like this, the singular thing on Kabuto's mind is what he can say to restore harmony to the household. He knows if he follows along with her suggestion that it was an automatic answer or that it was in fact someone else, that will just stoke the fires.

'You really don't listen to anything I say, do you?' she continues.

'No that's not – of course I listen to you.' All he can do is be evasive. 'I was just ... mistaken, that's all.' Evasive, but resolute.

'Dad's probably just mixing it up with a conversation he had with a client or something. Lots of people go camping in the mountains.' It's Katsumi, riding to the rescue. He sounds bored as he says it and he stacks another corn cob atop the pile.

'Yeah, that's probably what happened.' Kabuto sounds casual, but on the inside he's nearly sobbing with appreciation for his son's intervention. The prow on his boat is breached, the hold is taking on water, he had resigned himself to the end – and here comes Katsumi in a helicopter, tossing down a life-ladder. His son is heroically backlit, the radiance making the corn shimmer. *Thank you*, he wants to shout; he wants to squeeze Katsumi but he fights down the urge, instead flashing his son a thumbs up out of view of his wife: *Nice one*. Katsumi glances at it, then looks away, unmoved.

Thanks to Katsumi's explanation, Kabuto's wife seems to take it down a notch. 'Well. It's true that you're awfully busy at work.'

'Anyway – what was it you wanted to tell me about camping?' Kabuto recalls where the conversation started.

'Oh right, that. In three days, we're leaving early in the morning to go camping. We'll have to load our bags into the car.'

'All your camping supplies.'

'Right. So we'll have to open the trunk—'

'And then close the trunk.' Kabuto is only willing to contribute meaningless snippets of conversation, like an athlete who's just messed up and will only risk minor plays.

'Right, and the wasp nest is in the osmanthus tree just behind the carport.'

'Ahh.' Now Kabuto is starting to see what his wife is getting at. 'You're worried that all the opening and closing of the trunk will upset the wasps and they'll come after you.'

'I'm not worried about me, I just don't want Katsumi getting stung.'

'Exactly,' Kabuto says without thinking, intending to make a show of agreeing with her, but then he notices the sharp points in her eyes and he hastily adds, 'I mean, of course we don't want you getting stung either, that would be awful.' It's like she set a trap for him. 'That's why when we spoke on the phone I told you to stay in the house.'

46

'I want to get this taken care of by the time we leave for our camping trip.'

'Okay, tomorrow I'll take the spray and deal with it.' As soon as it's out of his mouth he realizes that she's likely to find fault with that too, saying something like *I thought I just told you not to try to handle it yourself, weren't you listening?* But luckily she doesn't go in that direction.

'It's dangerous; I'd rather you call an exterminator. If you get in touch with the ward office I'm sure there's someone there who can help you.'

Kabuto looks at the calendar on the wall. It's the start of the Obon summer holiday. The ward office will be closed, and it's not likely he'll be able to get in touch with an exterminator. Not in the next three days, anyhow.

'Let me do it,' Katsumi says again, but Kabuto waves him off.

'No,' he pronounces, getting up from his seat. 'First I'll go gather intel about the target.'

'Gather intel about the target? Wow, Dad, what are you, like an assassin or something?'

Kabuto looks carefully at his son's face, but it seems the kid was just making a joke.

'It's dark out now, you're better off waiting until tomorrow,' says his wife.

He agrees. 'You're right, honey. You know you really are a sharp cookie! I shall obey.' As he hears his own words he worries that he might have overdone it, but it doesn't seem to bother his wife. If anything she looks quietly pleased as she vanishes into the kitchen.

Later that night, in his study, Kabuto sits at his desk and fires up his computer. His wife fell asleep the moment she got in bed, and Katsumi is in his own room, probably studying. Kabuto sends him supportive vibes: *Keep up the good work.*

He opens the internet browser and searches for how to get rid of wasps.

A jumble of search terms: *wasp, extermination, elimination, how to*. They produce a flood of results so massive he feels like he's staring out at the expanse of the ocean. He jumps in, clicking on the first few links that catch his eye. Most are ads for exterminators. One particular block of writing stands out to him under the urgent header: 'If you find hornets, leave it to a professional!' He leans closer to read more.

Wasps are dangerous, but an encounter with hornets can be deadly. You should never try to deal with them on your own. Apparently.

The page also has some photos of different nests.

One is the kind with numerous holes. He imagines it's what someone might have in mind when they threaten somebody with a gun and say something like 'I'll fill you fulla holes like a beehive' thinking it sounds cool (although he's never encountered anyone among his fellow professionals who has actually used that line). It also kind of looks like a showerhead with all those little holes. Then the other photo is of a nest that's spherical like a melon, but with a coloring that makes him think of fine earthenware pottery. It only has one hole in it. The ball-shaped one is a hornet's nest, and the caption underneath it reads, 'If you discover a nest like this, don't even think about trying to take care of it yourself.' Of course an advertisement for an exterminator would say something like that, but he finds a number of other non-ad pages that say similar.

I guess hornets really are dangerous, Kabuto thinks with a swell of uneasiness, but then he tells himself, *It's okay though – we've got wasps.*

'You definitely seem to have a Hornet problem,' the doctor says in his usual toneless, medical-device voice.

'No, as far as my wife was able to tell, we're dealing with wasps.' As he says it Kabuto realizes that he forgot to check the garden this morning before he left. *Need to get on that.*

'I am not speaking about insects.' The doctor adjusts his glasses, his expression blank.

They're in his exam room, in the office building in the city. The chart in the doctor's hand contains information from their client, but it's all written in an indecipherable scrawl so Kabuto has no idea what any of it means.

Someone he knew from the business once told him, 'I'm a go-between also, so believe me when I tell you that this doctor of yours has a good system.' The guy's name was Iwanishi. He always sounded bored, but he was actually fairly high-strung. He worked with a young professional who specialized in knives, and he would often gloat about controlling the kid like a cormorant fisherman works his bird. 'Here's the deal with your doctor,' he explained knowingly. 'Doctors usually talk to patients in private rooms. Perfect for discussing a job, right? And they can use medical words as a code, so even if the nurses overhear something, nothing seems amiss. Am I right or what? And the toughest thing for us go-betweens is keeping records. You can enter it all into a computer, but if the cops get that computer, you're toast. Which is why using patient charts is so brilliant. Mix the job files in with the normal patient files, translate them into the medical code, and that's a pretty solid setup. He can put photos of the target and maps of their location in there too, disguised as x-rays.'

Because the doctor had been his handler ever since Kabuto first started getting his hands dirty in the business, he had never given too much thought to the particular merits of his system. But once Iwanishi pointed it out to him, he saw it – a doctor working out of a clinic was the perfect cover.

'I wonder who wants me to have surgery,' Kabuto muses. If

49

he's being targeted by the Hornet, that means that someone wants him dead and hired the Hornet to do it.

'Summer is when hornets are the most active.' The doctor's comment sounds like nothing more than small talk. 'Particularly now, during the Obon holidays.'

'Who hired him, do you think?'

'It will be a few more days before those test results come in.' The doctor is choosing his words carefully, his internal translation software hard at work.

'Maybe it's payback for one of my surgeries.' Kabuto has lost count of how many people he's killed. He could probably figure it out if he went through all the doctor's files, but at minimum he knows that it's more than he could tally on all his fingers and toes. It wouldn't be at all odd for someone connected to one of his targets to be carrying a grudge. 'That's happened before.'

There was a job once where a woman wanted her boyfriend taken out, but the boyfriend somehow got wind of the plot and hired a different professional to keep him safe. This other professional decided to get proactive and made a move on Kabuto.

'That amputation went perfectly.'

'It wasn't all that easy of an operation, doc.' Kabuto thinks back to his fight with that particular professional. Just then something occurs to him. 'Hey, I wonder if it had anything to do with that recent issue.' The criminal group plotting the bomb attacks, until he took out some of their key players. 'Could be someone's pissed off about that.'

'There is a non-zero chance of that, yes.'

'I wonder if they're planning to get their revenge on me.' As soon as he says it out loud, the idea takes shape in his head, inscribed in vivid relief, a matter of inarguable fact. 'It would make perfect sense. But why just me? Shouldn't they also have a problem with the patient who ordered the operation? And the physician too.'

In other words, the doctor-as-go-between could be targeted too.

The doctor's face remains impassive. 'That could very well be.'

I can never read this guy, Kabuto thinks with a sigh. He's known the doctor for more than twenty years, but they haven't exactly grown close in all their time working together.

'I've got wasps at home and the Hornet is after me. I'm doing just great.' It would be easier if it were just one thing at a time, but his problems are swarming.

'What do you intend to do about the wasps in your garden?' Surprisingly, the doctor asks a question unrelated to a job.

'The ward office's website says that if you get in touch they'll send you a list of local exterminators. But it's Obon, they haven't gotten back to me. The neighborhood association might have someone also, but same deal.'

'Then what will you do?'

'A certain someone is saying "don't try to deal with it your-self" while at the same time saying "take care of it by such and such day". I'm not really sure what they want from me.' He keeps it vague, not wanting to share more about his family than necessary.

'"Take care of it as soon as possible but not by yourself" is a difficult position to be in. I recall a similar passage in *The Merchant of Venice*.'

'Oh yeah?' For most of his life, Kabuto hasn't read much beyond manga, but once in a while he picks up one of the books that his wife or Katsumi leave lying around. These days he's been finding them enjoyable, at least some of them. He remembers reading *The Merchant of Venice*, but he can't recall much of what happened in it.

'The moneylender Shylock is told that he can have his pound of flesh if he can remove it without spilling a single drop of blood, which of course he cannot do. Similar to the order to secure your garden by a certain day without actually eliminating the wasps.'

This sparks a glimmer of recognition for Kabuto. But the main thing he remembers is the scene near the end of the play, where the wife demands to know why her husband took the ring she had gifted him and gave it to someone else. The husband explains himself, but reading about how the wife hectors and accuses him, Kabuto felt like he was the one being attacked, and his stomach began to ache. And the fact that the whole episode was a scheme on the part of the wife made it even worse. *Wives are terrifying.*

That afternoon when Kabuto returns home, he goes to the garden to check out the osmanthus tree. It's lush with vivid green leaves and blossoms. He leans in to sniff at the flowers – still too early for the full fragrance – when he hears the buzzing of little wings. He freezes.

A yellow and black striped insect flies past Kabuto's head and disappears into the thicket of leaves. Must be headed back to the nest.

Kabuto has been in life-or-death situations countless times. Facing down the barrel of a gun, or the blade of a knife, while he himself brought only his fists to the fight. He's used to the threat posed by another human, so much so that in a confrontation his pulse barely even quickens.

But now, a single wasp passing by roots him to the spot. He has to laugh at himself.

You're the first thing that's had that effect on me in a long time, little guy, he wants to say. *Well, you and my wife.*

He tries to shift his mindset. He tells himself it's not a wasp, but one of his fellow professionals. Just as he hoped, that calms him right down. His breathing steadies. He takes a step closer and presses his face in among the leaves.

When closing in on a human target, it's crucial not to let them sense you're coming. That goes beyond keeping silent – it also means minimizing any vibrations in the air. He tries to picture how his approach seems to the wasps. *I wouldn't even need to move a branch for them to get a bead on me; I bet they'd know something is up just from the movement of the leaves.*

But there's no way he can avoid rustling the leaves or bending the branches. He tries to keep his movements to a minimum as he gingerly works his way deeper among the tree limbs. Now he can see the trunk. In the crotch where one of the thicker branches originates is an earth-colored mass, a lump like a skin tumor.

The nest.

Kabuto thinks back to the images he saw online yesterday.

The ones that look like a showerhead are for wasps, and the ones that are shaped like a ball are hornets.

Even though the nest he's looking at is partially obscured by the branches and leaves, it's very clearly shaped like a ball, reminiscent of a little planetoid in space.

Hornets.

Kabuto's face twists into a grimace. At the same moment, there's a deep buzz like the thrumming of a large rubber band. A single hornet pokes its head out of the nest. The coloring on its face makes it look like it's a bandit in a mask. Black and yellow send a sharp signal that registers at an evolutionary level deep in Kabuto's being: *danger.*

Now he has two problems.

The first is that he's dealing with hornets. The second is that his wife was sure that they were wasps. So now he has to find the right way to tell her she was wrong.

There are some fundamental truths in this world. Even without proper schooling, Kabuto knows these truths. Actually, the fact that he learned them from experience means that he feels them all the more keenly.

One of these truths is that no one likes being corrected. Particularly not by their spouse.

His heart sinks.

He goes back to his house and gets on the computer. Still no response from the ward office, but he wasn't really expecting one, not during Obon anyway. He tries calling a few exterminators, but none of them answer. They probably take off for Obon too.

He doesn't blame them. The problem is that the hornets don't take the holiday off.

As he continues to search around, he learns that there are several types of hornets. The largest and most dangerous are the Asian giant hornets, but according to what he finds they usually build their nests underground. The ones that take up residence in urban trees and gardens are most typically yellow-vented hornets or their cousins the yellow hornets. Neither of these are especially aggressive; in fact, it seems that in general hornets don't randomly sting humans unless they perceive themselves to be under attack.

If an intruder gets too close to the nest, a squadron of scouts will fly out and threaten them. If you retreat, they won't pursue. The problem is if they're buzzing around your head and you reflexively wave them away and end up bashing one of them. Then the one that got hit lets loose pheromones that say 'This guy's after us!' Then the rest of the hornets from the nest join the attack.

So if you're careful and you leave them alone, you won't get stung. Reading this reassures Kabuto. But there's still the matter that his wife brought up, about the chance that they might run afoul of the hornet scouts as they're loading the camping supplies into the car, particularly the bigger gear that might get unwieldy. If only they had pheromones that could tell the hornets, 'Sorry, it was just an accident!'

His wife comes home a bit after five. Her work is closed for Obon so she was probably out shopping with a friend. Likely someone she met at the cooking classes she's been attending recently. From what she's been telling him they use gourmet ingredients and learn advanced culinary techniques, but so far she's shown no signs of debuting any of them in the home. It seems like the class is mainly about preparing the food for themselves and enjoying it together. Just once he asked her if she would cook something from the class for them at home. Although he didn't come right out and say it, it was more like a roundabout non-request: 'I'd love to try some of the food you're learning to make, I can't think of anything that would make me happier. But I'm sure it'd be too tough to make at home.' And he said it so softly that someone else might very well have thought they were just hearing things. But she pinned him with her needle gaze, and he made up his mind then and there never to ask about her cooking class again. In his mind Kabuto kept a box of taboos, full of subjects he must never bring up with his wife. He tossed the cooking class in with the others.

He can tell immediately when she gets home that she's in a good mood.

'I'm home. Oh, hi, honey, you're back already?' Her tone is light. 'I haven't prepped anything for dinner so I'm going to do it now.'

Without any hesitation Kabuto says, 'I think we have some of that fried rice in the freezer. That was good, I've been wanting to have it again.'

He's given serious thought to how he should answer when she asks what he wants for dinner. Of course, there's not one correct answer, but from past experience he's learned a thing or two. Saying 'anything's fine' is a losing move. There's not a single cook in the world who appreciates being told anything is fine. Suggesting that they order in or eat out is okay. Okay, but not great. Depending on how she's feeling, she might answer 'You think we can just spend money left and right? When it comes to running a home you really know nothing' and so on and so forth. It's happened more than once. She could go on for as long as it would have taken her to prepare a meal.

He's found it's best to ask for whatever will be easiest for her to make. If there's something quick, tell her that's exactly what he's been craving. Often it seems to please her and she happily agrees.

Now, just as he was hoping, she says brightly, 'Sounds good, if that's what you want – that'll be easy.'

'By the way, I took a look at the nest in the garden. Looks like it's not wasps but hornets.' He tries to slip it in casually.

'What?' She freezes. 'Really?'

'From the shape of the nest, yeah.'

'Guess I was wrong, huh . . .'

'No no, they look a lot alike, wasps and hornets.' He hopes this sounds natural. At the same time, he feels slightly embarrassed that he was so concerned about telling her this.

'Well, all the more reason to leave it alone and call a professional,' she says. 'Unless you've already dealt with it?' There's a slight edge in her voice.

'No, of course not.' This concerns him. Is she trying to tell him that he actually should have taken care of the nest? His habit of reading deeply into everything his wife says doesn't always help him.

Later in the evening, Katsumi comes home. He trudges straight up to his room as always, reappears for a moment only to get in to the bath, emerges again only to sprawl out on the couch in front of the TV. Kabuto wants to chide his son for being so easygoing, for leaving himself defenseless when an assassin could burst in at any moment, but he suppresses the urge and tells himself that his world has nothing to do with his son.

'More exam prep today?' Kabuto knows the answer but he

asks anyway. Even though he can predict the flat response he'll get, some genetic imperative makes him try to strike up a conversation with his son.

'Yeah. Self study.' Ordinarily, this clipped answer would be all Kabuto could hope for, but Katsumi goes on. 'I saw something today at the bus stop that I just could not handle.'

'What happened?'

'There was a mother with her kid. Young mom. The boy must have been in pre-school.'

Sounds lovely, Kabuto almost says, but holds it in. A mother and her kid isn't necessarily lovely. Much of the misfortune in the world happens between family or close friends.

'I guess their cat died the night before.'

'Oh, that's sad.' Kabuto has a hard time putting much emotion into his words. He spends his days killing human beings; he's not exactly sure how upset he's supposed to get over a cat.

'Sounded like it was a cat the mom had had for a long time. She was more upset about it than the kid was. She kept crying.' He purses his lips. 'The kid seemed to be doing okay, but his mom was a wreck, so he was trying to cheer her up.'

'Good kid.'

'I thought so too. So the kid says to his mom, "Mom, Callie just turned into a star, that's all."'

'Wow.'

'And the mom gets all sharp with the kid and says, "If Callie turned into a star, then go up into space and bring her back!" Can you believe that? So then now the kid gets upset.'

'She must have just been all twisted up about losing her cat. She got emotional and took it out on her kid. I'm sure she didn't mean it.' *Meanwhile, your mother's always taking her emotions out on me.*

'Yeah, but the kid doesn't deserve that. And as soon as she did it she made a face like, oh no, what have I done.'

'Parents are often thinking that.'

'The kid was so sad.'

'I'm sure. But I would also bet that somewhere the kid knew that his mom didn't really mean it. And then maybe that's the first time he had an understanding that his parents aren't perfect and that their behavior can change based on their emotions.'

This was also from Kabuto's own personal experience. His parents were always rough with him. Emotional, selfish – in fact, dealing with them was how he got so good at reading facial expressions. For the first time he makes the connection to why he's always scrutinizing his wife for signs of her mood.

'Katsumi, your dad says that we have hornets in the garden, not wasps,' she calls to her son from the dining table. 'Be careful out there, okay?'

'Oh, wow. Okay. Yeah, hornets are dangerous.' Katsumi looks out the window into the garden. 'Dad, did you call an exterminator?'

'They're all off for Obon.'

'I really don't think you should try to take care of it yourself, Dad. This one kid in my class, his grandfather got stung by hornets and it was pretty bad.'

Kabuto isn't quite sure how bad pretty bad is. And he's generally suspicious of stories that go around. Rumors in the business are always flying and getting embellished. Even if someone isn't trying to twist the story intentionally, they just tell the basic contours and people fill in the blanks. If there's an episode where five people died, it quickly turns into ten, and more often than not, fifty. When it comes to getting stung by a hornet, 'pretty bad' could mean the hospital or it could mean the morgue.

'From what I found online, the hornets we have in the city are usually yellow hornets, and their venom isn't as strong.'

'Still, it's scary.'

'They're also not as aggressive as some other kinds. If I don't mess with them, they should leave me alone.'

'Seriously, Dad. Come on.' Katsumi looks at his father. From Kabuto's perspective, the kid is clearly his junior, but his son addresses him like they're equals. Sometimes it's a little disorienting, but not altogether upsetting.

'What?'

'You're planning on using poison spray to destroy their nest. From their point of view, that's definitely messing with them.'

'Well, true.' As he says it Kabuto imagines his entire body being covered with hornets and having them all sting him at the same moment. His skin tightens into goosebumps. 'Yeah, let's just leave it to a professional.'

What changes his mind is a video he watches online late that night. Even though he had declared he wouldn't try to get rid of the hornets himself, he still stays up searching for *hornet* and *exterminate*. Eventually he finds himself on a site with user-uploaded videos.

The first one that catches his eye is a video of fights between a hornet and a praying mantis. Watching two insects clash until one of their lives is extinguished is unsettling to Kabuto, nothing like watching fight scenes in movies or anime, or even the fights that he himself engages in. Seeing it in nature is somehow frightening. It's also fascinating. What's particularly fascinating is seeing how evenly matched the hornet and praying mantis are. The video he watches has multiple battles. In some the hornet wins, and in the other the praying mantis comes out on top. Victory is decided by the barest of margins, the slightest opening or misstep.

He starts to see the two insects as natural rivals, vying for supremacy with equally matched power.

This makes him happy. There's nothing that upsets him more than the thought of one race or tribe or species calmly obliterating another. Striking from a risk-free position feels underhanded. It would be the same as killing a defenseless elderly person in their sleep. Too easy, too shameful. And he absolutely hates when people brag about doing that kind of easy, shameful work. Work should be hard. He feels that every day when he goes to his job at the office supplies company. The sweat he puts into making his sales rounds, the unreasonable requests from clients, the butting heads with middle management. It's spiritually exhausting and endlessly infuriating. He doesn't believe that there's any job on earth that's easy-breezy.

As he watches the video, hornet versus mantis, he tells himself: *This is how it's supposed to be – risking it all, equal risk on both sides. That's only fair.*

Then he finds another video with the title 'DIY Hornet Extermination'.

He clicks play.

It opens on a man in protective gear. The caption introduces him as a fifty-year-old office worker who decided to take care of the hornet's nest in his garden by himself. He borrowed the protective gear from his neighborhood association. It looks like a cross between a silver rain poncho and a spacesuit. The man is ready for liftoff.

He's standing in what looks like his yard. His car is parked off to one side. It's morning, and the sun shines down on the scene from a blue sky. He's in his silver outfit in front of a wild-looking azalea bush. The camera holds the shot steadily, as if it's on a tripod. It's showing a side view of the man approaching the azalea.

The man bobs his head to the camera as if to say, *Well, here goes.* He looks nervous. In his right hand is a can of wasp and hornet spray.

Let's see what he does, Kabuto thinks.

First the man sets the spray down by his feet and picks up a pair of gardening shears. They're the extra-long kind, used for cutting higher-up branches. He grasps the shears with both hands and takes his position in front of the azalea. Lowers his hips slightly. Extends the shears forward. The blades clack shut and a branch falls to the ground. Right away a small buzzing insect floats out from the depths of the bush.

He's gonna get stung, Kabuto thinks, and for a moment is seized by the sensation that he himself is standing there facing the hornet. But the man in the video stays steady. He holds the shears in his left hand and reaches down to take the spray can in his right. He aims at the hornet and lets loose a jet. Kabuto can see the insect drop out of the air.

Then the man goes through the same motions, again and again.

Cuts off a branch. A hornet appears. He lifts the can and fires. The hornet falls.

Before long, Kabuto has a handle on the method.

First, expose the nest. Unlike a wasp's nest, a hornet's nest has exterior walls, with only one hole as a point of entry. To attack the nest with spray you need to target that hole.

Which is why the man needed to cut back the branches that were in the way. Each time a branch falls, the disturbance brings out a scout from the nest. But they don't immediately attack the man. The hornets don't seem interested in picking a needless fight. They're just checking out the situation.

And that's when the man hits them with the spray.

Little by little, branches pile up on the ground and the nest becomes easier to see.

Once enough branches are pruned, the man in the protective gear gauges that he can make his move. He sets down the shears, takes a firm grip on the spray can and takes one last measuring look at the opening in the nest. *Here it comes.*

The man aims at the exposed hole and unleashes a long, steady stream. There's a prolonged noise like TV static.

Kabuto thinks about the times he's gone up against another professional and gotten his hands around their neck.

At the end of the video the man shears off the whole nest. His spray assault must have killed everything inside. He looks a bit uncertain as he picks it up off the ground, but is also clearly exhilarated as he turns to the camera and holds his trophy aloft in a victory pose.

Still staring at the screen after the video finishes, Kabuto murmurs to himself: *If that's all there is to it . . . why can't I do it too?*

Kabuto's eyes open at 4 a.m. and he's immediately wide awake. The nerves would have made it tough for him to sleep in anyway. He had read online that if you're getting rid of a hornet's nest, the best bet is to do it early in the morning, before they're up and about their business. He doesn't know if that's accurate or not, but it seems reasonable.

He washes his face and combs down his hair, then heads to the closet to select his outfit.

Without proper protective gear, he'll need to cobble together something from the clothes he has.

He pulls on a pair of sweatpants. Then a pair of jeans over that. It's tight on his legs, but he doesn't feel like he has a choice. He grabs a sharpened pencil from his desk and jabs at himself experimentally. It hurts. *Are hornet stingers stronger than this pencil?* He has no idea. Just to be safe he pulls out a pair of white ski-pants from the closet and puts them on. That seems like it's enough for his lower body. Putting anything else on top of that probably won't do much good.

Now for the upper body. First he puts on a sweatshirt. Then a knit turtleneck sweater that he pulls out of the box of winter clothes, to cover his neck. Then a jean jacket over that. Finally, a down jacket.

He can still stand straight, but he has so many thick layers on that he feels like a snowman. One misstep and he'll topple over.

Next he pulls on two pairs of socks. It's difficult to bend his body but he manages to flex his knee, reach down to his feet, and get the socks on. He has a pair of ski gloves that he'll put on once he's outside.

And next . . . He scans the closet and spots his full-face ski helmet in the corner. That should protect his head. He tries it on and lowers the shield. It's hard to breathe, but it's his best option.

He hasn't taken all that long to get his outfit together, but he's starting to worry about the heat outside. It's August, and the past few days the temperature has shot up past 90. News programs keep issuing heat warnings and urging people to take precautions. He figured that it wouldn't be so bad this early in the morning, but now he's uncertain.

He feels as jumpy as when he did his first job. The first time he ever killed someone.

As he starts to head outside, he realizes that his neck is vulnerable. He has the helmet on, but any time he moves his head his neck is exposed. The turtleneck is covering his skin but that might not prevent a hornet's sting from getting through.

Neck would be bad, he tells himself.

Most times he takes out his targets he does it by strangling them. The neck is familiar territory; he has some knowledge of the arteries in the neck and how they work. While he doesn't know how potent a hornet's venom is, when he stops to think about all the blood that passes through the neck on its way to the rest of the body, leaving it open to attack feels highly risky.

He searches around for his scarf but he can't find it anywhere. Then he remembers: he disposed of it after he used it to strangle a target last winter.

I don't have time to be messing around like this. He can feel the seconds slipping by. The hornets are probably already awake and buzzing.

Okay then, he decides, and grabs the duct tape from his desk drawer. He starts to tape up the gap between the helmet and the down jacket. It's hard to move with any precision thanks to all the layers he has piled on, but he manages to tear off several long strips and plaster them roughly on, forming a seal around his neck. *No need for it to look pretty.*

He steps out into the hall.

Before heading down the stairs, Kabuto notices that his son's door is ajar and he peeks his head in. Katsumi is in bed, fast asleep. Practice test materials cover his desk. Must have been studying late into the night.

Kabuto steps inside, forgetting that he's wearing a bizarre ersatz spacesuit. How long has it been since he's set foot inside his son's room?

He gazes down at the young man's face, eyes closed, mouth half-open, and has a flash of what Katsumi looked like as a very little boy. *He got so big, so fast.* The bittersweet pang rushes through him. From what his wife's been saying, depending on the school Katsumi gets into, he might be living on his own. Kabuto keenly feels that the time he has left living with his son under this roof is precious, and counting down.

Then he remembers that he's about to go do battle with a colony of hornets, and he tenses back up.

He brings his helmeted head close to Katsumi's face and whispers, 'You'll be a good man, son.'

According to what he found online, hornet venom isn't as dangerous as everyone seems to think it is. If you do happen to

64

get stung, a severe reaction isn't likely to occur until the second sting. There probably isn't that much cause for worry. Nonetheless, Kabuto somberly says to his son, 'Take care of your mother for me.'

It's a battle against fear, and a battle against time. He's been standing in front of the osmanthus tree for twenty minutes now, still unable to make his first move. Just a few minutes ago the sun first poked its head over the horizon, but already it's high in the sky.

It seems to be shining a spotlight directly onto Kabuto, emphasizing his absurd getup.

I really hope no one sees me dressed like this, he thinks. Both his down jacket and his ski pants are white, making him look like a bizarre, puffy, pale man.

The shears are in his hands as he squares off against the tree. In the end he decided to forego the ski gloves. He thought they'd get in the way of him using the spray properly. It wouldn't be good to accidentally drop the can. Instead he put on cotton work gloves.

Once he cuts the first branch there'll be no turning back. Same as in his usual work. As soon as he makes his first move against a target, he's fully committed. All other options disappear, and there's only one path stretching forward: eliminate the target. No retreat.

As he goes over this in his mind, time marches onward. Sweat starts to drip down his body. It's hard to breathe in the helmet and he keeps having to lift the face-shield to get any air.

Finally he works himself up to it. If he keeps standing here like this forever, his neighbor Mrs Kamata will come out and spot him. She just turned seventy-seven this year, and every day she wakes up at 5 a.m. and sits in her garden. He wants to finish his task and get out of this outfit before she sees him.

He takes a step forward and extends the shears. He's conscious of the fact that he's bent over in a ridiculous posture, head forward and ass jutting out. His back doesn't want to straighten.

He cuts a branch.

Just the end of it. He's being timid. The bit of wood falls to the ground, but the shape of the tree is largely unchanged.

No hornet comes to investigate.

He reaches the shears forward again, and though his body is resisting him, he puts them in deeper this time and closes them hard. The feel of the blades cutting through wood travels up his arm and the tree limb drops.

Without even waiting for any reaction from within the tree he grabs the spray can in his right hand. With all his thick layers it's difficult to move quickly. His hand is trembling slightly as he aims the nozzle straight ahead and pushes the button.

A gush of noise and pesticide.

A hornet falls to the ground.

No turning back now. Kabuto tries to empty his mind. *Just keep doing the job.*

Cut a branch. Grab the can. Spray.

Work the shears. Spot the hornet. Grab the can, push the button. Put the can down, cut another branch.

With every rustle of the falling branches, a hornet emerges from the nest, as expected. He takes them out with the spray. Their corpses start to pile up on the ground.

The more he gets used to it, the more his fear subsides.

But every so often, a hornet dodges the spray and floats off into the sky, showing him that his plan isn't foolproof. He doesn't know where these escapees are going, or when they'll come back. When they'll strike. The helmet cuts off his peripheral vision and even what he can see is less than fully clear through the visor.

66

He feels a slight breeze and his mind screams *Hornet!* He knows he's imagining things, but he flails, he lurches backward, he grabs the spray can and waves it. He thinks he hears a noise and he twists his body toward it.

Nothing he's ever done has made him feel this ridiculous.

He loses sight of one of the hornets that emerges, and, terrified that it might attack from behind, he retreats to the house and presses his back up against the wall. He flips open the face-shield and gulps air. Like a fugitive on the run.

The heat and the difficulty breathing combine with his fear and nerves, exhausting him. It's taking all his willpower not to close his eyes and drift off.

'The heat,' he groans, 'is gonna get me before the hornets can.'

Then he spots the one he had lost track of and sprays it. It drops out of the air. Kabuto feels a simultaneous sense of relief and guilt.

The hornets didn't do anything wrong. Nothing at all.

They were just following their nature: build a nest, run a colony. And the internet said that hornets aren't even that aggressive.

But I'm protecting my family. That's natural too.

Cut. Spray. Cut. Spray.

Hornets emerge one after the other. By now the whole colony must be aware of Kabuto's existence.

All he can do is shut down his emotions and see the fight through to the end. He hardens his resolve and goes through the motions like a machine at work. His breathing is heavy and he's dripping with sweat. *This is a test of endurance,* he tells himself. There's no guarantee that while he's pushing his limits the hornets won't lose their patience and attack, but he's not thinking about that.

It's been almost twenty minutes since he made his first cut, he realizes with a start. The osmanthus tree is looking quite trim. And right there in front of him, hanging like a giant swollen fruit, is the nest, exposed.

There it is.

The entrance hole is facing him. Assuming that it leads to the inner reaches of the nest, this battle is all over.

He feels a swell of emotion as he lays the shears down and takes the spray can in hand.

Time to finish it. He sprays the hornets as they emerge from the nest, readying himself.

Okay – go. Like the start signal on a race. He steps up to the nest and inserts the nozzle into the hole, then holds the spray button all the way down. He wants to squeeze every last drop of spray from the can. White mist billows out from the nest.

A powerful sense of wrongdoing takes hold.

He thinks about the video he watched with the contests between the hornets and the praying mantises. Deathmatches. Those hornets were the same as the ones he's fighting now – desperate to protect the colony, to keep their nest intact. These ones were just unlucky in choosing to build their nest in this particular tree. It's not as if Kabuto and his family made it clear that their osmanthus tree was off limits. The hornets didn't know they were trespassing.

I'm sorry. The apology he offers the insects is more than he's ever given to any of the human beings he's killed. Tears well up, to his surprise. He wants to wipe them away, but the visor prevents it.

Even after the spray can is empty he keeps the button depressed for several long seconds, so intent is he on finishing the task. Finally he snaps back to himself. He flips the visor up and takes a step backward, then another. There are no hornets buzzing anywhere.

Did I win? He stands there in a daze, his shoulders sagging.

*

Heaps of dead hornets lie piled at his feet. He surveys the scene as he steadies his breathing. Tiny corpses, brought down by poison spray. A mess of yellow and black and chemical fluid and dirt. *I'm sorry,* he thinks again. A snippet of an old poem flashes in his mind: *All that's left of warriors' dreams.*

He picks up the shears once more and approaches the nest. Extends the blades toward where it connects to the tree. The ground underfoot is swampy from all the spray.

He works the shears once. With a sound like cracking clay, the nest detaches from the tree. It hits the ground and splits open like an overripe fruit. After being saturated by the fluid pesticide it must have softened considerably. Kabuto sees something white on the inside and takes a closer look: larvae. A chill runs through him. The remorse of extinguishing so many young lives.

Could I have done this differently? . . . No, this was the only way.

He squats down and starts scooping dirt on top of the ruined nest. The least he can do is give the baby hornets a burial.

After finishing the makeshift grave he lets out a heavy sigh, then reaches overhead and stretches. His body aches from struggling against so many layers of clothing. He turns toward the house, wanting to get out of this outfit as soon as possible. As he walks he tries to take off the helmet but there's all the duct tape attaching it to the jacket.

He doesn't know exactly what time it is, but his neighbor Mrs Kamata hasn't come out yet, so it must still be before five.

That's when he catches some movement: near his gate, a man ducking just out of sight behind the wall.

Kabuto instantly determines that it's an intruder. Not because of the early hour. It's because they hid when they saw him. The speed, the easy movement. A fellow professional.

Without a moment's hesitation Kabuto charges out of the garden and through the front gate. Standing there is a man, tall and slim. Just standing – maybe caught in the act of trying to escape, maybe defiant in the face of being discovered, or maybe he planned to be caught. Kabuto isn't sure yet what to make of it.

The man stares steadily. He's wearing a black long-sleeve T-shirt and bootcut jeans. It's hard to say how old he is, but he's handsome, like a model. Both hands are in his back pockets, which would make it hard for him to defend himself. But Kabuto can tell the guy is a pro. He can feel the tendrils of threat and wariness emanating from the man's body, probing. The hands in his back pockets are probably holding some sort of weapon that he could whip out at any moment.

'You here for me?' Kabuto asks the man. He thinks back to what his handler the doctor told him: *You are being targeted by the Hornet.* 'You thought at this hour everyone would be asleep, huh?'

So is this the Hornet? As soon as the thought enters Kabuto's mind, he's certain of it. Which is typical for him.

He remembers pulling a job in a skyscraper one time, and there was a man who looked a lot like this in the elevator. At least, he's pretty sure he looked the same. And after that job he heard a rumor that the Hornet had been on site as well. *Yeah, it's got to be him. That's the only explanation.*

The man says nothing, just glares back.

Is he going to make a move? Kabuto readies himself. But as soon as he tries to engage his body he feels the fatigue from his battle with the nest. In his current state he'd have a hard time dealing with an ordinary civilian, let alone a professional. He tries to calm his pulse as it quickens. *What do I do?*

Failing anything else, he needs to keep his focus on the man's hands, in case they make a move and he has to react. But his body feels leaden, his vision fuzzy.

The attack still doesn't come. Kabuto can read some tension in the man's face.

Is he afraid of me? If that's the case, then it's a major failing as a hired killer. You can't afford to fear your target.

Then it dawns on Kabuto that he's still wearing his improvised anti-hornet protective gear. With his helmet taped in place and his body all puffed up from the multiple layers, he must look truly bizarre. Like some kind of mystery man.

Is that why he's on guard?

It does seem likely that encountering someone dressed the way he is would be confusing, possibly even unsettling.

Kabuto takes an experimental step forward.

The man retreats one pace.

'You use poison needles, right? Tough luck.' He raises the face-shield. 'Look at how I'm dressed. Needles won't get through it.'

The man looks Kabuto up and down.

'I knew you'd come.' Kabuto takes a long, deep breath, careful not to let his fatigue and agitation show. 'I was ready for you. I was waiting.'

Of course he's just bullshitting. The showdown he had planned for was with actual hornets.

The man says nothing, just keeps staring hard.

Kabuto realizes it's the same expression he himself must have had when he was about to attack the nest. The fear of facing an unknown lifeform.

'Why don't you head on home.' Kabuto tries to make the words sound as cutting as he can.

The man shrinks back another step, then turns to leave.

Kabuto watches him go, then takes another deep breath. But before he can savor his relief he hears the sound of his neighbor's door opening. Mrs Kamata must be up. He scurries back through his gate and makes for his own door, wanting to get out of sight.

Then he stumbles: his shoe was untied, and he tripped on his laces. He tips forward, loses his balance, scrambles to keep his footing, and staggers several steps tipped at a crazy angle. His forward momentum is too much and he tumbles down to the ground.

His whole body goes limp, drained.

Exhaustion and overheating have finally gotten the best of him. He can't move a muscle. He lies on his back with his arms and legs spread wide, staring up at the now-bright morning sky. A well-deserved break. The urge to sleep steals over him. It doesn't feel wonderful lying there all soaked with sweat, but spending some more time resting on the ground like this also doesn't seem like the worst idea.

The woman steps out of her condo and locks the door behind her, then takes her son by the hand and leads him down the open-air fifth-floor walkway.

Her travel plans to go home for the holiday have her and her son leaving early in the morning, but even at this hour the sun is already high in the sky, getting ready to broil Tokyo for another day.

'I hope it's cooler at Grandma's place,' her five-year-old son says as he looks out over the railing. Ordinarily he'd be fast asleep at this hour, but he's up and excited about the prospect of seeing his grandmother.

'Oh, I think it's a good bit cooler in Aomori,' she says. He asks her about what trains they need to take and she explains the route.

They wait for the elevator to come up from the ground floor. Her son squeezes her hand and she looks down at him. He's small, just a little kid, but he stands straight and sturdy. It's somehow reassuring. She thinks back to what she said to him yesterday, how she snapped at him, and her heart hurts a little.

Then she finds herself looking out over the railing, not for any specific reason – and she spots it.

Five stories below them, the house next door to her condo building, there appears to be someone in the garden, lying on the ground. She can't quite make out what's happening, but it doesn't look right, and she fishes her camera out of her bag. The zoom should help her get a better look. She looks on the screen and sees a human form sprawled out on the ground with arms and legs spread wide. Right there in the middle of the garden, face up toward the sky.

It's too big to be a doll, but it doesn't exactly look like a person. Maybe it's a mannequin?

'What is it?' her son asks. The elevator arrives and the door opens, but she ignores it.

'There's some weird person asleep down there.'

'A weird person?'

She hands the camera to her son and lifts him up so he can see. Careful not to hold him too close to the railing, she directs him to look down at the house next door.

'Where?' her boy wonders, shaking his head. But then after a moment he makes a happy little noise of discovery. 'There it is!'

'You see it? I wonder if it's a doll.'

'It moved a little. It looks like a spacesuit!'

'Hm, yeah, I guess it does.' She lowers her son and takes back the camera so she can look again. It looks like someone wearing a motorcycle helmet, but she can see how her son would think it's like a spacesuit.

He asks to see it again and she hoists him up once more. As she holds him she thinks for a moment, and then says, 'Maybe that person went up to space to bring back Callie after she turned into a star.'

Her son laughs. 'Yeah, maybe they did.' He's smiling so broadly it's hard to tell if he's playing along or if he believes it. 'It looks like they fell down to Earth from space.'

'Well, that would be dangerous. Maybe better they didn't bring Callie after all. She can stay up in the sky as a star.'

Her son likely hasn't forgotten her sharp tone from yesterday, but he smiles at her like none of it happened, and she feels a deep appreciation for the generosity of his young heart. She couldn't stop crying her eyes out whenever she thought of losing her cat friend of eleven years, but that was no excuse for her to be a bad mother. She's ashamed of how she behaved. She wants to apologize, but she's embarrassed, or her pride is making it hard. Instead she says, 'Still, I wonder if they met Callie up there.'

'Maybe they did,' he answers.

'I'm really sorry about yesterday,' she finally manages to say.

And of course she has no idea that nearly an hour later the wife of the man who was lying in the garden next door would come outside and scold him; 'What are you doing wearing all of that? Don't tell me you got rid of the hornets yourself!'

CRAYON

HE LOOKS UP AT THE wall. It's covered with rock-like objects in all different shapes and colors – holds for bouldering. Each hold has a piece of colored tape affixed next to it. Kabuto locates all the holds with blue tape, confirming his route to the top. He sets his stance and places both hands on the starting hold, then pulls himself up onto the wall. There aren't many rules in bouldering, but you do have to put both hands on the starting and ending holds.

Before he started, all he knew about bouldering was that it was a sport that involved climbing up a wall using these funny little rock-shaped objects as handholds and footholds. Once he tried it, he found that it was actually quite deep and required creative problem solving.

He grabs on to a hold that looks like a giant clam, gripping it with both hands so that it looks like he's praying. Whenever he clings onto the wall in this position he finds that he actually does send up little prayers. He knows that there's no forgiveness for the violent work he does, so far astray from any righteous path – instead he prays for a peaceful home. For his wife and son to live safe, quiet lives.

He reaches his left arm up and to the right, hugging the wall as he tries to get to the next hold. The muscles in his upper arms bulge with the effort. The wholesome ache of exertion makes him feel alive. His hips follow his arm up and to the right as he grabs the light blue hold he was aiming for. Another prayer enters his mind: that he can retire one day soon.

The doctor doesn't seem to want to let him retire. He keeps saying that Kabuto needs to save up more money.

He reaches directly overhead toward the next hold and pulls himself up. His left hand closes tight around it. Another prayer: *Please let my wife see my worth.*

'Wow, Miyake-san, you really raced up that time!'

Kabuto is sitting in a chair next to the crashpad below the wall when a man in a suit calls out to him. He's used to being called Kabuto in his underground work, and Dad or honey at home. Hearing his actual name anywhere other than at his office job feels somehow new.

'Oh, hi Matsuda-san. Did you stop in on your way home from work?'

'Yeah, I just got here. I promised myself today I would clear the purple route.'

There are lots of holds on the wall in bouldering. Climbing up using any hold you want would be too easy, so one of the other rules is to aim for the goal following a certain route, using only specific holds. The colored tape next to the holds indicates the route, and the difficulty. The pink tape, for example, is a beginner route.

Matsuda pats some chalk powder into his hands, steps up onto the crashpad, and approaches the wall. He grips the first hold in the purple route with both hands, leans in, and starts climbing.

There wasn't any particular reason why Kabuto chose this climbing gym over the other ones in the city. One of his jobs required him to kill a pharmacy owner by inducing anaphylactic

76

shock, and it so happened that opposite the building where he did the hit was a sign for this bouldering gym. It read 'Check out the hot niche sport!' He laughed at that – apparently not hot enough to avoid being called niche – and walked over to learn more. The gym wasn't very close to his home, but he could get there on an easy subway ride without any transfers.

Matsuda started at the gym around the same time that Kabuto did. He said he worked in sales at an ad design firm nearby and had been eyeing the gym for a while but the timing kept not working out. Eventually he made up his mind to make it happen.

For safety purposes, only one person is allowed on the wall at a time. Everyone else waits and watches. Sort of like in bowling how only one person bowls at a time, but unlike in bowling there are no points or opponents to compete against. It's a solid workout, but there's none of the narcissism of body-building. It's just about the climb, and the sublime sense of satisfaction when you make it.

'It's funny how great you feel, even though all you're doing is climbing up a wall.' Kabuto remembers Matsuda saying that in their first conversation.

The gym was crowded that day, so he had to wait a fair amount for his turn. Matsuda just happened to be standing nearby and struck up a conversation, maybe because they were about the same age. Naturally, Kabuto was wary at first. He thought maybe this man knew about his work, his double life. Or maybe he was another professional. Kabuto's replies were clipped. But over time they kept running into each other at the gym, and he saw that this man was genially making conversation with other people as well. Figuring that he was just a friendly kind of guy, Kabuto began to open up to small talk, surface-level stuff.

He didn't typically make small talk. It felt kind of nice.

Then one day they found a deeper connection. They were talking about something or other, maybe about a big typhoon that was making its way toward Japan, when Matsuda's phone rang and he excused himself to take the call. Kabuto did his climb, and when he was done he noticed that Matsuda was still gone. He glanced over toward the bathroom and saw the man, still on the call, phone pressed to his ear, bobbing his head deferentially to the person on the other end. Kabuto figured the man had made some error at work, but when Matsuda came back looking sheepish and explained his long call, Kabuto felt a surge of empathy.

'Sorry, that was my wife. You know, I'm the top salesman at work, they respect me there, but at home it's a whole different story.'

Before Kabuto even knew what he was doing, his hand was extended to shake Matsuda's.

Matsuda looked taken aback, but in an instant he realized that it was the handshake of an ally.

'You too, Miyake-san?'

'Yeah.' Kabuto pulled his chin back.

'So, what, if you work late she gets mad at you?'

'She's always asleep by the time I get home,' Kabuto answered. 'But if I make any noise she wakes up and gets on my case.'

Matsuda's face was a picture of both dismay and relief, smiling and even welling up a little. 'Same! She even says it's too loud when I come home hungry and open the fridge.'

'Oh, I can tell you the best food for late night snacks.' Kabuto's voice was almost buoyant. 'It's quiet, and it doesn't go bad.'

'I go for fish sausage.'

Kabuto was stunned. This must have been what it felt like when a mathematician who solved a proof that had been befuddling people for centuries met another scholar who had found the same solution. He shook Matsuda's hand again, even more vigorously.

From that point on he looked forward to seeing Matsuda at the bouldering gym. He never imagined that he would meet someone like him.

Now he's watching Matsuda work his way up the purple route to the top. Matsuda reaches the last hold, which he has to grab with both hands. But he loses his grip and falls. He lands in a heap on the crashpad, then hops down to the floor, looking slightly deflated.

'Almost had it,' Kabuto says.

Matsuda squeezes his hands together as if gauging how much grip strength he had left. 'Ha, yeah,' he says with a grin. 'Whenever I get to the last hold I start to think of my family.'

'What do you mean?'

'All our neighbors always call us the happy family. And, I mean, we aren't unhappy, but sometimes I feel like I'm holding on for dear life just to keep us happy.'

'Aha.'

'It's not like things are terrible at home. I love my wife and my daughter. But sometimes I feel like my grip strength is running out, and it would be easier to just let go and fall.'

'I see.' Kabuto had never felt that himself, exactly, but he understands what Matsuda is getting at: *Why am I willing to put up with so much stress just to keep my family happy?* Kabuto had certainly had similar thoughts.

'Emotions don't cancel each other out,' Matsuda goes on.

'What do you mean?'

'When something good happens, it doesn't wipe away the bad things that happen. You can't balance emotions like a checkbook.' They discuss that for a bit when Matsuda asks, 'How old is your son?'

'He's in his third year of high school. Studying for his college entrance exams.' Saying it makes Kabuto tense up momentarily. *I wonder where Katsumi is going to land.*

'Oh that's funny.' Matsuda blinks several times. 'My daughter is in her third year of high school too. Also busy with exams.'

'Huh, imagine that.' Kabuto is pleased at the coincidence. And when they compare notes a bit further they find out to their surprise that Kabuto's son and Matsuda's daughter are at the same school. At first they're both taken aback by the unexpected confluence. Then they shake hands, thrilled.

'I guess we're like . . . dad friends,' Matsuda says.

A warm feeling spreads through Kabuto when he hears Matsuda say this. He never imagined he would make a friend.

When he returns home he finds Katsumi in the living room eating cup ramen. 'You're a growing boy, eat something with some actual nutrition' is something Kabuto would never say. When he was in high school his diet was horrendous, and that was the least concerning aspect of his wild lifestyle. He doesn't feel like he has the right to tell his son what to eat. But more than that, if he gives Katsumi a hard time for eating instant noodles, it could very well come off to his wife as him hinting that she should make her son a proper meal. Wives, and really all women – actually all humans is probably more accurate – are highly sensitive to hidden meanings. They think that behind anything anyone says there might be a second meaning, or a criticism, or an ulterior motive. For human beings, who developed language as the ultimate form of communication, this wariness is probably a survival mechanism. What troubles Kabuto is that he's never putting hidden messages into his words, but somehow his wife always thinks he is. He can't bear it. When it comes to finding the hidden meaning that isn't there, she's a genius.

Katsumi slurps his noodles as he's flipping through vocabulary flash cards. Kabuto thinks about his own teenage years, when he was doing his best just to stay alive. He had more than a few run-ins with the law.

A question pops into his mind: 'What meal is that?' It's three in the afternoon. Late for lunch, early for dinner.

'Lunch, I guess.'

'Don't push yourself too hard.'

'Yeah. I dunno. I figure I'll just do what I can do and that'll have to be that.'

'And if it doesn't work out, at least you tried your best, huh?' Kabuto's wife was always saying that. People can only do what they can do. Once, years ago, Kabuto had asked if that wasn't just another way of saying that man isn't in control of his own destiny. *My way of putting it is nicer, and doesn't sound so self-important,* she said self-importantly. 'Where's Mom?'

'Upstairs. She started cleaning up the clutter and it doesn't look like she can stop.'

Kabuto sighs. Once his wife gets into something, like a book or house cleaning, she seems to completely forget about the passage of time. Especially cleaning. She's tidy by nature, so when she gets fired up with cleaning she really goes for it. Which of course isn't a bad thing in and of itself. But it does tend to upend the family schedule.

Just then he hears footsteps coming down the stairs. His stomach tightens.

'Oh, hi, honey, you're home.'

'Just got back.'

'I started cleaning and I can't stop. There's so much stuff to put away that's been bothering me for a while. And then I had some ideas about where things should go and started rearranging everything. Can I store some stuff in your study?'

'Of course!' She calls it his study but it's really just a slightly renovated closet. Might as well be called Dad's Closet. When he said he wanted to update the house and put in a study, she suggested they build out the closet for him.

'All that cleaning must be tough,' he says.

'It sure is.'

'Thanks for doing it.'

Showing appreciation is rule number one. The other day at

the bouldering gym, Matsuda said the same thing. 'That's what I've learned over nineteen years of marriage. Whenever my wife tells me anything, I tell her that it sounds like it must be tough. That's really the best option. Obviously this applies when she's complaining about something, but also when she's uncertain about something, telling her it sounds tough is the best thing to make her feel better.'

Kabuto agreed. Say for example that she asks him which outfit to wear, he'll usually say, 'Tough choice,' and make a show of sympathy for how difficult a position she's in. Of course, sometimes she yells at him to tell her what he actually thinks. But giving his honest opinion is far from guaranteed to maintain peace in the house.

'I was thinking of making tonkatsu for dinner tonight, does that sound good to you, honey? I have some pork cutlets in the freezer.'

'Sure, sounds great. I was just thinking I wanted to eat tonkatsu.' It's true enough – he had been out doing recon for a job and got hungry for a hearty meal.

'Okay. But I'll be straightening up for a little while more, and then I'll have to go out and buy some panko, so we probably won't end up eating until later.'

'I can go get the panko.'

'Oh, would you?'

'Sure. You're working hard, that must be tough, let me pitch in.'

As she goes back upstairs, Katsumi gives Kabuto a chilly look. 'Dad. Isn't it hard for you to always be bending over backwards to please Mom?'

'Bending over backwards? I'm just trying to help.'

'But you work hard too. You offered to go out and get the panko and Mom just like, assumed that you would do it.'

'That's not true.'

82

'If I get into college and go live somewhere else, I'll be worried about you.'

'What's that supposed to mean?'

'I mean I'll be worried about it just being the two of you together.'

This fills Kabuto with emotion. *You're worried about me?* He wants to wrap his son in a bear hug, but of course he doesn't.

'There's this guy at school, in my class, who's been flipping out a lot recently. He's usually so calm.'

'Is he being bullied?'

'No, no. He's a quiet kid, studies hard, but he's, I dunno.'

'I dunno either.'

'He's lacking social skills.'

'So am I.'

Katsumi laughs at that. 'In the middle of class this guy just starts yelling at the girl next to him. "Don't act like you know! You don't understand!" I don't know the details but apparently he's got like a complicated home life. It must have all built up inside. The girl next to him tried to say something nice to him and he just exploded at her.'

'What's this got to do with me and your mother?'

'I have a feeling that you'll blow up too, sooner or later. You and Mom get along well enough, but it's always you catering to her.'

'Is that what it looks like?' Kabuto's voice gets a touch louder and he leans toward his son. *He can tell! It's obvious to anyone who's watching!* He wants to send up a benediction to heaven. But at the same time another thought occurs to him: The work he's been doing all these years, the work that he can't seem to escape from, the unforgivable work he does trading human lives for some coin – maybe that's obvious to anyone who's watching too. In which case, retribution will come for him. It's only a question of when. One day, he'll have to pay for what he's done. All he wants is for his family to be spared any of his punishment.

'I mean, you're always apologizing to her.'

'I guess that's just my nature. You should be careful not to end up the same way, Katsumi.'

'Though it's also not cool for the man of the house to order everyone else around.'

Kabuto remembers that he needs to go get the panko and lifts himself out of his seat. As he's getting up he asks Katsumi, 'Do you go to school with a girl named Matsuda?'

'Matsuda? You mean Fuka Matsuda?'

'So you know her?'

'Yeah, we're in the same homeroom. Actually, she's the girl who tried to be nice to the guy and he yelled at her.'

Kabuto feels a little bubble of joy at hearing this – Matsuda's daughter and his son don't just go to the same school, they're in the same class, and she organically came up in Katsumi's story. It feels less like coincidence and more like fate. Almost like they're destined to fall in love.

He hears his wife coming down the stairs again and has a sudden feeling like he's doing something wrong, even being unfaithful, though of course he isn't. He's about to ask her if she's done cleaning but before he can she says, 'It looks like I'll be another while,' pointing back upstairs.

'That's tough, dear.'

'I wonder if instead of tonkatsu we shouldn't have something a little lighter. Somen, maybe.'

Kabuto's stomach was already excited about tonkatsu and had been getting ready to receive a big juicy breaded pork cutlet. His wife turns her idea into a question: 'You don't mind, do you?' A normal person would say what they wanted and tell her, 'Actually, I really was in the mood for tonkatsu.' But that's an amateur move. After long years of experience, Kabuto knows exactly how to answer, and wastes no time in doing so:

'I was just thinking that somen might be better.'

Katsumi smirks and goes back to his vocab cards. 'Piteous: worthy of sympathy. Pathetic.'

It's the middle of the day on a weekday, and the clinic waiting room is mostly empty. Just one elderly woman who eases herself slowly into a chair as if her knee is hurting.

'This doctor really doesn't have a good bedside manner, does he?' she says to Kabuto.

He's momentarily surprised at being addressed but then answers, 'No, he doesn't, you're right. If you wanted to put a good spin on it you could say that he's very even-keeled.'

'But he's so cold, like that old saying about not having any blood or tears.'

'If he has a medical degree and experience, then it's not an issue.'

'Well, I suppose that's true. Blood and tears won't fix his patients.'

As she chuckles, Kabuto's name is called and he gets up to go to the exam room.

The doctor is there in his round glasses and white coat. 'Any change since we last met?' he asks vaguely.

'Not much.' *Actually I did make a friend,* Kabuto thinks, but keeps that to himself.

The doctor flips through some charts. 'I recommend this procedure for you.'

Kabuto takes the offered file and looks it over. He doesn't need much time to consider it before he answers. 'I'll pass. It's high risk. Doc, I told you, I'm not interested in any more high-risk operations. I'm really not interested in any more operations.'

'But lower-risk procedures do not involve as much remuneration. And as you have said before, you feel less guilt when you perform a high-risk operation.' The doctor's skin is smooth and his expression is blank. Like a doll. Or an android. Kabuto imagines that one day physicians will be replaced by androids that process test results, calculate probabilities, diagnose illnesses, and print out prescriptions. This doctor seems like a prototype.

'Well? What do you say?' The doctor pushes the file toward him again.

It has the name of a professional who specializes in using bladed tools – scissors, box-cutters, gardening sickles. His physical attributes, his usual territory, a record of the jobs he's pulled. It's all disguised as a patient file, so much of it is coded in medical German. It takes Kabuto a few minutes to translate it.

'When I think of blades I think of Cicada.'

'Ahh, Cicada. I remember him fondly,' the doctor says with zero fondness in his voice.

He goes on to give more details on the job. The target, the professional in question, was trying to cut ties with the group he was affiliated with, and the leadership of the group decided that they wanted him taken out. They didn't put an open bounty on his head, that would be too high-profile, but they did make inquiries with various professionals and go-betweens. It's an old story: death to traitors and deserters.

For Kabuto, who's been wanting to get out of the game ever since Katsumi was born, this might as well be his own story. It's hard for him not to identify with the target.

'Got anything else?' The doctor often has multiple jobs available. Kabuto is hoping one of them is on the less dangerous side. He's gone up against professionals who wield blades in the past. It's not fun. One time he nearly clashed with Cicada, the aforementioned master of knife fighting, but they ended up parting ways without coming to blows. 'And I've been meaning to ask this, but doesn't our industry have any kind of talent turnover?'

'Meaning what?'

'I've been doing this for a long time. But I don't hear much about any up-and-coming young professionals. I get it that experience and well-honed instincts are important, but all the rumors and stories floating around are the same old names. Isn't there any promising new talent?' If there is, he'd be happy to step aside and make room for the next generation of skilled assassins.

'Clients place more trust in those with experience.'

'Sure, but no one has any experience when they first start out.'

'That is true enough. Still, as with all things, there is increasing polarization. The famous gain more fame, and the nameless wallow in obscurity.'

'It's a vicious cycle.'

'Indeed. And that is why those with no renown seek to gain renown. They take on high-risk jobs, seeking famous adversaries.'

Some guys want to get out, and some guys are dying to get in. Kabuto has to laugh at it.

'What about this surgery?' The doctor proffers a different file. 'The parameters are slightly out of the ordinary.'

Kabuto looks it over as he listens to the doctor's subdued explanation. Basically, the job is to furnish the client with a corpse. Out of the ordinary, to be sure. The goal isn't to get rid of any person in particular, but rather to kill someone in order to get a body. The client is apparently looking for a decoy, so they can fake their own death to throw off some pursuers. The file specifies height, blood type, and other identifying physical characteristics.

Find and kill someone who matches all of this? Does this kind of a perfect match even exist?

Before the thought can fully form in Kabuto's head, the doctor tells him that as long as the sex and general age match, the rest can be fudged by manipulating the body. No need to check all the boxes.

'In that case . . .' Kabuto has an idea. 'What if we put it together with the other job? The pro who wants to retire?'

'DIY,' the doctor says, seemingly out of nowhere. For a moment Kabuto has no idea what he's talking about, until he remembers that there's a professional who goes by that moniker. The guy uses tools as weapons, so maybe the name is because he reminds people of a home-improvement enthusiast, or maybe he actually buys his implements at a DIY store.

'What if someone were to take out DIY and give the body to the client on the second job? Two birds with one stone.' Kabuto doesn't want to be the one to have to do it, but he does think it's pretty clever.

'You propose using the tumor extracted in the first surgery for the second case?'

'Exactly.'

The doctor shakes his head from side to side, slowly, as if expressing pity for Kabuto. 'The two operations cannot be handled together.'

'Why not? I think it's perfect.'

'The client for the second procedure is the target of the first.'

In other words, DIY wants to get out of his organization and is looking for a body to fake his death.

That means that the doctor received requests from both sides – kill DIY, and also locate a decoy corpse on behalf of DIY. It strikes Kabuto as humorous, but it also means that they can't take on both contracts.

'Are you interested in either procedure?'

Kabuto shrugs. Coming up with a corpse would be the easier job. He could just kill any civilian. But taking out DIY would be less guilt, and more money. Killing an innocent person is more likely to attract attention, and on top of that, choosing the target would take time and consideration.

He tells the doctor that he needs some time to think about it and takes his leave of the exam room. The old woman is still sitting in the waiting room. She grins and bobs her head in his direction. *Wonder if she's a professional too. Or she could just be a regular patient.* He'd be fine with either one.

'I met up today with some women I haven't seen in a long time,' his wife tells him.

'Who's that?'

The three of them are sitting at the dining table, eating sukiyaki.

'Some of the other mothers on the PTA from when Katsumi was in elementary school. Four of us, including me. We thought we would get together for lunch, it'd been so long.'

'That sounds tough.'

'How'd you know?'

He isn't quite sure how to answer and stuffs his mouth with the leek he had in his chopsticks.

'It got me to thinking.'

Uh huh, mmhmm, he says, showing that he's listening. Inside he's praying that whatever happened didn't stress her out too much. Meanwhile Katsumi deftly cracks open an egg with one hand while the other flips through his flashcards.

'Do you remember a Suzumura? In Katsumi's class?'

Kabuto looks up from his food and says as little as he can. 'Girl?'

'That's right. So her mom was there. It turns out her husband just died. He was a pharmacist.'

Kabuto almost chokes on the meat he had just shoveled into his mouth. 'How?' He pictures the pharmacist he had killed on a recent job, trying to remember his name. Had he unknowingly killed one of Katsumi's former classmates' fathers? And shouldn't he be upset about killing anyone, period, whether or not it was one of Katsumi's classmates' dads? He tells himself in no uncertain terms that he needs to get out of this line of work, and fast.

'She said it was a car accident.'

'Oh! Oh, that's . . . that's awful.' Kabuto feels a rush of relief. He quickly starts stirring the contents of the hotpot, hoping that his relief doesn't show.

'Mrs Suzumura looked so upset, none of us knew what to say.'

'Yeah. I can imagine.' Kabuto isn't especially sad about it, but he tries to make it sound like he is.

'But then Mrs Hisamoto – Katsumi, do you remember Hisamoto, in your class? Energetic boy?'

'Yeah, sure. Hisamoto. We used to hang out.'

'So Mrs Hisamoto said something she thought might make her feel better. And I thought what she said was totally fine. Completely natural. But Mrs Suzumura got so mad. "What would you know about it," she said. "*Your* husband didn't die in a car accident!"'

'Oh man,' Katsumi says with a grimace.

Kabuto thinks about the story Katsumi told him the other day, about his high school class. Someone going through something difficult snapped at someone else who tried to comfort them, saying they would never understand. It's basically the same situation.

'I guess I know where she's coming from. I mean, she just suddenly lost her husband.'

'I know, that's terrible, her husband is gone.' Kabuto says it emphatically, hoping that the idea takes root in his wife's mind. He wants her to wonder, what if I lost my husband? He wants her to picture herself wishing that she had been nicer to him.

'But then I was thinking, if someone yells at you and tells you that you have no idea how tough it is, I mean, what are you supposed to do about that?' She sounds upset. 'Mrs Hisamoto was only trying to be nice.'

'You're right. That's tough to navigate.' He gets up to refill his empty bowl from the rice cooker. His wife raises her eyebrows and tells him that she would have gotten him rice if he had asked her, but he knows better than to expect her to pamper him. Doing it himself is the safest course of action.

'But wait,' Katsumi says as Kabuto resumes his seat at the table. 'Did Hisamoto's mom say anything?'

'What do you mean?' She doesn't follow, and neither does Kabuto. 'It's because Mrs Hisamoto said something that Mrs Suzumura got angry.'

'No no, I mean, I guess she didn't, like, talk about her own situation. Which is kind of impressive.' Katsumi nods, processing the information.

'What are you talking about?' Kabuto asks.

'Hisamoto's sister and dad both died in an accident, a while back.'

Kabuto's wife freezes, except for her eyelids blinking in disbelief. Then she turns to look at Kabuto, her head swiveling robotically. He flinches, thinking he's about to be criticized, and tries to sit up straighter. His heart is pounding. *I should say something.* 'That's crazy.' He turns to Katsumi. 'Is that true?'

'Yes, it's true. Hisamoto told me about it when we were in middle school. Apparently they don't talk about it much.'

'So then it's just him and his mother?' Katsumi's mother asks.

'Yeah, a mother-son household. Which explains why Hisamoto has always been so close with his mom.'

'So then today when Mrs Suzumura said, "You wouldn't understand how I feel," then Mrs Hisamoto . . .'

'I'd say she probably understands.' Katsumi is a little brusque, a little bored-sounding.

'I wonder why she didn't say that her husband and daughter had died too.'

Kabuto just sits there listening to his wife and son. For so long he's been doing his best to stay alive, he's never had room for any emotions when someone else dies. He's never even thought how someone might feel when they lose a loved one.

'Maybe she didn't say anything because she knows exactly how Mrs Suzumura feels, and she knew that it wouldn't help.' Kabuto's wife seems to say this to herself. Suddenly she starts to cry. Her eyes are shut tight and the tears come like they're being squeezed out, one after the next. Kabuto just watches. 'It must be so hard for them.'

'That is really tough,' Kabuto says, his expression blank. He doesn't have a perfect grasp on the feeling behind his wife's tears, but he's starting to understand. He wants to understand more. He's like an alien steadily observing human behavior in order to comprehend their thoughts and feelings.

I have to get out of the game, he thinks while chewing another piece of meat. He knows it might be too late, but he doesn't want to fade away without understanding the way people's hearts work.

The bouldering gym is mostly empty, so Kabuto can climb again and again. He climbs and prays, for his family's health and safety, for his wife to be forever in a peaceful mood. He hops down off the crashpad to catch his breath and reapply chalk.

Standing next to him is a young woman. 'You're amazing, you just shoot right up the wall!' She smiles, revealing a neat row of white teeth. She's objectively good-looking – short hair, workout clothes, seemingly made entirely of wholesome ingredients.

'I guess I've gotten the hang of it,' Kabuto replies, immediately feeling a stab of nerves. He knows there's nothing wrong with him chatting with other women, and he has no illicit intentions. But it could be a trap set by his wife. A test. While that doesn't seem likely, he can't escape the feeling that his wife is watching him, gauging his reactions.

This has to do with your guilty conscience from all the bad things you've done, an internal voice opines. *You've broken the rules and taken people's lives, so you don't deserve to have a happy home life. The things you've done are unforgivable, and your life could fall apart at any moment – at least that's what you're scared of, which is why you can never relax.*

Kabuto argues with himself: *No, I'm just scared of my wife!*

He's relieved when Matsuda shows up, as if his friend were a family doctor paying a visit to help settle his unstable nerves.

'Hi, Miyake-san.' Matsuda comes over and starts warming up.

It's after he falls off the wall near the end of the blue route, which he normally never has a problem with, that Kabuto notices Matsuda's face is drawn and pale. 'No good today,' Matsuda says, scratching his head. His eyes are puffy. He looks exhausted.

'Are you feeling okay?' Kabuto asks.

Matsuda knits his brows. 'That obvious, huh?'

'Obvious enough.' *After all, we are friends,* Kabuto wants to add.

'My wife and I were up late last night arguing.'

'Arguing?'

'Yeah. Which we don't typically do. I guess because usually I don't push back at all. So maybe I should say that I don't argue with her. But this time, I don't know, we got into it about her parents.'

He goes on to explain that his in-laws run their own business, and business hasn't been good. They came asking for some money. Matsuda wasn't unwilling to help them out, but their attitude was so high-handed and entitled that he lost his temper.

'My wife works too, and together we make decent money. So neither she nor her parents took what I was saying seriously at all. I just felt, I don't know, awful.'

'Hmm.' Kabuto doesn't quite know what he should say. He's at a bit of a loss because the particular friction Matsuda is experiencing has never come up in his own home. 'That sounds tough.'

'So for a change I spoke my mind, and she got angry with me. But here's the weird thing – I was doing my best to choose my words carefully, but she just blew her stack and said some things that she can't really take back.'

Kabuto considers saying that men and women are wired differently, though that feels a little reductive. Instead he just encourages Matsuda to go on.

'I mean I guess it was just an argument. But I'm just feeling so worn out. I'm questioning what I'm doing with my life. And when I start thinking that way I get too stressed to sleep.'

Listening to Matsuda, Kabuto tries to characterize the feelings that are welling up inside of him. Sympathy? Empathy? Or something different – the pity he feels toward his victims on a job?

'But, hey, you know what, Miyake-san?' Matsuda's face crumples into something Kabuto would almost call a smile. 'When I couldn't sleep I was doing some cleanup and I found a picture my daughter drew of me when she was little.'

'Oh yeah?'

'It's in crayon. I think she did it when she was in pre-school, for father's day. It even kind of looks like me.'

'That's great.'

'It says "You're the best, Daddy".'

'Nice.' Kabuto thinks back to when Katsumi was in pre-school. He recalls getting a similar picture. It's probably somewhere in the house now. *Maybe I'll look for it when I get home.*

'Then today when I got here I thought,' Matsuda says, pointing to the climbing wall, 'those colorful rocks look they were drawn on in crayon.'

Kabuto can see it.

The two of them climb, clinging fast to the colored rocks,

trying earnestly to hold on to the memories of when their children were young.

How about we go for a drink, Matsuda suggests, and Kabuto is thrilled. He usually only goes out to bars with other professionals, killing time on a job, or because the target is a patron. Outside of work, this is probably the first time anyone has ever invited him out. He used to go out with his wife, before they were married. But nowadays that period of their relationship, when they were young and newly in love, seems like ancient history, as distant as the Bronze Age.

Matsuda suggests they go to his regular place and tells Kabuto the location. It's not somewhere Kabuto has ever been before but he doesn't mind. The only potential snag is that he realizes he hasn't told his wife that he'll be home later than expected. He's about to excuse himself to get in touch when Matsuda takes out his own phone and makes an apologetic gesture. Since they're both cut from the same tending-to-wife cloth, they both immediately understand. *Like telepathy!* Pleased, Kabuto calls home.

He tells his wife that he's going out for a drink. 'Oh, you are?' She almost sounds happy about it. She must be having a good day, or maybe she hadn't gotten started on dinner yet and the extra time helps.

'Okay, I'll see you later,' he says, glancing over to see Matsuda nodding and bowing on the phone. Kabuto realizes that he himself is also bobbing his head up and down. *We really are two of a kind.*

The main drag of the bar district is lively. Salarymen in suits stagger about and young people pass by, shouting and laughing.

Kabuto enjoys his conversation with Matsuda. They talk about finding the right timing to bring up something their wives might not want to hear about, they talk about the importance of putting on a cheery face no matter how hard a day they've had at work. Topics that most people would find uninteresting, but to Kabuto it feels like they're discussing the secrets of the universe.

'You know, Miyake-san, I keep a log with all these tips and tricks.'

'Really? For what?'

'Not to show it to anyone. But when I run into trouble it helps. Sometimes when I'm dealing with my wife I forget a key technique, and it's good to be able to reference it.'

'Smart.'

'And it makes me feel good to get down in writing what I've learned. Like I've accomplished something.'

Kabuto thinks it's a great idea, and he decides that he'll give it a try himself.

The conversation is bouncing along and they haven't even gotten to the bar; Kabuto imagines that once they sit down and have a few drinks they'll lose track of the time enjoying themselves.

As they walk, they pass by a group of unsavory-looking younger guys, one of whom bumps shoulders with Matsuda.

Matsuda immediately apologizes, but the guy rubs his own shoulder and says threateningly, 'You think you can just say you're sorry and that's it?' The two other guys he's with, dressed similarly, line up next to him, facing down Matsuda and Kabuto. 'Watch where you're fuckin' going, old man!'

Kabuto has no intention of mixing it up with these youngsters. 'Come on, let's go,' he says, pulling Matsuda along. As he tries to walk off, though, one of the guys grabs his jacket from behind.

'Hey, where'dya think you're going?' The guy gets up in Kabuto's face. *What a pain in the ass.* The only emotion Kabuto feels is annoyance. But he also doesn't want to waste any time with these punks.

Matsuda, looking concerned, tries to get between Kabuto and

the guy, but Kabuto holds a hand up to block his friend. 'Let's get out of here.'

The guy just holds on tighter to Kabuto's jacket, which is completely expected. Kabuto takes a handkerchief from his pocket and drops it near Matsuda.

Matsuda bends over to pick it up, and in that moment Kabuto slips out of his jacket and wraps it around the guy's hand in one smooth movement, then twists his body and breaks the guy's finger. The guy's eyes widen at the sudden pain, but before he can make a sound Kabuto clamps his other hand down over the guy's mouth. He brings his mouth close to the guy's ear and whispers, 'Leave, now, or I'll break the rest of your fingers. I'll break them in multiple places.' The guy's face goes white and the other two look rattled. Kabuto unwraps the jacket and deftly pulls it back on.

Matsuda stands back up and holds out the handkerchief, which Kabuto accepts. The young guys have already beaten a hasty retreat.

They turn off the main drag onto a side street and come to an intersection, where they stand waiting for the light to change. They're chatting with each other when someone from off to the side says, 'Um, excuse me.' Kabuto tenses up, ready. It could be those punks back for revenge, or it could be another professional targeting him.

It turns out to be a young woman, very pregnant, asking for directions. He doesn't let down his guard entirely, knowing that she could be an assassin just pretending to be pregnant, but after sizing her up he decides that she's not dangerous.

Matsuda politely gives her directions. Standing there listening, Kabuto thinks back to when his wife still had Katsumi in her belly.

Then he notices that the street they're on is otherwise deserted. There are a few streetlamps, but it's fairly dark. And out of the darkness appears a lanky man in a mask. Gripped in his hand is a kitchen knife, about fifteen centimeters long.

Matsuda's eyes go wide and he reflexively steps in front of the pregnant woman. Kabuto gets into a loose stance so he can act quickly if he needs to, gauging the distance to the masked man. The knife makes him think it's an attack targeting him, but the masked man seems more interested in Matsuda and the pregnant woman. 'Gimme your money!'

'Okay, we'll give you money.' Matsuda starts to reach for his bag but the masked man shouts at him and starts waving the knife around. Then he slashes at Kabuto, who dodges backward a step.

The woman stands there rigid, plainly terrified. Matsuda has both hands over his head in a gesture of surrender. Kabuto puts his hands up too. The masked man is leaving himself open in so many different ways, it won't be hard at all for Kabuto to make a move. On the other hand, he doesn't want to get into a fight in front of Matsuda.

To neutralize an armed opponent as agitated as this man is, he'd have to be fairly violent. He's worried that after seeing that Matsuda wouldn't want to associate with him anymore. *I finally made a friend. I don't want to mess that up.* He can't decide what to do.

The masked man seems to think that Matsuda and the pregnant woman are together. His shrill scream sounds from behind the mask: 'Well aren't you the happy couple!'

Matsuda says falteringly, 'No, no we're not that.'

The woman also waves her hand in denial, but she's too frightened to say anything. She has a ring on her finger, which catches the light as she waves. The glitter in the dark seems to enrage the masked man even more.

'I'll kill you and your baby!'

Matsuda shouts to the woman, 'Run!' She's too pregnant to really run, but she starts to move away as fast as she can.

The masked man is furious and starts toward her but Matsuda intercepts him. Kabuto is right there on his other side. The man's hand is trembling from fear and excitement. *This guy doesn't know how to use a knife,* Kabuto realizes. Definitely an amateur. Looks fairly young too. *Giving in to despair, I guess.*

'You have no idea what's it like for someone like me!' the masked man wails.

The same line of thinking Kabuto has heard a couple times over the past few days. People telling someone that they have no idea how they feel.

'You're so happy, it makes me sick!' the masked man says viciously.

'You think I'm *happy*?'

The words ring out hard in the air.

Not from Kabuto.

From beside him. From Matsuda.

'You think *I* am happy? Maybe *you* have no idea what it's like for someone like *me*!' Matsuda is furious, nostrils flaring and face turning scarlet.

The masked man looks momentarily taken aback, but he didn't have such a firm grip to begin with, and he starts making stabbing motions in Matsuda's direction. 'What the hell would you know about it?!' His voice is strained.

'What makes you say that I'm happy? You can't imagine the stress I carry around with me every day!' Matsuda looks like he's about to launch into a fiery monologue. He seems to have forgotten that Kabuto is even there. He lays out in detail all the persecutions he suffers at his wife's hands, even down to the fact that it's been years since she let him touch her.

His shoulders heave like he's an animal menacing its prey. All the toxic sludge that had built up and built up inside of him has

99

become superheated, boiling over. Kabuto wouldn't be surprised to see steam pouring from his ears.

'You're still better off than me,' the masked man says, but Matsuda shouts over him.

'You think I'm happy!' It echoes down the dark street like a battle cry. Matsuda slams into the man.

Kabuto doesn't react in the moment. It's not that he's surprised at the attack, but rather that he was powerfully affected by Matsuda's emotional eruption. They're allies: both cowed by their wives, both spending their days stressed and worried, but what Matsuda's dealing with is clearly on a different level.

Matsuda knocks the man to the ground and mounts him, punching him savagely in the face, over and over again.

Kabuto carefully approaches, looking around to make sure that no one is seeing this. Matsuda is gasping for breath as he brings his fists up and down. Kabuto pats him gently on the shoulder. He looks up with a start. Seeing Kabuto, he comes back to himself, his eyes opening wide.

'Easy.' Kabuto helps Matsuda up to his feet. 'Right now the best thing is to calm yourself down. Take a deep breath.'

Matsuda listens like an obedient child, inhaling and exhaling, while Kabuto steps over and inspects the masked man. He's not moving. Kabuto slides off the mask and sees that the mouth is gaping like empty space. No light in the eyes. Definitely dead. Checking the pulse confirms it.

Probably died when he first fell and hit the back of his head on the ground.

'Miyake-san.' Matsuda sinks onto his knees. He looks like he's in shock. 'How did this . . .'

Kabuto is used to seeing dead people. More often than not they're dead because of him. But he has zero experience talking to someone who's just accidentally killed somebody, let alone trying to comfort them. He has no idea what to say.

He ends up going over to Matsuda and telling him, 'This wasn't your fault.'

'What?'

'Anyone would get angry if someone talked to them like that. Like he was the unhappiest in the world and everyone else was just fine.' Kabuto isn't just saying it. He actually believes it.

Matsuda is still stunned, unable to properly form words. He looks at his hands, then over at the dead man. His breathing starts to speed up again.

Kabuto has seen people in this condition before. Unable to process what's happening, unable to understand how their life has brought them to that point, with no warning or planning or preamble. They don't accept the reality of the situation; somewhere in their hearts they believe that it can still be fixed. He's seen it in the people who do a thing and in the people who have the thing done to them.

He crouches down next to Matsuda, who turns to him. 'What do I . . . ? How did this . . . ? Miyake-san, what's going to happen?'

'You didn't do anything wrong,' Kabuto says. 'That guy was the kind of asshole who would go after a pregnant lady. And for no reason! He brought this on himself. I think he was dead before you even started hitting him.'

'It's all over.'

'What's over?'

'This is going to ruin my life. And my daughter's! What's going to happen?'

He looks at his hands, shaking violently.

'I'll take care of this,' Kabuto says. 'Go home. What you did wasn't really that bad. Remember that.'

Of course Matsuda doesn't accept this, twisting his head back and forth and sputtering for a few moments, but Kabuto knows they can't just hang out here. He walks them a short way to hail a cab and has to half-force Matsuda to get in. 'We'll go for a drink next time.'

Now on his own, Kabuto knows what to do.

He takes out his phone and places a call: the doctor's night-time emergency line. He doesn't imagine the doctor is sleeping, but it takes a while for him to answer.

'I did the DIY job.'

'Which one?'

'The one DIY contracted. I don't know if he'll be able to use it, but I got my hands on a dead body double.'

'Did you perform the surgery yourself?'

'I found it on the side of the road.' He gives his location.

The doctor doesn't laugh. 'I will send someone immediately.' He hangs up.

In less than ten minutes, a white car blaring a siren pulls up.

'Hey, Dad, didn't you say that you knew Fuka Matsuda's dad?' Katsumi asks while they're sitting in the living room watching TV.

'Yeah.' Kabuto has an idea of what Katsumi might be about to tell him.

'She changed schools.'

'Oh yeah?'

After that night, he hadn't run into Matsuda at the bouldering gym. He thought that maybe their schedules just weren't match-ing up, but when he asked the gym attendant he found out that Matsuda hadn't been by at all.

Kabuto can guess why.

Either he didn't know what to do with himself after the events of that night, or else he was scared of Kabuto after he offered to handle the body but gave no explanation.

'And just before exams. That's really tough.'

'Yeah. I also heard that her parents got divorced.'

102

'Huh. Wow.' *He left his wife. He set himself free.*

Matsuda must have realized that he couldn't keep his grip on the wall anymore. *I hope he's in a better place,* Kabuto can't help thinking.

His wife comes downstairs. Lately she's been reorganizing like it's the new fashionable thing to do. Any free moment she has she spends moving things around.

'Look what I found.' She places an old box on the table and removes the lid. Inside are stacks of folded up drawing paper. She takes one out and spreads it open. It's a drawing in crayon. 'From when Katsumi was in pre-school.'

It's a man with a big head, and letters that are just barely legible: 'Thank you for taking care of us Daddy.'

Matsuda-san, my son drew one for me too! He wishes he could tell his friend.

'I should probably hang on to these,' she says.

'Of course you should!' Kabuto surprises himself with how forcefully he says it.

He gazes at the picture for a little while longer, unable to form a proper thought. His chest aches, and at the center of the ache is a hole. He wishes he could paper it over with crayon drawings.

'Dad, what's up?' Katsumi hugs one knee as he looks through his textbook.

'Oh,' Kabuto says, his voice a bit husky, 'I had just gotten friendly with her father.'

Kabuto spends less and less time at the bouldering gym, but when he's there, gripping the holds, once in a while, he sends up a prayer that he might see Matsuda again.

EXIT

HAVING LOTS OF FRIENDS IS not necessarily a good thing. Kabuto's wife said that once a while back, maybe when Katsumi was getting ready to start at elementary school.

Some might respond to that by saying, 'You're absolutely right!' But Kabuto had learned that this isn't the best idea. It's important not to give automatic and unconditional agreement. Far better to ask, 'Oh really, why not?' and solicit the speaker's reasoning, listening along and saying that each point is sensible and logical and finally saying, 'Ah, I see,' being sure to nod firmly. That's what Kabuto did when his wife first weighed in on friendship.

'I just think that you're better off with one close friend, some-one you really get along with. I've got this one friend, and a different friend of hers asked to borrow money. Caused all sorts of problems. And then another friend of mine, one of her other friends stole her boyfriend. And another of my friends has a friend who's so jealous of her and treats her so badly.'

Sounds like you actually have a lot of friends, Kabuto had wanted to say, but he didn't. He got the point she was trying to make.

What's the point of quantity for quantity's sake? Far better to aim for quality. The same critique that's been made so many times since the industrial revolution and the advent of mass production.

Saying 'We should all make lots of friends' is basically the same as saying 'We should try to be the kind of people who don't cause any friction and can more or less get along with everyone.'

To Kabuto, who has lived his life with very few significant relationships, and who makes his money killing people (which goes a bit beyond causing friction), this seems like an idea from another world.

His day job at the office supplies company has given him experience interacting with other people. He makes plenty of client calls and has participated in no small number of happy hours with his coworkers. But none of that goes any deeper than surface level. He just goes through the motions, copying what he sees around him as a model for how people are supposed to behave when they're friendly.

'I find it somewhat odd that you have no close relationships besides your wife.'

The doctor had said that to him recently. The doctor typically only talks about work, and he conceals that as medical consultation and explanation of symptoms. He almost never brings up anything personal, so this comment seemed to come out of nowhere.

Kabuto understood what it meant.

For a long while the doctor has been saying that it would take some time before Kabuto could retire, that he needed to work until prior investments made in him had been paid off. *And if not . . .* Kabuto knows that the advice to keep working conceals a threat. *If you don't keep working, it could put your family in danger.* The doctor's only reason for bringing up Kabuto's wife is to remind him of the possibility that he could lose his family. He made the comment when Kabuto was hesitating about taking on a job – which, to be fair, has been the case with all his prospective jobs of late – and the doctor no doubt wanted to emphasize this point. *Your family is important to you, isn't it?*

'I enjoyed spending time with her.' That's all Kabuto answered. He said it in the past tense, although he still enjoys his time with her. What's different is that when they first met he was more relaxed. Nowadays he's suffused with a prickly concern over how to keep her happy. It's difficult for him to get in touch with his more easygoing younger self.

'Given that you are able to get along with your wife, have you never thought that you might be able to get along with other people as well?'

'I've thought about it.' Kabuto didn't mean he's thought about a relationship with another woman. But he has asked himself if he might not be able to enjoy being a bit more social. 'My wife's around though. That's enough for me.'

'You share a very admirable matrimonial love.'

'At least I hope we do.' It's also true that he spends his days on edge, watching her mood. 'How about you, doc?'

'What about me?'

'Have you ever made any friends?'

The doctor made a disdainful face, saying nothing.

'Miyake-san, are you sure I'm not disrupting your work? I do appreciate you giving me some time.' Sitting across from Kabuto, Nanomura dips his head in gratitude. Chilly winds have been blowing in the Kanto region, signaling the approach of winter, but the man uses a handkerchief to wipe sweat from his brow. He's on the shorter side, slightly paunchy and with a face that's vaguely block-shaped.

He's a security guard. About six months ago he had been assigned to this department store, and he and Kabuto started to run into one another when Kabuto would come by on sales calls to the stationery section. Over the past month they had grown closer.

It started with a kid trying to shoplift.

Kabuto had just finished going over the new product line with the stationery manager in the back room when he went out onto the floor and noticed a kid who looked to be about middle-school age testing out the pens. It was immediately clear the kid was going to try to lift some merchandise. Nothing he was doing was overtly suspicious, which was likely a testament to his comfort with stealing. But to Kabuto, it was plain as day that the kid was up to something.

He had no intention of stopping the kid. After all, when he was this kid's age, he was involved in much more serious crimes than shoplifting. What right did he have to tell some kid how to live?

That's when Nanomura showed up.

In civilian clothes rather than his security guard uniform, he walked over to the kid. A moment later he staggered – the kid had pushed him. Then the kid fled, scowling as he went.

'Are you okay?' Kabuto called to Nanomura.

'I messed up.'

'You know, if you want to catch a shoplifter, you should prob-ably call him out once he's left the store.' It seemed pretty dumb to confront someone about theft before they'd even left the store. And then to not go after him – Kabuto was genuinely curi-ous why this man didn't take the most basic steps to catch the kid.

'If I waited until he'd left the store then he'd have already stolen it.' He smiled good-naturedly.

'But he *did* steal it.'

'I thought maybe I could get him to change his mind.'

It's not too late, you can still put that back. Or something similar – Kabuto doesn't know exactly what he said, but whatever it was made the kid shove him and run.

'I suppose I was too hopeful.'

'Maybe, but it's not a bad hope.' Kabuto meant it. 'Yelling at kids doesn't necessarily make them learn wrong from right.'

'He was the same age as my boy,' Nanomura said, sheepishly explaining the source of his hope.

It turned out that the shoplifting kid was caught by a maintenance staffer who was loading drinks into a vending machine near the stairs. The kid was in a rush and kicked a box of plastic bottles out of the way, and when he didn't apologize the maintenance man got angry and chased him down.

From that day on, whenever Kabuto and Nanomura encountered one another, they exchanged the greeting of comrades who were in on a secret. Kabuto knew how to interact at the surface level, going through the motions of small talk and pleasantries, and at first that's how it was with Nanomura. But before long he realized that he was enjoying their conversations.

They had in common being the father of a single son, and on top of that Nanomura mostly talked about the weather, or the seasons, or other innocuous topics. Kabuto appreciated that.

'Nanomura-san, you're a very considerate fellow.'

'Oh? Considerate?'

'You always choose easy conversation topics. No sharp edges.'

He laughed self-consciously. 'As long as we're talking, the topic doesn't matter so much. The important thing is just saying hello and sharing some words together. People have different religions and ideologies; to some people sports is like religion. It just seems like it's quite easy to run into friction. The weather is much safer.'

'The weather is a safe topic. For sure. Although it doesn't usually go anywhere.' Kabuto was just saying what was on his mind. But Nanomura burst out laughing.

'That's exactly right!'

Though there was one time when they were talking about the weather, which led to talking about the seasons, which somehow got them onto talking about insects. Nanomura said, 'I raise *kabuto mushi*.' For some reason he seemed embarrassed to have a beetle hobby. He started out doing it with his son, but he got more and more interested, and now he's just like a breeder, monitoring the temperature in the nest to incubate the larvae and raise especially large specimens. Kabuto had an odd feeling listening to Nanomura talk about his rhinoceros beetles, given the link with his underworld alias, but the more he heard the more fascinating he found it. It got to be that every time they met he would ask about how the beetles were doing.

Huh. I guess we must be friends.

The understanding grew gradually stronger. It occurred to him that this must have been what Helen Keller felt like when her teacher poured water on one hand and spelled out w-a-t-e-r on the palm of her other hand – *so this is water* – but then he immediately felt guilt for comparing himself to someone so inspirational.

He almost had another friend, once, a few years ago, someone he'd met at the bouldering gym who had disappeared.

Whenever he thinks about it Kabuto feels a pang, like a lonesome wind is blowing. But he can't even remember the man's name now.

In any case, he felt lucky to have met someone else he got along with, so when Nanomura asked if he could talk to him about something, Kabuto happily agreed. To be precise, first he noticed that Nanomura was looking downcast and asked if he was feeling alright.

'Oh, yes, I'm fine,' Nanomura said, but then after a moment he spoke up again. 'Actually, Miyake-san, I wonder if I can talk to you about something.' And here they are now, seated facing one another at a four-top in the café on the third floor of the department store.

'I'm about to go on my night shift,' Nanomura begins.

'That's tough,' Kabuto says politely.

It doesn't especially matter what makes it tough. Everyone in the world has something tough to deal with, so it's always a safe bet to make people feel like their struggle is noticed and appreciated. He's learned that from living with his wife. Since they started living together, and especially since Katsumi was born, most of her discontent can be boiled down to the notion that he doesn't know just how tough things are for her. Or at least that's his read on it.

'The work itself isn't so bad.' Nanomura mops his brow again. As he moves his hand, it nearly knocks over his glass of water. Also, when the café waitress came to take their order he kind of mumbled it so that she had to ask him to repeat it twice. It gives Kabuto the sense that Nanomura hasn't had the smoothest ride in life, although to be fair he's not basing that off of much.

'It seems like it would be kind of tough to patrol the whole building at night. I bet it's a little scary.'

'Oh no, I like the way it feels in the department store at night. It has a special kind of feel.'

'But still.'

'I do feel responsible, though. If there were some trouble, or some kind of loss or damage, I would just feel terrible. They're putting their faith in me.'

'You're very committed.' Kabuto says it sincerely. Naturally, security guards need to take responsibility for what happens on their watch, but to feel that invested in it, to put it in terms of faith and trust, that doesn't seem like something just anyone would do.

'Commitment is my strong point,' Nanomura replies. 'But I can't help but feel that my son doesn't think much of me.'

'Why is that?'

'Well, I'm not very good with people, and I've always been rather quiet. Basically, I'm just not that impressive. Certainly not the kind of father a son would feel any respect for.'

'Come on, I'm sure that's not true.' Kabuto's voice is firm and he leans in as he speaks. He's thinking about his own son. 'What's an impressive job, anyhow? And quiet, that just means you know how to enjoy your days peacefully, that's all.' People who insist on being bright and upbeat can't enjoy their life without involving other people. 'I would think that your son would be proud to have a father like you, who lives his life with a sense of commitment.'

Nanomura looks uncertain. 'You're being too kind, Miyake-san. What's making you say all this?'

'I mean it!' At the very least, Nanomura's job is far more worthy of praise than the things Kabuto does for money.

'Well, I do appreciate you saying so. But, you know, as a father, the respect of my son . . .'

'I hear you. You don't want him to be disappointed in you.'

That's one of the reasons why he wants to have a friend. *My dad doesn't even have a single friend* – if that's what Katsumi thought, no doubt he'd think less of his father. The thought makes Kabuto feel very small indeed. Having lots of friends is not necessarily a good thing. Even having one friend isn't a guaranteed good thing. Kabuto knows this, but he can't help feeling the pull.

'So the other day my son said he wanted to come see what my job was like.'

'Oh yeah? Well, that's encouraging. You do a great job as a security guard.'

'He said he wanted to see what it was like to patrol the department store late at night.'

'It does seem like it would be fascinating to see the store after

111

hours. He's in middle school, right? My boy's in college now, but I remember middle school being the toughest years.' He doesn't actually recall much of it, but his wife is always saying *This is nothing compared to when he was middle school,* and *the middle school years were the roughest,* often enough that he's started to feel it himself. 'You should let him come.'

'I should, shouldn't I?'

'Are you worried about getting permission?' Kabuto could imagine Nanomura getting tripped up on that point.

'I don't expect they'd be thrilled about it. If my son is with me and there happens to be any trouble, that would make it worse, and it's mixing business with personal, which isn't ideal. What if a Shinkansen conductor wanted their kid to see them working and brought them into the control room? That wouldn't be good at all.'

'Sure, but patrolling a department store doesn't involve so many people's safety in the same way.'

'I suppose that is true.' It seems like Nanomura is too worried to make up his mind. 'It's always just me here by myself, so it wouldn't be hard to sneak my son in. Maybe the next time I have night duty . . .'

'I think that sounds like a great idea.' Leaving aside standard operating procedure and professional responsibility, from the standpoint of fostering a son's admiration for his father, it's obviously a green light.

But Nanomura's face sags in his block-shaped head. 'There's something else that's on my mind, though.'

'Dad, did you say something to piss off Mom?'

Kabuto is reading a book in the living room when Katsumi comes in and asks, keeping his voice low. Kabuto immediately sits up ramrod straight.

'Why? What happened?' he asks searchingly.

'Nothing really. She just seems crabby.'

'Where is she?'

'She's out. Something about the neighborhood newsletter.'

Kabuto's mind begins spinning, going back over the past few hours of everything he and his wife talked about and everything she might have seen him do. It's like an emergency summit inside his head. *Did I screw up somehow?*

Maybe I spent too much time taking it easy this morning? But that's his normal Sunday routine. An hour earlier she had asked him what he wanted for lunch. Naturally he wasn't stupid enough to say he'd be fine with anything. He gave a few suggestions for things he thought wouldn't be much trouble for her to make. Shouldn't have been any problem there. *Did I give too automatic an answer to something she said?*

'Dad, you're way too worried about it.' Katsumi laughs and sprawls out on the sofa. 'I was just asking. If nothing comes to mind, forget about it.'

Kabuto marvels at how his son went from being so little once to taking up the entire couch.

'Hey, I'm reading that book you recommended.' Kabuto holds up the paperback in his hands.

'Which one?'

'By Komao Furuyama.'

'Did I recommend that? I know it was on an exam I had.'

Come to think of it, Katsumi might not have specifically recommended it. He just mentioned that it was a story of the horrors of wartime. He said that the novel paints a picture of the terror and anguish, but somehow with a light touch, and even a bit of humor, which only makes the story more poignant.

To Kabuto, who had spent so much of his life working in the shadows, grisly stories were nothing new, but he appreciates the warmth and resilience the author conjures up in this book.

'Did you read the part yet where the guy warms up the prisoner?' Katsumi asks.

'Yeah, I did.'

A naked prisoner of war was freezing, and the main character found himself hugging them to keep them warm, which upset the main character's commanding officer. The protagonist thought he was helping, but he only made it worse. – *I just thought that I could do something to keep him warm. But then they hurt him even more badly, and then they killed him.* The narration is straightforward, unadorned. Katsumi didn't go out of his way to memorize it, but somehow it had stuck with him, and he told his father about it.

It didn't seem to Kabuto like he was reading a war novel. It felt much closer, more relatable, like an allegory that would work just as well in a contemporary setting. No doubt something to do with his entanglement in work where life and death hang in the balance. – *A person's whole life can just be snuffed out on the merest whim of some stupid general.* When he read that line, he pictured the face of the doctor who arranges his jobs.

He had just been reading the section that begins with *Tell me the difference between a friend and an acquaintance.* The author gives a non-answer to the question: *An acquaintance with whom you are close is a friend. A friend with whom you are not close is an acquaintance.* This frustrates Kabuto, and he looks up *friend* in the dictionary. What he learns is that there is no word more vague than *friend*. Except for maybe *closeness*.

Either way, given his current state of longing for a friend, he wishes he could shake the hand of the now-departed author for writing such a timeless story.

'Katsumi, do you have any friends?' he asks without thinking too much about the question.

'Huh? What's that supposed to mean?' Katsumi looks dubious.

'Ah, nothing, I was just thinking about a friend of mine.'

'You have friends?'

It feels like a nail being driven into the most vulnerable part of his body. Kabuto is momentarily paralyzed. *Why does that upset me so much?*

Katsumi doesn't seem to notice that his father is quietly stunned. He goes on casually: 'I guess not having a lot of friends is part of being an adult.' He sounds convinced by his own observation.

'Yeah, I guess so.' Kabuto has no idea if it's that way for most adults. 'Oh, I wanted to ask you something.' In fact he does – he isn't just trying to change the subject. 'Were you ever bullied? Or did you ever bully anyone else?'

Katsumi stiffens for a second. 'Um. Well, it's not like it didn't happen.'

Kabuto sits up a bit straighter. 'Oh yeah? And when was that?'

'Ha, you don't need to look so tense about it, Dad.' Katsumi smirks. 'I've never been the one doing the bullying.'

'So you got bullied?'

'Maybe it was like one step before full-on bullying.'

'Is there such a thing as that? One step before?'

'They had their eye on me. This was in middle school.'

'Why?' Katsumi is sitting in front of him, perfectly calm and easygoing, so he obviously made it through all right. But Kabuto suddenly feels protective.

'Who knows? Probably just something they didn't like about me.'

'I suppose that people don't really need any logical reason to dislike someone.' He thinks about the jobs he's pulled. The clients had their reasons, of course. But, objectively speaking, their reasons weren't often based in logic. It could be a grudge, or a misunderstanding. He had once heard about a person who wanted someone killed because they looked just like an ex-friend and seeing their face was too infuriating. Maybe they thought that it was the victim's own fault for looking the way they did. But from Kabuto's perspective, it was obviously the person who contracted the hit who was in the wrong. 'So how did you deal with it?'

'I don't even remember now. I guess I just got through it somehow. Standing up for myself, sucking up to them, nothing really made a difference. It's like what Mom's always said: you can only do what you can do. Beyond that, it's out of your hands.'

'Yeah. I guess so.'

'I mean, I did what I could. It was no use worrying about what I couldn't change. At the time it seemed like it would go on forever, but looking back now it was just a little while.'

'What were their names? What'd they look like?' If Katsumi remembers, Kabuto would be happy to find them, stalk them a bit, put a little fear in them.

'Dad, you've got the crazy eye.'

'What would you do if you ever met them again?'

'If I met them? I don't know, what should I do? I've thought about it. If I ever ran into them, would I be nice to them, or give them a hard time?'

'Good question.' Before Katsumi raised the possibility of being nice to them, there was only one option in Kabuto's mind, but he pretends that he had been wondering the same thing.

'You know what JFK said? Forgive your enemies, but never forget their names.'

'Huh.'

'Which I suppose means, you can forgive them, but don't let your guard down.'

'Or maybe it means you should remember them so you can get back at them in the next life. But hey, look at you, quoting Kennedy. Pretty impressive.'

'Ha, it's not like he said it directly to me. He might not even have really said it at all.'

'Smart. Hard to believe you're my kid.'

'Come on, you're much more impressive than I am, Dad.'

This hits Kabuto like a surprise attack. The thing that happened yesterday at the bus stop was surprising too, but this is even more so.

The surprise at the bus stop happened on the outskirts of Machioka. Still within the boundaries of Tokyo, but far from the center of the city, much closer to the border with the neighboring prefecture. A quiet area, still full of nature. Kabuto headed there for work.

Not his job with the office supply company though. It was a job from the doctor. The work he does that's less compatible with humanitarianism, or the law.

At first the doctor tried to get Kabuto to take on a surgery. Kabuto replied that if possible he would prefer not to do that kind of job.

'It is a high-risk procedure.'

'I've told you over and over again, I especially don't want anything like that.'

The doctor's expression didn't change. 'You feel guilty?'

Kabuto wasn't sure he knew exactly what guilt felt like. 'Maybe,' was all he said.

He tried asking himself what was bothering him so much. When did this kind of work become so distasteful to him? Not that it was ever enjoyable, but it had always just been how he survived: a job would come in and he would do it.

'Life is precious,' he ventured.

'Is that some sort of slogan?' The doctor's eyes flashed with contempt. 'I am a doctor, and you want to tell me that life is precious?'

'You're one of those "do as I say, not as I do" doctors, huh?' Kabuto just tossed out the first thing that came to mind. *Life is*

117

precious. Of course it is. He had known that for years. But it's also true that we as humans take the lives of other beings so that we can eat them. And it's true that when masses of children in some far off country die it doesn't really affect us that much. Which means that the preciousness of life is relative. He understood that too.

'Your love for your family is impressive,' the doctor said.

'I don't have any illusions that I can wash away the things I've done.'

'Naturally.'

'The only thing I can do is not add any more.'

'Any more what?'

'Any more things that I wouldn't be proud of telling my kid.'

'Surgically removing malignant tumors is by no means a bad thing.'

'Yeah, well, I've had enough.'

They kept going around in circles. Kabuto had lost count of how many times they'd had the same conversation, the same negotiation, the same back and forth. What he did know is where the discussion would end up.

'But you realize, Mr Miyake, that you cannot yet cut off your regular treatments.'

Investments have been made. If you quit now, someone will lose out. No one likes losing out. In all likelihood, they will become angry. If you try to wash your hands of this, the angered party will no doubt move ruthlessly, and not just against you, but your family as well. So keep working, just a bit longer.

You must comply. Income and expenditure must be balanced.

Always the same explanation. The doctor chooses his words carefully, but it never changes.

'If you prefer to avoid surgery, then perhaps there is a different treatment.'

With that, the doctor proposed another job: Go to a factory in Machioka and retrieve a certain item.

Kabuto understood that this was a compromise, and he accepted.

The factory was at the foot of a mountain. No security to speak of. Kabuto went around back and found a window with a rusty frame that he was able to break open with no trouble. Squeezing his body through the narrow opening was a bit tougher, but still easy enough to get inside. There was a long conveyor belt in the middle of the space with mechanical arms installed on either side. The arms looked to Kabuto like over-sized dental implements, and he pictured a gargantuan human riding along the conveyor belt, mouth open wide.

Based on the map the doctor had shown him, the office he was looking for was further into the building. He found it with no problem and opened the door. That's when he sprung the trap.

As he pulled the door toward him there was a sudden noise. He ducked backward, bending all the way down to the ground. Overhead something whizzed by like an arrow. Then he saw that it actually was an arrow. It thunked into the wall, quivering.

It turned out there was a tactical crossbow mounted in the room, rigged to go off when the door opened. Ever since Kabuto got into this line of work, people have told him that he does things the old-fashioned way, but sometimes the old-fashioned way still works. Just like how you can still rely on the multiplication table, or crying to get someone to lend you money. In sports the rules can be revised so that certain classic plays are no longer allowed, but in Kabuto's business, anything goes.

He got up carefully and hugged the wall as he entered the office. There was the crossbow, on top of a table facing the door.

It was covered in dust. This wasn't a freshly set trap. The cross-bow had been waiting a long time for its moment.

In the corner of the room was a cabinet, locked, but a solid blow opened it up enough that Kabuto could fish out the box he was looking for. A small box, the size that might contain a fancy watch or a ring. He tossed it into his backpack.

The crossbow trap was unexpected, but beyond that the job seemed to be as simple as grabbing the box and returning home. Kabuto was thrilled to have such an easy job, easier than any he'd ever done before. But he knew not to let his guard down completely. He had heard the story of the professional who took another easy job, to steal a suitcase on the Tohoku Shinkansen and get off at the next stop, but somehow he just kept being unable to get off the train and got entangled in a whole mess where the bodies kept piling up. Kabuto knew that danger could still strike at any moment.

And in fact, it did, while he was waiting for the bus home.

When Kabuto got to the bus stop there were three older men. He wondered if that was a local thing, that people here preferred to ride the bus than take a car. Then from behind a younger man appeared and asked him, 'Did I miss the bus? It didn't leave yet, did it?'

'I think you're okay.'

'Oh good. The next one's not for an hour.'

'There's only one bus per hour?'

'Yep. This is the countryside.'

'. . .Then shouldn't it be obvious if the four of us are waiting here that the bus still hasn't come?' *Why would he ask such an obvious question?*

'Sure, buddy, sounds right.' His tone suddenly familiar. The young man's hair was dyed brown and curled into a perm. He looked like he could be an artist, or a musician, or maybe a sleazy pickup artist. But Kabuto didn't think he was any of those.

This guy was just playacting being an easygoing character. Kabuto could tell that he was keyed up.

Maybe he's after the box. Kabuto was suddenly focused on his backpack. This guy might have been looking for a chance to sneak up and slash it open with a razorblade to get at the contents. Kabuto has done that move himself.

Or else maybe this guy was planning to attack from behind.

Either way, Kabuto kept his awareness trained behind him, which is why he was slow to react when one of the older men in front of him launched a kick.

He managed to get his right arm up, just in time.

The man's leg crashed into Kabuto's arm, now bent in a defensive position. Kabuto had to steady himself. He realized right away that these men were working together with the young guy behind him. Twisting his body, he rolled out of the bus stop and out into the street, then got right up to his feet. The four men moved to surround him. All three older men who were lined up waiting for the bus, and the one younger guy, together.

Nerves primed, Kabuto backed further away, trying to maintain some distance.

Who's first?

They formed a half-circle and crept closer to him, moving as one. It didn't seem like they had teamed up just for that day, but rather that they'd been practicing joint maneuvers.

Kabuto wondered where they would do something like that. He realized he had very little frame of reference, since he'd barely ever worked in a team. Then he pictured these men reserving space in the town recreational center and practicing fighting in formation late into the night. *Good, I'm glad they're dedicated,* he thought, all the while fending off their attacks.

A reverse spin kick, followed immediately by a snaking punch, then a blade slicing sideways, one attack after the next.

Kabuto dealt with each assault, dodging at the same time he was blocking, batting away one incoming blow and then hopping out of range of another, fully absorbed in keeping the attackers at bay.

But, alas, people in motion eventually lose their breath. Kabuto knew this to be true. The more involved the synchronized play they were running, the more it relied on them staying in rhythm; when one starts to slow down, the formation falls like dominos. Or like when the man pounding the mochi with the hammer and the man folding it by hand fall out of sync – not a pretty picture.

The young man with the dyejob was the first to show signs of fatigue. He aimed a kick but couldn't raise his leg as high as he wanted to, leaving him open.

Kabuto seized the chance to attack. Twisting among them, he took them down one by one. Of course, he was starting to breathe heavily too, and could feel his movements gradually getting slower, but he knew how to account for his flagging pace. It wasn't long before they were all incapacitated.

The four men were on the ground groaning, but otherwise the area around the bus shelter was quiet. No sign of the bus. The wind blew through, rustling the red and yellow leaves and livening up the scene.

Kabuto decided to give up on the bus. Just as he was about to leave he sensed something was wrong and wheeled around to see one of the older men, still on the ground, reaching his hand out toward him.

He darted over to the man and grabbed his hand. Something small fell out of it, like a toy. A tiny gun. Small enough to wrap your hand around it entirely. 'Swiss mini gun,' Kabuto muttered. There was some buzz around it a little while back – apparently designed using Swiss watchmaking techniques, and commonly touted as being no bigger than your thumb – but this was the first time that Kabuto had seen one in real life. This one appeared to be modified.

He turned it over in his fingers a few times, sizing it up. It would make for a great hidden weapon.

As for his four assailants, the old Kabuto would have killed them without a second thought. Anyone who tried to take him out was highly likely to try again if they got the chance, especially if they were the ones who instigated in the first place, which meant that they already knew they were risking their lives.

Forgive your enemies. That's almost never how it goes.

But this time, looking down at his four opponents, helpless on the ground, he didn't once think about doing them mortal harm. Far from it – he actually started thinking about how these men were all someone's child, trite though it may seem. He didn't know about their childhoods or what kind of parents raised them, but he could imagine that at some point when they were younger they must have been at least a little more endearing. Then he started thinking about his own childhood, which brought on a complicated mix of feelings.

His own parents had more or less left him on his own, and he had almost no memories of being a little boy.

'Dad, what's with the surprised face?'

Katsumi's voice brings him back to reality. 'Oh, just something from work yesterday that caught me off guard. But more than that, I was surprised by what you said.'

'What did I say?'

'That I was impressive.'

Katsumi made a noise of recognition. He scratched the top of his nose, blushing a little. 'Well, I mean, you are. You work hard and provide for the rest of us.'

'It's not often you hear a kid your age saying things like that, is all.' Kabuto is genuinely moved.

'And on top of that, you're very, um, kind, to Mom.'

'Kind, huh?'

'. . . Attentive to her mood.' Katsumi laughs.

'Come on, everyone wants their family to be happy. It's probably instinctive. When someone's upset around you, you get upset too. You try to find a way to make them feel better.'

'Even if you end up sacrificing yourself?'

'Sacrifice might be overstating it a bit. Is that really what it looks like to you?'

'I wouldn't say you're totally obsequious, but you could stand up for yourself a little more.'

'Hmm.' Kabuto keeps himself from smiling, and instead ends up scowling. 'I guess some people can appreciate a less flashy solo play too,' he says softly.

'What's a less flashy solo play?'

'Oh – ah, nothing.'

'Anyway, you do seem to have a knack for plugging away at whatever you're doing.'

'Oh yeah?'

'Sure. I see you solving those crosswords once in a while.'

'I don't hate the crossword.' He found it peaceful, not competing against anyone, just bending his brain this way and that to fill in all the squares. 'I like working on things that fit together neatly, the way someone planned it out. You don't see that too often in the real world.'

'No, you don't.'

'What do you know about the real world?'

'I mean, I have a part-time job. That can get complicated.'

'Ah, yeah, I guess it can.'

'It's like you're doing a crossword and you expect everything to be vertical and horizontal, but then diagonals and other directions pop up.'

'So your job is doing crosswords?'

'It's a metaphor, Dad. I'm saying that in life there are lots of problems with no easy answers.'

'You got that right. You think you're doing a crossword and it turns out to be a Rubik's cube. Happens all the time.'

Katsumi laughs again.

'What's so funny?' Kabuto asks.

'That's how it is with you and Mom, right? Her moods come at you from an unexpected angle.'

'What's this about angles?' His wife suddenly appears in the living room. Kabuto nearly squeaks.

'We're talking about math.' Katsumi is completely unruffled.

'Well then!' She sounds fine. She even sounds upbeat. Hearing that makes Kabuto feel relief down in his core. He wonders if something good happened to her, when she says, 'On my way back from shopping I found a new little restaurant. It just opened.' There's a bounce in her voice.

'That's nice.' Kabuto hits on the best thing he can say: 'Let's try it.'

'Yeah, we should!'

'I'll pass,' Katsumi says. 'The two of you enjoy.'

She presses, her voice pitching upward. 'Oh, but we're still all together. We won't always get to enjoy meals together.'

'I don't feel like it. It's fine, you two go without me.' Katsumi digs in.

Normally Kabuto would be inclined to respect Katsumi's wishes and just let him do what he wants, but in this case it's clear which side he should be on. 'Why don't we go try it out together, just this once.'

His wife jumps in. 'The meal's on us, Katsumi, you should take advantage of it. Come on. Or if you don't want to, you can come with me to Fuji-Q Highland.'

'You want me to go with you to the amusement park?' Katsumi wails.

'I want to ride the scream machines and I need someone to go with me!'

'Dad can go with you.'

Yeah, I could go with you, Kabuto might have said, but he knows it's not what his wife wants to hear.

'If you don't want to come with us to the restaurant, you have to come with me to Fuji-Q. Your pick.'

'You sound like a scam artist,' Katsumi says wryly. 'Trying to make me think I only have two choices.'

The department store after closing time is darker than Kabuto had anticipated, and silent. He imagines that a giant beast of some kind is sleeping in the inner reaches of the store. If he listens hard he might hear it snoring.

He came in through the rear entrance on the ground floor. That took him past the security office, but that was no problem, since he was invited to be here by the on-duty security guard.

From years of working jobs he's used to moving through the dark. But in the department store he has a bit less of a sense where things might be. Shining a small flashlight around, he makes his way.

The light catches in the mirrors of the makeup counter. Each time it flashes it looks like animals blinking at him from the darkness.

Nanomura and his son must already be on the top floor.

Kabuto starts up the stairs that Nanomura had directed him to take.

Apparently the standard procedure for security patrol in the store is to start at the top floor and check each level, working downward. Kabuto thought this was interesting. He would have expected the patrol to focus on the lowest floor so that if some-one breaks in they could be chased up to the higher floors and they'd have nowhere left to run. But the thinking is that corner-ing an intruder could be dangerous. They might get desperate, or they might hole up and occupy an area. Instead it's better to start at the top and chase any intruders out the door. Rather than trying to catch and punish them, the policy favors minimizing trouble.

Kabuto continues up the stairs, keeping his footfalls silent. As he continues upward he starts to hear Nanomura's voice. He reaches the fourth floor. Keeping in mind the timing so that they don't run into each other, Kabuto steps out onto the department store floor.

'Will you be the only guard on duty?' The other day in the café, Kabuto had asked this, among other questions. He was all for Nanomura bringing his son along on the patrol, but there were several points he needed to clarify.

'No, there's another fellow. But I imagine that if I explained the situation to him he'd understand. He's older, this is a retirement job for him.'

'And I guess he trusts you?'

'I hope that he does.' Nanomura's smile was a mix of embarrassment and self-deprecation. 'Doing the job well enough to earn people's trust is my secret weapon.'

'Sounds like a good one to have.' To Kabuto, who had used all kinds of weapons and implements in his jobs over the years – and had them used against him as well – it really did seem like the most important thing to settle a conflict is trust.

Now he sees another flashlight shining out over the fourth floor. Nanomura and his son, walking down the aisles. Turns out it's easy to hide in a department store. He's in the women's apparel section, so there are racks with clothing and mannequins everywhere, making it a perfect setting to conceal himself.

Listening for their footsteps, he picks his way across the floor on a diagonal, little by little closing the distance. Now he's close enough that he can make out what Nanomura is saying.

'The main thing is to look out for intruders, but we also have to check to see that there's nothing wrong with the fire extinguishers, make sure there isn't any trash lying around, that sort of thing.'

'Wow.' Nanomura's son is clearly distracted. *If you're trying to pretend you're interested, you'll have to do better than that,* Kabuto can't help thinking.

They come to the end of the aisle and turn right. The beam of light shines back and forth, then flips up to the ceiling momentarily, sending a shadow sliding off in one direction like a monster skittering away in retreat.

Kabuto's phone buzzes in his back pocket and emits a single tone. He takes it out and sees that it's a message from his wife, asking if he'll be home late. He had told her he was taking a client out to dinner.

Looks like I'll be a while, don't wait up, he writes back. She normally doesn't, but on the occasions when he does come home to find her still awake and waiting for him, he feels a heavy guilt, as if he's asked her to help him pay off a massive debt. He considers putting his phone on silent, but he doesn't want to miss any emergency messages. He lowers the volume and puts it back in his pocket.

Just as he does that he hears Nanomura's son say, 'Dad, hang on, I need to go to the bathroom.'

'Sure. Do you know where it is?'

'I think so. I'll be right back.' No sooner are the words out of his mouth than he's off running down the stairs.

'You need a flashlight!' Nanomura calls after him, but the boy ignores it, keeps going as if he's trying to escape his father.

Kabuto follows. The restroom is on a landing by the stairs, but Nanomura's son runs right past it, continuing down to the lower levels.

Based on the map of the department store's layout that Nanomura had shown him, Kabuto can guess where the boy is headed: a service entrance on the back side of the building. The kid opens the door from the corridor and disappears into the employee-only section. Kabuto goes after him, listening for the boy's footsteps to make sure he keeps enough distance between them. Slipping through doors and creeping down dark hallways is nothing new for him. He uses a tiny light clipped to his finger to show the way.

There's a rattling sound up ahead like a rusty door opening. Kabuto ducks behind a stack of cardboard boxes.

'Took you long enough, we've been waiting out here forever!' The voice is young, even a little childish. 'It's cold out, I thought we were gonna freeze to death.'

'You really are a worthless piece of shit,' says another voice.

'Sorry, sorry.' Kabuto figures this is Nanomura's son.

None of them notice him as they walk past on their way to the store floor. There are three of them besides Nanomura's son, each one shaped a little differently but all basically similar.

When they enter the store, Nanomura's son points around them and then holds his finger up to his lips. Kabuto is too far to hear any of what they're saying but it's clearly a warning to the others to keep quiet. Probably also reminding them that there are security cameras. Kabuto hadn't noticed when they first walked past him but now he sees that the boys have surgical masks or something covering their faces, no doubt as precaution in case they get caught on tape.

Nanomura's son says something, to which one of the other kids holds up a fist as if he's about to throw a punch. Probably some threat like *Who do you think you're talking to*, or something like that. The other boys all snicker meanly.

They wave Nanomura's son away, like they're telling him to

go back to daddy. Looking uncertain, he heads back to the stairs.

'I hope that I'm wrong about this.' That's what Nanomura had said, but unfortunately his hunch turned out to be true. 'I'm worried that he's being ordered around by some bad friends.' He lowered his voice for this part of their conversation at the café, seemingly pained at having to say it.

To Kabuto, the idea of a 'bad friend' was a contradiction that didn't fit in with the very concept of friendship. He thought back to Komao Furuyama's definition of friendship being acquaintances that you were close with.

'It just seems odd to me that he would suddenly take an interest in what my job is like. And that he's so focused on coming along for a night patrol. I've lived long enough to know when there's something going on.'

'And so you think your son . . .'

'He's a good boy, he studies hard, but he's rather meek. He was bullied in elementary school.'

'Oh, that's too bad,' Kabuto said earnestly.

'If there are boys taking advantage of him, it's not hard to imagine what they're thinking. They find out that someone they're pushing around has a father who's a security guard at a department store . . .'

'They figure they can get into some trouble . . .'

'Maybe they're hoping to get in at night and steal something.' Nanomura looked sad. 'It's easy enough to picture it. They would force my son to have me bring him with me to work, and while I'm showing him how the job goes he finds some way to let his bad friends in the back entrance.'

'You're probably overthinking it,' Kabuto had said, but now he sees that Nanomura was right on the mark. He's watching it unfold in front of him.

'Get to where they keep the video games, they're on the fifth floor,' one of the kids says as they clamber up the stopped escalator.

Kabuto considers for a few moments and then starts after the kids. They seem to be using their smartphones as flashlights, illuminating the area around them as they head for their target.

From the way they're carelessly shining their lights everywhere, Kabuto guesses that they had told Nanomura's son to make sure his father didn't come back to that floor.

Any floor that Nanomura had already patrolled should be wide open. That's why his son let them in once he and his father had made it down to the fourth.

It's a common tale: one side is so afraid that they won't fight back despite having been humiliated, while the other side assumes that they're completely secure, untouchable. It might even be the basic structure of society, the foundation of human relations. But Kabuto doesn't like it one bit. It doesn't strike him as fair.

Which is why, before he's even fully aware of what he's doing, he finds himself creeping up to where the masked teenagers are riffling through the videogames and asking them: 'What's so good about these games anyway?'

This wasn't what Nanomura asked him to do.

'I imagine my son will try to lead me to a part of the store away from where his friends are going, so that they can steal whatever it is they're after,' Nanomura had said. 'That's why I'd like to ask you, Miyake-san, to stand in for me and keep track of what they do.'

'Keep track?'

'If you can, it would be helpful to take some photos of them, for proof.'

'Aren't there security cameras?'

'There are, but aside from the ones by the entrance, most of

131

the cameras in the store are rather old and don't take very high-quality footage. If someone conceals their face even a little then there isn't much hope of identifying them. So if you can get some photos or video of them from a little closer up, or record their voices . . .'

'And you would use that . . . ?'

'Yes, if it comes to it, we could stick it to them.' Nanomura had smiled bitterly, maybe because he was talking about sticking it to children, or maybe because he knew that 'if it comes to it' was basically a certainty.

'So you don't want to confront these kids in the moment?'

'Well, I'm not sure exactly what they'll do, and I certainly don't want to put you in any danger, Miyake-san. It would be best to avoid any kind of conflict. To the extent that you can, try to avoid letting them spot you.'

Kabuto broke that almost right away.

He wasn't intending to go against Nanomura's wishes that he stay hidden. But seeing how these kids bossed Nanomura's kid around as if he were their underling pushed him past the point of restraint. It reminds him of a war movie he watched once, with a scene where the soldiers play games with their prisoners' lives. He found it deeply upsetting. Not because he was the kind of idealistic person to be bothered by every unpleasant thing that happens during wartime. It was because he imagined his son Katsumi as one of the people being tortured. As soon as the thought entered his mind he nearly boiled over.

The kids are stunned at Kabuto's sudden appearance, looking wildly at one another, yelping and squealing. 'Shit, it's security!'

He knows that they'll try to run for it. When people who are caught up in the moment suddenly find themselves in trouble, they drop whatever they're doing and try to escape. They don't worry about past or future, only the immediate situation they're in. They don't care about what might happen to anyone else, so desperate are they to avoid any harm to themselves. They just go, unthinking, uncaring. Later, once some time has passed, they look for a scapegoat, someone to pin the blame on.

They believe that only other people should suffer, and that only other people need to take any responsibility.

Kabuto makes his move before they can run.

He doesn't know which of the three is the ringleader, so he grabs the nearest one by the shoulders. 'Don't move,' he says to the other two. 'Running will only make things worse.' One of them stands rooted to the spot, and the other flees, taking off without a moment's hesitation. He must be convinced that all he needs to do is get out of there in one piece and then it'll all be okay.

'What the hell, man?' The kid twists himself loose from Kabuto's grip.

Kabuto tries to decide whether to get mean or to be polite. 'I'm patrolling this area,' he ventures.

The two kids look at each other. Probably wondering if this is Nanomura's dad.

'You guys in middle school?' Kabuto asks.

The one kid rubbing his shoulder seems to register some warmth in Kabuto's tone and decides it's an opening to either plead or act tough, and chooses the latter. 'Hey, that hurt. Don't mess with me, man.'

'Oh, it hurt?'

'Yeah, it did! What's your deal, anyway?'

The kid must be used to this sort of lame performance working on the teachers at school. Kabuto is even a little impressed. He grabs his shoulders again and squeezes even harder.

The kid screams and his knees buckle.

The other kid's face tenses up, visible even under the mask.

'How fast can you run fifty meters, huh?' Kabuto turns his

133

attention to this kid while still gripping the other one by the shoulders. 'If you think you can run faster than me, then go for it. But if you do, make sure you get away. If you try to run and I catch you, you'll be sorry. I won't go easy on you. So I'm telling you – if you decide to run, you need to be sure you can outrun me. You'll need to break all your personal records.'

It's clear that the kid won't run. Kabuto is suddenly thrown off, and questions himself. *What the hell am I doing? I'm much more powerful than they are. Isn't this just more bullying? These kids were using force to control someone weaker, and I'm using force to control them.*

Although there is a logic to it.

It's okay to use force on those weaker than you, as long as they're using force on someone weaker than them.

This makes sense to Kabuto. It seems reasonable enough. But when he looks at the middle schooler's surprisingly skinny wrists and his face contorted with pain, he feels a crushing guilt.

The next thing he knows, the kids are running away. He must have let go.

What should I do now?

He had put some fear into them, a little pain, that should be enough for them to learn their lesson. But there's still the possibility that they'll take out their frustration on Nanomura's son. He decides he'll catch up with them and make sure they get the message that they need to do better. Meanwhile he's also wondering what's going on with Nanomura.

He tries to listen for any sounds in the dark. The fifth floor is quiet, seemingly deserted. Then he thinks he can hear something one floor down, some barely audible footfalls. He cross-references where the sound seems to be coming from with the map he's memorized: the bathrooms.

As he walks down the long corridor on the fourth floor he can hear voices coming from the bathroom. It's the kids, shouting 'What should we do?' and 'Who the fuck is that?'

They must be panicked if they're hiding in the bathroom, which has only one way out. Feeling a little sorry for them, Kabuto debates for a moment whether he should enter the bathroom or wait here for them to emerge. Before he can come to a decision he hears a scream. Followed immediately by another voice, apologizing again and again.

Maybe the stress is too much for them?

He enters the bathroom. It's dark. Without hesitating he flips the light switch.

The kids appear in the sudden illumination. They scream even louder.

They're standing in front of the innermost stall, rooted to the spot, mouths agape. When they see Kabuto they go pale. They have their phones in their hand, as if they had been using the LCD screens as flashlights.

They had been about to go into the stall to hide, when they saw something that made them freeze.

There's a person in the stall. A man, sitting on the ground. Kabuto recognizes the red jacket from somewhere. An instant later he has it: it's the maintenance man from the department store. Kabuto has seen him plenty of times.

Something is sticking out of the man's chest. It looks like a kitchen knife. He's very clearly dead.

For the kids it's like being between a rock and a hard place, only it's between a corpse and a killer. They probably figure the corpse is safer. He wonders if they would think differently if they knew it was a choice between a corpse and a stressed-out family man.

'We, we didn't –' The kids are standing shoulder to shoulder, visibly trembling.

Kabuto is concerned about the body, but he decides that he needs to deal with the kids first. 'Okay, guys, just take it easy.' His voice is kind, and he's never once given any advice to anyone he was up against, professionals or otherwise, so for him this is actually extremely kind. 'Now listen, you guys might be tough enough to act big in school or in your day-to-day lives, but you know that's a tiny little world, right? Everyone lives in their own little worlds. So you have to learn your place. Some people are weaker than you, and –' But here Kabuto cuts himself off. *This doesn't quite fit.* Here he is menacing people weaker than himself. Not really a good position to be giving that particular lecture. 'Look, nothing in this life comes easy, okay? Never do what you did here tonight again.'

They shake their heads vigorously.

'And don't tell anyone about any of this.'

They might be feeling remorse now, in their moment of terror, but it's possible they'll go home and digest what happened and then forget the lesson entirely. Now Kabuto starts to think about the body in the stall.

'Get out of here, now.' He waves the kids away. They toddle off, looking like their legs can barely support them.

The man in the red jacket is leaned up against the toilet, eyes closed, not breathing. Kabuto inspects the body carefully, trying to touch it as little as possible.

It doesn't look like he's been dead long.

This happened here in the department store. What is going on?

He decides he should go connect with Nanomura and starts to leave. But just before exiting the bathroom he stops and looks back again at the dead man in the stall. *He had parents too. He was once a little kid. And this is how he ended up.*

Kabuto offers a silent prayer for the man, blinking a few times. Then he turns off the lights. The moment he does,

136

though, he thinks he notices something, and flips the switch back on.

He goes back over to the stall and squats down next to the man's body. There by his feet: a gun. Looking at the man again, he sees a holster on his belt. Not the kind of equipment normally needed by a maintenance staffer who refills the vending machines.

Kabuto leaves the bathroom and walks several paces before he realizes with a start that he left the light on. His wife is always yelling at him, 'The power bill!' He hurries back to switch it off. *Can I be done in here?*

He steps out of the bathroom once more and looks around, wondering again what exactly is going on. It makes him think of the sudden call he got the other day from the doctor, that prompted him to go pay a visit to the clinic. Things seem to be getting complicated. Looks like the crossword wasn't just verticals and horizontals after all.

'Miyake-san,' he hears from behind. A flashlight beam moves in the dark, letting him know that Nanomura is there on the same floor as him. 'What are you doing over there?'

Kabuto turns around and nods toward the juice vending machine beside him. 'I was checking to see if anyone had maybe forgotten to take their change.' He shrugs. 'Coins add up.' He raises his arms, like a fugitive caught in a searchlight. 'Where's your son?'

'He went home,' Nanomura replies. 'He said there was something he needed to take care of.'

'So watching Dad at work is to be continued?' As he speaks Kabuto tries to follow Nanomura's movements. The flashlight on him is blinding. *There's something I need to ask you*, Kabuto is about to say, although there are a number of things he'd like to know. But before he can say anything Nanomura says the same thing:

'There's something I need to ask you.'

'Go ahead.' Kabuto keeps his hands held up.

'When you accepted my invitation tonight, was it because you had something specific in mind?'

'Something specific?'

'Because you thought it would be a perfect chance to try and take me out.'

The flashlight is in Nanomura's left hand. His right arm is held up high, elbow bent, hand behind his ear. He's holding a blade. A kitchen knife.

Kabuto glances to one side at the store guidance signs. *Kitchen Supplies*, it says. Kabuto sighs mournfully. 'You probably shouldn't use the goods without paying for them.'

Nanomura sighs as well, sounding similarly sad. 'I suppose it's true after all.'

'Suppose what's true?'

'If you're so calm in this kind of a situation, you must not be just an average man.'

'I'm a salesman for an office supply company.'

'On the surface, yes.'

'Do you have a surface and an underside too?'

'No, no, I'm retired. Well, actually, I'm about to retire.'

'So this security guard job . . . ?'

'It's my last job before retiring. At first I wasn't told why I was supposed to pose as a security guard, only that it would be revealed to me eventually.'

'And the whole thing with your son wanting to see you at work?'

Nanomura frowns and raises his eyebrows. 'That was true. And so was the fact that my son is being led astray by some bad friends.'

Kabuto had actually been wondering if the boy was even really Nanomura's son. There are people in the industry who can supply actors to play roles, from young boys to old men. But Nanomura appears to be telling the truth. The words 'bad friends' stick in Kabuto's ears. Friends are different from acquaintances. And bad friends are different than real friends.

'Speaking of which, what happened? With my son's friends?'

'I owe you an apology on that score.' Kabuto's arms are starting to ache from holding them up. 'I was planning to take some photos and videos for evidence like you asked me to, but they spotted me. And I lost my temper and scolded them.'

'You scolded them?'

'Yeah, I yelled at them, a little.' Kabuto shrugs again. 'Sorry about that.'

'So they really did force my son to come here tonight.'

Nanomura looks so crestfallen that Kabuto can't help feeling bad for him. 'It could be that both things were true. He actually wanted to see you at work, and his bad friends glommed on to that.'

'You're a kind man, Miyake-san.'

'First time anyone's ever told me that.' It really does feel like the first time. Kabuto realizes that his tone with Nanomura has shifted somewhat, mixing their normal polite register with greater familiarity. He's starting to lose track of the line between surface and substance. 'I found a body in the bathroom. What's that about?'

Nanomura lets out another little sigh. 'He's on the maintenance staff. One of the vending machines is out of order. I knew he'd be here working late tonight.'

'So, what, he couldn't fix the machine and got so frustrated he stabbed himself in the chest with a kitchen knife?'

The flashlight suddenly seems to grow a bit brighter. At the same time, Kabuto thinks he can see Nanomura's expression soften slightly.

'It seems the maintenance man was a late addition to the mix.'

'Late addition?'

'I received my instructions just a short time ago. Right before I began my patrol with my son. They said that someone would be here tonight, targeting me. I was supposed to eliminate that person.'

'And that was the maintenance guy?'

'No.' Nanomura's face barely moves. But now it looks colder, harder to read. 'It's you, Miyake-san.'

'Ah.'

'I was told you came here to take my life.'

Kabuto had gotten his instructions from the doctor the other day. He reluctantly went to the clinic, where the doctor briefed him on a high-risk surgery he was to perform. The x-ray image showed details of the 'tumor,' that is, information about the target. When Kabuto saw that it was Nanomura, he fell into shocked silence.

'Is this someone you know?' the doctor asked. But he probably already knew everything.

'I'm not sure.'

'He works at one of the locations where you make sales calls.'

Kabuto couldn't bring himself to dissemble so he just stayed quiet.

'If you perform this operation, you may retire.'

'I can retire?' Kabuto didn't mean to say this. So many times he had heard that he needed to keep working, that he needed to amass more money, but this is the first time the doctor had ever plainly said that doing a job could clear the way to him retiring.

'Correct. If you perform this surgery.'

'This must be . . .' There aren't many scenarios Kabuto could imagine. 'This must be pretty high risk. Or else someone pretty big must be contracting it.'

The doctor said nothing.

Nanomura continues speaking evenly. 'Once I began my patrol with my son, I saw someone moving in the darkness, and I thought it must be you, Miyake-san. That you had come for me after all. But I was wrong.'

'It was the vending machine guy.'

The flashlight bobs up and down once, as if standing in for Nanomura nodding. 'Most stores have theft prevention netting over the displays at night, but not here. With all the clothing racks and mannequins, it's ideal for sneaking around and hiding.'

'I was thinking the same thing myself, earlier.'

'The maintenance man was doing just that, creeping closer to me, very obviously looking for a chance to make his move.'

'I wonder . . .' Kabuto recalls a conversation he had previously with the doctor, about the polarization in the industry. Well-known professionals get more and more work and become even more well-known, while the unknown can't break out of their anonymity. They may be good, but they still need to find a way to attract attention. That means they try to pull off one or two high-level jobs. 'He might have been a no-name professional butting in to win some recognition. Or maybe someone actually hired him to take you out.' It was easy enough to imagine the man pretending to be a vending machine maintenance man in order to get closer to Nanomura. Either way, if multiple parties are trying to get rid of Nanomura, that's just a testament to how dangerous he is.

'I was hoping he wouldn't try to attack when my son was still with me, but then when we got down to the fourth floor my son left to go to the bathroom.'

'He didn't go to the bathroom. He was letting in those bad friends of his.'

'I thought he was gone too long for just going to the bathroom. But it worked out.'

That was when Nanomura dealt with the vending machine man.

'Just like that?'

'We were right by the kitchen knives, so . . .' Nanomura relates how he tore open a box, grabbed a knife, and hurled it at the man. Kabuto pictures the blade flying through the darkness and sinking into the man's chest.

'So I guess it was a two-knife set.' Kabuto eyes the knife held aloft in Nanomura's hand.

Nanomura ignores that. 'I hid his body in the bathroom stall. I certainly didn't think you would find it.'

'It was the kids. They went into the bathroom and discovered it.'

Nanomura says no more. He just watches Kabuto. The blade is still held high, ready.

'You may not believe me, but I had no intention of moving on you. It's true that I was given a contract, but I never had any intention of doing anything about it. The reason I came tonight was because of what we discussed, so I could help with your son's situation.'

'You know, I thought you and I had a lot in common. With regards to how we care for our families, and how we approach our jobs. But I was surprised to find out that we have this line of work in common as well.'

'It really is too bad.' Kabuto's shoulders sag. 'I'm not intending you any harm, Nanomura-san,' he says again. 'I would hope you know that.' *So you can feel free to put down that knife.*

It seems highly unlikely that Nanomura is any run-of-the-mill professional. Based on how the doctor was talking about

142

him, it seemed apparent that he wasn't the standard sort of high-risk target. Facing him down like this now, Kabuto knows it beyond a shadow of a doubt. His stance is relaxed and his tone is polite, but his presence fills the whole space, probing. It's clear that if he detects the barest sudden movement he'll strike like lightning.

'I want to believe you, but I can't.'

Kabuto understands perfectly.

A professional will use any means necessary to advance their agenda. Especially when their opponent has the drop on them, weapon poised. What's a lie or two in a situation like that?

There's a fundamental difference between life and death. Surface and substance, heaven and hell. No matter who you have to betray, no matter what values you have to subvert, the most important thing is survival. The longer someone works in this industry, the more times they've had to lay their life on the line, the more absolutely they know this.

'I'm not going to fight you.' Kabuto says this, but he's aware that in a situation like this it's hard to take such an assertion as genuine. There's no room for logic or analysis. They're operating on instinct alone. If Kabuto were to lower his hands and make a move that looked like he was going for a weapon, Nanomura would throw his knife before even thinking. The same if Kabuto tried to dash to the side and take cover. When survival is on the line, the body acts before the mind.

'I'm sure you realize that it's hard for me to believe when you say that, Miyake-san.'

At this moment, the only thing in the minds and bodies of Kabuto and Nanomura is getting home alive.

'I can't die here,' Nanomura says. 'I need to live, for my son.'

Me too, Kabuto thinks, but keeps it to himself.

The exit sign glows green in the dark, emitting a low hum.

If there's any question that your opponent might be

dangerous, the sensible thing to do is eliminate them. That's the trick to survival in this business. It's not even a trick, it's just common sense.

All he has to do is flick his wrist, and I die. The thought of death doesn't upset him. But never seeing his wife again, never seeing Katsumi, that would be painful. Just the thought of it makes his chest tighten. Let's go to that new restaurant together, he had said, but that might never ever happen.

In that moment another thought comes to him: *How many people have felt the same pain, the same loss, because of you?* His body suddenly feels leaden.

In the face of all the things he's done, the desire to stay alive seems like the height of selfishness.

'Nanomura-san, can I go collect the coins from the vending machine?' He gestures vaguely to the machine with his still-raised hand. 'I forgot my change.'

'Sorry to say, but no.' Nanomura isn't leaving a single opening.

A mosquito needs to be swatted, whether or not it's trying to bite you. Once it's bitten you, it's too late.

There aren't many moves for Kabuto to make. All he can really do is try to dodge the knife when it's thrown at him. The flashlight beam makes it hard to see, but he squints and focuses all his attention on Nanomura's hand, watching for the slightest movement.

Like a standoff in a western, they face each other, silent, trying to sense one another's breathing.

With the maintenance man's body, the kitchen knife was sunk deep into his chest, exactly where the heart is. Given that it was likely thrown from some distance, Kabuto has a sense of just how good Nanomura is.

If he were throwing it himself, he would use the flashlight to blind his opponent just before attacking. So now, if the light moves at all, he'll try to jump to the side. *When will it come?*

Now? Now? . . .Now? A succession of nows flows past. He tries to keep himself from blinking so that he doesn't miss anything. His senses are fully activated. Any second the knife could plunge into his chest, and he won't be able to think about his family anymore, he'll just be swallowed up into a pitch-black void.

His phone chimes with an incoming message. The volume is low, but it hits both of them as unexpected input. For the barest of moments, Nanomura is distracted.

Kabuto leaps to the right. In the same instant the knife slashes his shoulder. He doesn't have any time to register the pain. As he's dodging out of the way it whizzes by, taking a chunk of him with it.

He gets up and turns back to Nanomura. From that point onward his head is empty of thought. His body just attacks. He lowers his hips into a fighting stance and launches blow after blow.

Nanomura defends, backing up steadily.

There's no room to exchange any words. Only their breath escapes their lips.

Nanomura catches Kabuto's right arm and pins it under his own arm. He wrenches it upward, forcing Kabuto to twist his body around to free his trapped arm. Kabuto ignores the pain in his left shoulder and aims a punch at Nanomura's face. Nanomura skips backward, out of reach.

Kabuto narrows his eyes.

The flashlight is on the floor. Its beam spreads outward, vaguely outlining the shapes in the darkness.

Nanomura's eyes glitter, sharp. Kabuto sees himself reflected in them. They're both breathing hard, but, frustratingly, there's no sign that Nanomura's movements are slowing down at all.

As if there were a signal to switch attacker and defender, Nanomura advances. Kabuto falls back, evading.

He doesn't have any opening to look around for something he might use as a weapon. For better or for worse the kitchen section is on the other side of the floor. Maybe for the better – if Nanomura got another kitchen knife, the fight would be over pretty quickly.

Kabuto launches a counterattack. Nanomura deflects. They advance and retreat, gaining ground and giving it up, like they were in a fencing match.

Kabuto knows that his shoulder is bleeding, but he didn't expect that he would end up slipping in his blood on the floor. He pitches forward and catches himself on his hands. Moving with his momentum, he whirls around, launching a reverse spin kick at Nanomura's head.

Despite the fact that Kabuto falling changed up the rhythm of their fight and that the kick came in from an unexpected angle, Nanomura doesn't miss a beat, blading his body and dodging the blow.

Kabuto's leg sweeps through the air and slams into a mannequin.

The mannequin crashes to the floor causing both of them to look down at it. They suddenly stop moving.

In the course of their combat they had traveled across the floor to the back-to-school section. It's full of backpacks and child-sized mannequins. Kabuto had kicked one of these.

It's on the floor, face down. One of its arms has popped off.

Kabuto is momentarily taken aback and finds himself staring at the mannequin. Nanomura has dropped his fighting stance as well. Their breathing settles to the same rhythm.

The mannequin looks like a real child.

After a few moments, Kabuto steps over to it. It's designed to look like a western boy. He gently stands it back up. Nanomura collects the missing arm.

Kabuto returns it to the place it had been. They reattach the arm and put the backpack that had tumbled off back on again.

Kabuto is thinking about when Katsumi was starting elementary school. His backpack seemed bigger than he was as they watched him go off to his first day. Kabuto remembers feeling a pang of anxiety and intoning a silent prayer that nothing bad would ever happen to his son. More scenes swim up out of memory: Katsumi packing up his books, worrying that he might forget something, and his wife saying soothingly, 'We'll check everything together, and if you do forget something, then we'll just make sure you take it next time.' The memories keep coming.

When they finish returning the mannequin to the way it was, the two men turn to face one another again.

Kabuto doesn't have any illusions that they can talk things out. Both of them are experienced professionals. When it's time to act, you act. When you have a move, you make it. That's the way it works. They both know this. It's burned into their bodies. So when Kabuto speaks up, it's not because he thinks it will stop the other man from attacking. All he wants is to honestly communicate how he's really feeling.

'Nanomura-san. I don't want to fight you anymore.'

Nanomura says nothing. But neither does he attack.

They look at each other. Time passes.

Eventually Nanomura speaks. 'I was told you were hell-bent on killing me.'

'That,' Kabuto begins, 'was a false option.'

'What do you mean, a false option?'

Kabuto thinks back to the conversation with his family the other day, where his wife told Katsumi that if he didn't want to go to the restaurant then he had to go with her to Fuji-Q. Katsumi had said that it was a scam technique, making it seem like there were only two choices. *Which of the two will you choose? If you don't do one, you have to do the other.* It's a way to make someone think that they have to pick one of the two options. Kabuto can picture a sleazy guy telling his girlfriend who wants to leave that she has to stay with him, or else she can leave but she has to pay off his debts. Two bad options. But it often works. He's heard stories of women getting trapped like that plenty of times.

It's exactly what the doctor had been offering all along.

'Even though there are plenty of other options,' Katsumi had said sadly.

If you want to leave this line of work, you need to keep going a bit longer, until the investments are paid off.

'There are some choices where neither of the options on the table are any good,' Kabuto says to Nanomura.

He recalls the line he read the other day in his book. *A person's whole life can just be snuffed out on the merest whim of some stupid general.*

Nanomura watches him steadily. Kabuto puts his hands up again, emphasizing that he has no intention of fighting. The bleeding from his shoulder is heavy, but his clothing is absorbing enough of it that not much is dripping down to the floor anymore.

Kabuto turns around, showing Nanomura his back. He takes a step away.

A small, quiet movement. But to Kabuto it seems like it takes all the courage he's built up over his whole life.

It's very possible that Nanomura will attack him while his defenses are down.

A knife might sink into his back at any moment.

Another step, then another, slowly walking away, one step at a time.

There are things he wants to ask. What's the difference between a friend and an acquaintance? How can you go from being an acquaintance to a friend?

After a bit, he turns around. Nanomura is nowhere to be seen. Maybe he left as well.

Just his voice, seeming to float across the floor to Kabuto. 'I wanted to hear more about your son.' Kabuto can't tell if Nanomura actually said it or if it was just his imagination.

He comes to a stopped escalator and decides to walk down. Then something occurs to him. 'Nanomura-san, there's some change left in the vending machine.' His voice rings out through the store. 'I want you to have it.'

When he exits the department store, Kabuto takes out his phone to check the message that came in. It's from his wife. *Katsumi wants to move out. I want to talk about it so I'm waiting up for you.* A jolt of nerves shoots through Kabuto, sharper than anything he felt during his fight with Nanomura. He's about to write back but his fingers are slick and he can't properly input the characters. It's only then he realizes that his hands are covered in blood. The pain in his shoulder comes back to him in a rush and he drops his phone. He picks it up and wipes it off, remembering when Katsumi fell down as a little boy and he fastidiously wiped away the blood from his son's cuts.

He knows he can't get into a taxi bleeding like this and thinks for a moment about what to do. It occurs to him that he can't go home either, looking like he does.

He tries to think of an explanation – he fell down, or a drunk bicyclist crashed into him. That might make her feel sympathetic.

But he managed to end it without killing Nanomura. This makes him happy. Through the force of his will, he broke the chains that bound him.

He goes to the clinic one week later to declare his freedom and cement his victory. Your two options were a scam, and I chose neither. The doctor is shaken. Not long after, Kabuto falls from the roof of an eight-story office building, and dies.

After Kabuto leaves the department store, Nanomura does what he needs to do to clean things up. He goes back to where they were fighting among the mannequins and checks to make sure there's no visible damage, then makes a call to have someone come in and deal with the body in the bathroom. After that he looks around for any other damage or mess. Finally he scans through the security tapes and erases anything incriminating. As he goes about his tasks by the light of his flashlight, he thinks about the situation with his son.

Thanks to Kabuto intimidating the boy's friends, it's possible that his son's situation might change for the better. But Nanomura also knows that there's no guarantee his son will work to change himself in any significant way.

He's worried about his son.

But he's also glad to be able to worry.

He could have easily been killed just a short while ago. If Kabuto had taken his life, he'd never be able to worry about his son again. *I'm grateful for my life,* he thinks, and while it seems like the sort of thing someone might write on a decorative strip of paper to hang at a temple, his feeling is sincere.

It's only when he's wrapping up and ready to head for the stairs that he senses someone behind him.

For a moment he thinks that Kabuto might have returned, but almost immediately he knows that's not it. He turns around to see his coworker, the other security guard on the night shift, a man almost twenty-five years his elder. White hair, medium build. Usually his eyes look sleepy both day and night, but now they gleam in the darkness.

It's when Nanomura notices the gun in the man's hand that he realizes his coworker is after his life. *Another one.*

It's turning out to be much harder to retire than he had hoped.

He suddenly thinks of the man who gives him his contracts. The doctor. *Is it possible that he was pitting me and Kabuto against one another, trying to get rid of us both?* Or maybe he would have been satisfied if just one of them was out of the picture. Either way, it seems likely that he was the one who set up their confrontation. Then they both bowed out of the match and left it at a draw. At which point the doctor sent orders to his coworker to finish the job. At least, that's how it all seems to make sense to him.

'Hands up,' says his coworker. The man seems relaxed, his voice steady.

Nanomura steps backward. He has no intention of doing what the man says, at least not yet. He doesn't raise his hands, either. Another step back. Another.

The gun remains aimed directly at his chest.

Is this where it ends? Did I only get a brief extension?

'Hands up,' his coworker says again, advancing.

'Wait. Why are you targeting me?'

'You know why.'

'No, I really don't.'

'If I take you out, my stock goes up.'

'What are you talking about?'

'I'm old. The only jobs that come my way nowadays are delivering messages. If I do you, people will know I can still pull a proper job.'

'Wait. Please, wait.' There's real entreaty in Nanomura's voice.

'I won't wait.'

'Please. There's just one thing I need to ask you.'

'What?'

'I need to get my change from the vending machine.' At this point he's backed up far enough that the machine is right behind him.

'Your change?'

'From when I bought a drink before.'

His coworker laughs. 'You need your change now? You can't spend your coins when you're dead.'

'I just don't want to leave it there.'

'Fine. Only reach for the change slot. Don't touch anything else.'

At his coworker's pronouncement, Nanomura feels a wash of gratitude.

And that's where you and I are different, he thinks. The man didn't fall into obscurity as a professional because of his age, but because of thoughtless decisions like this one. Nanomura would never have let Kabuto reach into the change slot, no matter how much he asked. You can never let your opponent set the agenda.

His back still to the vending machine, Nanomura reaches his right arm behind and hooks his fingers into the coin return.

He knows there's no guarantee he'll find anything.

But it's his only hope.

His fingers find an object. At first he's not sure what it is. He has to grope at it a bit before he can ascertain its shape.

'How much change is in there?'

Nanomura nods at his coworker. 'Enough to save me.'

He thrusts his arm forward and fires.

It's a gun, small enough to fit in the palm of his hand. He's never held one of these before. But it works.

There's a short, sharp bang.

No bigger than your thumb, but still powerful enough to kill. The famous foreign-made miniature gun.

A red hole appears in his coworker's forehead. The man stands stock still, then topples over backward.

Nanomura exhales. *Miyake-san really is good after all,* he thinks. The best professionals make all sorts of provisions. If they have a chance to go to the scene of a job beforehand they'll invariably conceal something they can use in case they lose their weapon. By stashing a blade or a firearm they can turn the tide of a fight. Just like how Kabuto hid a miniature gun in an unlikely spot.

Miyake-san. You saved my life.

Nanomura resolves to thank him personally the next time they meet. It may not be for a long time, but he hopes that they can go back to the way things were before, when they were friendly acquaintances.

FINE

KATSUMI

IT'S THE DAY OF THE big test, but I'm totally unprepared, and on top of that I'm late. I thought I could at least cram on the way to school but as I flip through the textbook every page is blank. There's also construction everywhere blocking the way; just as I realize that I won't even be able to get to school, I wake up. I look at the clock and see with a jolt that it's past eight. Late for work. And I have a meeting today.

'Daddy!' My son Daiki is standing in the doorway. 'Mommy, Daddy's awake!' He runs off to her. I get out of bed and check the date on my phone.

'Thought it was Monday.' My smile is sheepish as I enter the living room.

'You must really love your job,' my wife Mayu teases. 'Don't forget, I have a hair appointment today.'

'Ah, that's right.' She's been wanting to go for a while. Not even for a perm, just a cut, since her hair has been getting long. Most days she's at home with Daiki, who's just turned three, so she doesn't get much time to herself.

I eat breakfast and watch my son as he watches his favorite

anime like he's glued to the TV. Meanwhile Mayu walks back and forth with loads of laundry, then she's washing the dishes, and then she's running the vacuum cleaner, seemingly every-where at once. I start feeling a little bad for sitting here, which reminds me of my father. Mom would be busy cleaning the house and Dad would notice that she maybe wasn't in the best mood and then he'd get all fidgety and awkward, not sure what to do with himself, which would end up making my mom get annoyed with him.

'Oh, Katsumi, your mother called,' Mayu says. 'She wants to know if we'll be visiting your father's grave for New Year's.'

It's only autumn, and Mom's already worried about the holi-days? We've got our hands full with work and the kid, we can barely think a couple weeks ahead. But I get that this is import-ant to her.

'You should call her, she sounded a bit down.'

That's no good. The past couple of years she's been doing a lot better, no more visits to the therapist, going about her daily life more or less normally. A lot of it must have to do with becoming a grandmother. She's been off the meds a while, happy to say. But maybe something happened that put her in a bad place. I remember how she was when Dad died. Blank, expressionless, not doing much besides sitting there breathing. I feel a flash of fear that she could get that way again.

'What's with the extra-concerned voice?' Mom says on the phone, sounding bright and chipper. When I hear that I'm relieved, but also a little nonplussed. I had been concerned enough that I was starting to think about taking time off work to go be with her.

'Oh, nothing, Mayu just said that you sounded a little down and I was worried.'

'Well, of course I'm down. It's only been ten years since my

155

husband killed himself.' I would hesitate to make a joke like that even among the family, but if she's doing it then I guess she really is fine. They say that the best medicine for grief is time, and I suppose ten years is a long enough time. She may well have decided that if it hurts whenever we think about Dad then it's best to talk about him more often, so that we get desensitized.

'I'm planning on coming home at the end of the year, like always.'

'And Daiki's coming too?'

Daiki is her top priority. At this point I'm just an add-on.

'Of course. So, hey, everything's okay, right?'

'Ah, right, I wanted to tell you.' Mom's tone changes. 'The other day someone showed up at the door. A young guy.'

'A young guy. Lucky you.'

'No, it was weird. You know what, I think when I spoke to Mayu it was still on my mind, which is why she thought I was feeling down. She's a sharp one. Careful, kiddo, or she'll catch you cheating on her.'

'You're just assuming that I'm cheating?'

Mom is quiet for a moment. I say, 'Mom,' and she begins again, only now her voice is low, almost flat.

'I thought your father was cheating, and look what that led him to do.'

'What are you talking about?' I notice my own voice has gotten more forceful.

It's not that I was desperate to get all the details of some never-before-heard story, but still, on my way back from work to our condo in Saitama I stop at Mom's house, where I grew up.

She seems fine now. In a teasing mood. 'So eager to hear about your father's cheating episode, Katsumi, are you sure you aren't cheating too?'

I don't rise to her taunt. 'Was Dad really cheating?'

I steal a glance at Dad's photo on the family altar in the corner. Is it true, Dad?

'It was the day before it happened. The morning. I was pressing him a little. A girl from work had sent him a text, and I wanted to know what it was about.'

'A text from another woman? And you read it?'

'I just happened to.'

'Just happened to, huh?'

'Yep,' she insists. 'The text came in at night. The ringtone woke me up so I switched his phone on silent, and I ended up reading the message.'

This is surprising. Ever since I was in elementary school I had been aware that Dad would hang on Mom's every word, watch her every move, but I never really knew Mom to pay that much attention to what Dad was doing. 'And what happened?'

'What happened? I asked him about it.'

'An interrogation?'

'No, no, nothing like that. But then the next day he took the day off of work to . . . And I wondered . . .'

'You thought he did it just because you suspected him of cheating?'

Her face darkens, and I worry that I went too far. I was mostly joking, but I guess what I thought was a gentle poke might have felt to her like I was piercing the scab of a still-healing wound.

Then I realize she might have been tormenting herself with that very question after Dad died, and that's what made her need medical care. She might have felt it was her fault.

'But I don't think Dad would actually cheat.'

'He was a very handsome man.'

'Sure, maybe, but . . .' Based on how he always bent over backwards to make her happy, I just can't see him doing something like that. But then again, love and lust aren't usually governed by

157

calm, reasoned decision-making. There are so many examples throughout history, all that drama and tragedy. 'Well, so, what happened?'

'When I asked him if he was cheating on me?' Mom is suddenly much older. Or at least it looks that way to me. I realize that I've opened a box that shouldn't be opened, asked a question that should have been left unasked. 'He said the woman had made a mistake. That she probably meant to send it to someone else but entered the wrong number.'

'Kind of a flimsy excuse.'

'I thought so too.'

But apparently after Dad died she found out the flimsy excuse was true. She doesn't explain it to me in detail, but I imagine that the woman later sent a message explaining that the first text was meant for someone else.

'And what's this thing with the young man who came by?'

'Did I say he was young?'

'You did. Did he strike you as suspicious? Was he selling something?'

'He just showed up and asked about your father. Is your husband in, ma'am? But he knew his name.'

'He was looking for Dad?'

'Yeah. At first I thought for a second that he was an illegitimate son.'

'How old was he?'

'Maybe twenty.'

At that Mom reaches into a postcard holder on the dresser – and I realize that this postcard holder is the one I made in elementary school art class, decorated with engraving, impressively still in use, like an old player still in active rotation, though it's not like there were any new players trying to take this one's place – she takes a small piece of paper out of the postcard holder. 'He left his card.'

Ryoji Tanabe, Personal Trainer.

'What did he want to see Dad about?'

'I didn't like it, so I told him to leave.'

'Without hearing what he had to say?'

'Why should I listen to him?'

'Hm. I wonder what he wanted.'

'You know, you really have grown up.'

'Huh?'

'You're a father now too, Katsumi. It happens so fast.'

'I don't think we're talking about the same thing anymore.' Maybe Mom's mind is starting to go.

'You look just like your father.'

Ryoji Tanabe certainly has the body of a personal trainer. Plus silky hair and a wholesome vibe. Like a fresh-faced college student.

'I'm very glad you took the time to meet with me.'

'Oh, um, sure.' I keep my answer noncommittal. My wife was worried about me meeting him. She thought he might be part of a cult or something and she kept insisting that I be on my guard. 'What exactly were you looking for when you visited my parents' home?'

'I apologize for showing up so suddenly. And for upsetting the lady of the house.'

The lady of the house? Weird. 'She wasn't upset, she—'

'No, I didn't have a chance to explain myself. All I wanted was to pay my respects to your father. My story is a bit detailed, I hope you won't mind.'

I do mind, but I can't exactly tell him that, so I ask him for the short version. He agrees, but the story he launches into ends up being astonishingly long. It starts with him entering elementary school and not quite fitting in, then little by little growing into a happier kid, then becoming a bit physically stronger and getting really into handball as a teenager, then winning a sports scholarship to college – he just goes on and on. A best-man's speech at a wedding wouldn't have this much detail on the groom's life story. It's like he wants me to write his biography.

'Now I work as a trainer, and my life is fine, but, you know, just fine.' I feel certain he's about to launch into all his current anxieties and concerns. I wish I had a remote control that could put him on fast-forward. 'So, here it is. Not too long ago I went to a fortune teller who has a pretty good reputation. I wanted to ask what to do to level up my life.'

'Level up. Right.'

'And the fortune teller says to me, there's something from your past that you've left undone. You've forgotten something that you need to do.'

I feel bad for young Tanabe, his eyes shining as he tells me about the fortune teller, who was obviously just doing a standard routine. It's like telling a salaryman that they're caught up in a web of problematic relationships. Ninety percent of them will feel that it's right on the money. Then the fortune teller says, 'You'd rather live a quieter life,' and most of them will agree. But the words in the reading Tanabe got – something from your past that you've left undone – it's just abstract mush. A masterclass in vagueness. Basically any interpretation will fit.

'And that's when I remembered. Amazing, right? This episode from ten years ago, it hit me like an electric shock.'

'I'm hoping this is the part where any of this has to do with my family?'

I let my irritation show, but he doesn't even seem to notice. 'Ten years ago, when I was still in elementary school. Sixth grade. I skipped school that day. Like I said before, I didn't really fit in at school. So I was just wandering around that day, wasting time, when some scary older boys, I mean they were only in middle school, but they surrounded me and told me to give them my money.'

I have no idea where this is going, and it's starting to annoy me, but I nod, pretending to be interested. 'A shakedown.'

'I was so scared, I didn't know what to do. But then a man appeared and chased them off.'

Come on, I think, but Tanabe confirms it: 'That was your father. Such a respectable man.'

'Dad? Dad did that?' It's hard for me to imagine him facing down a bunch of juvenile delinquents. He was just an ordinary man holding down a company job. He never gave me the impression that he had such a strong sense of justice that he would do something like that. Although I do remember it being important to him that things be fair. He always used to tell me that we may not know what's right or wrong in this life, but at least we should try to be fair.

'As he was leaving he took a piece of candy out of his pocket and gave it to me, and that's when he dropped this. I picked it up, meaning to give it back to him, but he was already gone.'

Tanabe reaches into his own pocket for his wallet and takes out a small rectangular card. It's old-looking, the corners bent and worn down.

It's an appointment reminder card for a doctor's office, with Dad's name on it.

'I took it home with me and kept it all these years.'

Hard to imagine holding onto something so easily replace-able as an appointment reminder like it was some kind of prized possession.

'I was just a kid,' Tanabe goes on. 'I kept thinking I needed to return it to him, but I never did.' The look on his face is like he's confessing an old sin.

'Huh.'

'Then when I visited the fortune teller, I realized that *this* was the reason my life feels so stuck.'

Sounds to me like Ryoji Tanabe took the fortune teller very seriously and decided he needed to find the thing left undone from his past. I can picture him turning his room upside down looking for the one thing that caused all his current woes, thinking that there had to be something, eventually digging out this appointment card.

I would think he'd understand that returning a card to the person who dropped it after ten years isn't going to turn his life around. That's just not the way things work. But the hopeful gleam in his eyes says otherwise. It's the sparkle of a true believer, an adherent to the theory that life is surprisingly simple after all.

'Well, that's considerate of you.' I don't see any harm in thanking him. 'Thank you.'

'No, it feels like a big weight off my mind.' I can tell he thinks that the binding seal has been broken and that it's only rosy days ahead.

It feels like we've finally concluded the Good Fortune Ceremony of Young Tanabe, but then I flip the appointment card over, and something shifts. 'Wait.' I wasn't prepared for what I see on the back of the card: the date of the appointment. 'This is for . . . the day after.'

'The day after? Day after what?'

The day after my father died, I tell him. One day before this appointment Dad killed himself.

Tanabe is visibly shocked. 'Your – your father – took his own . . . ?'

'Yeah. He did.' By jumping off a building.

'When I met your mother the other day and she said your father had passed, I just assumed it was from an illness or something like that.'

'At least that would have been –' But I cut myself off. It's not really a question of which is worse, losing someone to suicide or to illness. They're both awful.

'Wait, hold on. That means that the day I met your father was the day he died.'

'Really?'

'When I picked up the card I looked at the date. I remember thinking, oh, this is for tomorrow. That's why I wanted to give it back to him as soon as I could.'

I peer at Tanabe. Did he really see my father just before he died?

'I can't believe this,' he says.

'We couldn't either.'

'No, I'm telling you I actually don't believe it.'

What, he's more shocked than we were?

'Because I remember – I remember what your father said.'

'What did he say?'

'He said being a kid is hard. Hang in there and do your best.'

Tanabe had told Dad that he didn't have any friends, and Dad had laughed and said that he didn't either. But even without friends, he was happy. His life was a gift, every day.

'So for me to hear that someone who said that to me died right after. And not just died, but . . .'

Yeah. Threw himself off a building.

In that moment, I feel something change. Like the fog in my mind has burned away all at once.

Mom accused Dad of cheating, and she carries that regret with her. She blamed him for something he didn't do and she wouldn't believe his explanation, and she's convinced that it was all too much for him. I half believed it myself. But if I really think about it, Dad wouldn't kill himself over something like that.

In fact, Dad disappearing without any explanation and leaving Mom angry is something he would never do. He was always so focused on not upsetting her. I'm sure that even after death he's still watching her, trying to gauge her mood. He would have done anything he could to clear his name from beyond the grave.

Mom's interpretation was completely illogical, but I had been ready to accept it.

These past ten years I've kept a little box in my heart, a box stained the color of grief and regret. Only now it's starting to look like the contents of that box are completely different than what I had thought.

I thank Tanabe sincerely.

He looks like he might still have some feelings he wants to get off his chest, but I'm overcome with the need to get out of there.

How did my father die? And why?

'Mr Miyake, do you want this belt cleaned as well?'

For some reason there are multiple cleaners in our neighborhood, which sparks some fierce competition. It's like the Cleaning Wars. Although I think my wife and I are the only ones who call it that. They're all clustered in the same area, and every household has some reason for picking the one they use – whether or not it has a point card, whether or not they're nice to the customers, how fast they are, things like that.

We started going to Nano-chan Cleaning for no other reason than the fact that they have a cute vegetable mascot on their sign and our son would always point at it whenever we walked by. We have no complaints about the staff or the cleaning or the price.

'The belt?'

'The belt on this coat comes off, so we treat it like a separate garment. We have to charge separately for it.'

'Ah, I see.' I don't give it that much thought. 'Sure, go ahead and clean the belt too.'

'Sounds good,' says the man behind the counter. Recently I realized that it's his shop. He looks like he's in his late forties or early fifties, quite friendly and plain-spoken, easy to talk to.

I pay him the fee and exit the shop. Out of nowhere I start thinking about Dad. An episode from when I was a kid pops into my head, from when I went with him to the cleaners and a similar situation cropped up.

When he handed over Mom's coat, the staff asked the same question: the belt is separate, what would he like to do. Just like me, he quickly said, 'Yes, let's do the belt,' but before the words were even out of his mouth he started to have second thoughts. He was worried that if it cost extra money Mom would get mad at him, *Why would you pay extra money for the belt,* and so maybe he shouldn't do it. At the same time, he was afraid of what Mom would say if only the belt went uncleaned: *You left the belt dirty? Who leaves the belt dirty? Did you do that specifically because it was my coat?* I was only in elementary school, but I could tell he was worrying about what Mom thought way more than he needed to. I think I remember suggesting that he call her and ask. But either he did and she didn't answer, or he muttered something about not wanting to annoy her with a call like that. Either way he never got an answer from her. Instead he took out his own money and used that to pay for the belt instead of the money Mom had given him for the cleaning. 'See, Katsumi? Easy, right?' I remember he seemed pleased with himself. 'We'll see what Mom says, and if she thinks that the belt didn't need to be cleaned we just won't tell her it cost extra.'

I couldn't imagine Mom actually cared that much about a

little extra money for belt cleaning, and it seemed bizarre to me how Dad was always so careful with her.

'I bet your dad didn't know how to interact with other people when he was a kid,' my wife once said. Dad was already gone by the time she and I got together, so she only knows him from my stories, most of which involve me laughing about how he used to act. 'I didn't have a lot of friends when I was little, so I feel like I understand where he was coming from. Once you find some-one who means something to you, you get worried that the littlest thing might push them away.'

'Nah, I doubt there was anything so sophisticated going on with my dad.' He was just a regular submissive guy.

When I was younger I used to think that I would understand where he was coming from better once I grew up and had a wife and kid of my own. But now that I do, more often than not I just feel like Dad was being silly.

What if his death wasn't suicide?

After going back and forth on it, I decide to only tell Mom part of what I heard from Ryoji Tanabe. It doesn't feel right to stir up her feelings, and anyway, I don't have any real answers. That said, when she asks what I heard from Tanabe, I know that I have to tell her something or it would just worry her more. So all I tell her is that Dad saved him from a bunch of bullies. 'He did?' she asks, her eyes welling up.

As the days go by, my doubts about Dad's death only grow.

He didn't seem like someone who would opt for suicide. I had always thought that, over these last ten years. Then again, I couldn't deny the reality of it. My only choice was to push down those thoughts.

I was never in as bad shape as Mom, but his death hit me hard. I blamed myself – I lived my whole life with him, yet somehow I never sensed his urge toward death, so I couldn't do anything to stop it. There was a while where I was in a very low place. He seemed the same as always, right up until he died, which I interpreted to mean that he had been depressed for a long while; all the times he seemed to be enjoying himself with me, all the everyday conversations we had, he had been suffering through it all. Once I had that in my head, I didn't know what to believe, and I turned inward. Probably the only reason that I didn't need to seek medical help like Mom did was because I met Mayu. If I hadn't, I'm sure I would have had to go along with Mom to see a doctor.

But maybe it wasn't suicide after all. And if not, how did he die? And why?

I don't have much in the way of clues. Just an appointment reminder card, returned by Young Tanabe ten years later.

I look online and find that the clinic is still in business. It feels like if I call out of the blue and ask, 'Excuse me, do you recall a patient named Miyake from ten years ago,' that they would think I was some kind of crazy person.

I turn it over and over in my head, unsure of what to do, until I find myself standing in front of the clinic. I was out making sales rounds. To be precise, I planned a sales route that would take me nearby the clinic. I found the placard among the tenant listings. Third floor, corner office. The name of the clinic on the door matches the one on the appointment reminder card. Same doctor's name as well. Internal medicine and cardiology. What did Dad need to go see a doctor for?

No, actually, the bigger question is why he would come to see this particular doctor.

Our family doctor was close to our house. At first I thought maybe it was easy for him to get here from work, but this place is pretty far from his office at the time. So maybe he had some specific malady that he needed to come here for? But as far as I can tell it's just a normal neighborhood doctor's office.

So why here?

Maybe he had some connection through work. He was in sales for an office supply company, and there's a non-zero chance that they sold to this clinic and Dad was in charge of the account. Maybe he had something small he needed checked out and planned to do it here.

'Can I help you?'

I turn to see a woman in a white coat, actually a slightly pink coat, who must be one of the medical staffers. She looks to be around Mom's age. She stands up straight, good posture. Probably coming back from some errand.

'Ah, no,' I say, but then I realize that I won't get anywhere if I don't come out with it. 'Um, actually, I think my father might have been a patient here, ten years back . . .'

I was expecting any overture like this to come off as odd, but she seems totally unfazed. 'And what was his name?'

Hearing such a calm response, I'm the one who's flustered. 'This was ten years ago, mind you.'

'I was here ten years ago.' Her voice is crisp and clear. Even a little cold. 'I have a very good memory.'

The words appear in my mind: *android nurse*.

I must have handed her the appointment reminder card because she says, 'Ahh. Mr Miyake. I remember him well.' Her expression doesn't show any signs of recognition, but she's probably not lying. Why would she be?

'Well, I wanted to know about my father . . .'

'You don't know your father?'

'I recently came across this appointment card. The date on the back of it . . .'

'The appointment date is written there, yes. Nowadays our cards are a bit sturdier stock.'

'This date – it's the day after my father died.'

She peers at me for a moment. It feels like her eyes are x-raying me.

'He killed himself,' I tell her. Not a pleasant thing to tell someone, but I get the feeling that not much would rattle this lady. 'And I was curious to know what he might have been sick with.'

'He killed himself because he was sick?'

'I don't even know that.'

She looks at me, then the card, then at me again. 'Would you please wait here a moment?' Then she goes into the clinic. I wait there, like a kid who's been told to sit still.

'Mr Miyake? It was ten years ago, so I cannot say I remember him well, but, yes, I have some recollection.'

The doctor could be fifty or seventy. His short hair is fully white, his face has no flab or folds, and his lines look like they didn't come from age but rather were carved into him. His gaze is sharp and his back is ramrod straight. The only thing about him that seems relaxed is his voice. He feels robotic, just like the nurse.

It's the middle of the workday but we're in an exam room and he's speaking with me, leaving me to wonder if I'm not getting in the way of other patients' appointments, or maybe this is in violation of some law or statute, and I'm hunching my shoulders with uncertainty, but he says, 'The clinic has an afternoon break,' as if he had seen right through to my anxieties.

I feel his eyes moving over me like the pressure of an ultrasound machine.

'I do see the resemblance. Looking at you brings back memories of your father.'

'Was he a patient here? Or did he come for work?'

The doctor regards me steadily, as if he's about to tell me I have a serious disease. It makes me nervous. 'Work?'

'He was in sales for an office supply company.'

'Ah, I see. That work.'

'That work . . . ? Uh, yes. A salesman.' I look over at the desk to see if maybe there are any supplies from Dad's company.

'Your father was a patient here.'

'What was wrong with him?'

'I am not permitted to discuss that sort of thing, but I can tell you that it was not a very serious ailment. The kind I might prescribe headache or stomachache medicine to treat.'

I had my doubts that he killed himself because of some serious illness that he couldn't bear any more, and now it seems I can safely rule that out. 'I was just wondering, because this office isn't close to where he worked or to our house, so I wasn't sure why he would have come here.'

'And why are you looking into this now?' His voice is hard. It feels like he's scolding me for letting my symptoms go for too long before seeking medical attention.

'I happened to come across his appointment reminder card. It just struck me as odd – he had an appointment here for the day after he died, so.'

So? What am I trying to say? It's not like I'm here on a tour of my father's favorite spots.

The doctor stares at me. It feels like he's about to ask, *Is there anything else that's been bothering you?* But instead he says, 'Well, thank you for coming. This is the first time anything like this has ever happened to me. A fresh experience.' It seems like something that a researcher would say, but devoid of any of the curiosity or excitement that drives the desire to do research.

I stand up and start to leave the exam room when the doctor calls out, 'Wait a moment.' He takes a step closer. 'Did your father ever tell you anything?'

'Anything?' He raised me, so, yeah, he told me lots of things. Although mostly it was his worries about Mom, or rather his gentle grumblings. I'm pretty sure that's not what the doctor is asking about.

'Ten years ago, or thereabouts, your father said to me that he had something he wanted to pass on to his son.'

'Something to pass on to me?'

'But if that does not sound familiar then perhaps I am wrong.'

I leave the exam room. The waiting room is empty, kind of dimly lit. Half of the lights are off. It makes me wonder if this clinic actually sees any patients.

I wonder for a moment if I need to pay, but the woman at the reception desk is looking down at something else, so I just bob my head and murmur, 'Thank you,' then make my way out.

It's only when I'm on the elevator down that I realize the doctor didn't ask whether Dad died of an illness or in an accident. Did I even mention the cause?

'Why this, all of a sudden?'

'Sudden? It's been ten years.' But I imagine what Mom is asking is why I'm looking through things now that haven't been touched in a decade.

It's the weekend, and I'm at Mom's house poking around Dad's study, searching for any clue as to what he might have been thinking back then. If he was thinking about death. Or if he was specifically not thinking about death.

I give Mom a kind of vague excuse. 'After I talked to Tanabe the other day I just started feeling like I wanted to clean up Dad's study.'

She tells me she hasn't gone in there once in the last ten years.

Dad's study, we called it, but it's basically just a closet that we built out a bit.

Ha, I remember how it happened.

I think it was when I was in middle school, and Dad suddenly started saying that he wanted his own space. He was all excited about it. He said the house was old enough that it was reasonable to think about renovations. But Mom said that we should be using the money it would cost to renovate on my education instead, and if he really wanted a study we could just expand the closet a little bit; Dad clapped his hands at that. 'Wonderful idea! Why didn't I think of that myself?'

At the time, seeing Dad act like that, I remember thinking that he was being shrewdly opportunistic, but that's not quite right. Strictly speaking, opportunism means staying flexible and picking the direction that looks the most advantageous. In Dad's case, he would go along with whatever direction Mom suggested, even if it put him at maximum disadvantage.

Like if they were watching a baseball game and the umpire called a ball and Mom carped about it, 'No way, that was in there for sure,' Dad would chime in, 'Seriously, that was a strike any way you look at it, get your eyes checked, ump!' But then Mom would say, 'Well, I don't know, maybe it was a ball after all,' and Dad would smoothly change course, 'Yeah, it's a close call, but maybe it's just a hair out of the strike zone.' I saw it happen a million times.

Seeing me going through Dad's study now, Mom must have felt like it was time to finally get it a bit more organized, because she brings over a big trashbag and says, 'Toss out anything we don't need to keep.' None of the emotional reaction she had a few years ago when I last suggested we clean out his room.

It goes smoothly enough. Being more of an oversized closet than an actual room, it doesn't take too long to work through all of it. I inspect everything in the cabinets and separate it out into stuff to keep and stuff to get rid of.

Each item recalls some episode with Dad; there's a gentle tug of sentiment, deciding what to do with the item, then pulling the next one out and getting a fresh wave of memories, over and over again, slowing to a crawl – thankfully none of that happens. I'm able to work through it efficiently. Most of the things Dad had in there are nondescript office supplies, samples he got from work, magnets and paperclips, documents. Nothing that would pull at the heartstrings. Mostly just stuff.

I'm starting to feel like this will end up being just a closet cleaning, when I find it: behind a heavy cardboard box is a paper bag, seemingly hidden back there. I haul the box out of the way and dig into the bag.

The first thing I pull out is a piece of drawing paper, with a picture in crayon. It says 'Thank you for taking care of us Daddy' in messy letters. Must be something I made when I was little. I don't remember drawing it, but it has to be something I gave him. And he kept it . . .

Then I take out three notebooks with college ruled paper. Each one is numbered on the cover in simple, blocky text.

I flip through them and see they're filled with Dad's handwriting, neat lines like they were exam study notes. At first I assume that they're his notes from his student days, but when I read more closely I see that it's not that.

When asking 'Why are you angry?' and the answer is 'I'm not angry,' assume anger.

It reads like a bunch of aphorisms. But actually they're all more like practical instructions, guidance for how to get through life. He worked at the office supply company, maybe they were notes on how to deal with claims from his clients. But then I read some like 'Always respond enthusiastically to everything she says, but don't be too over the top or she might get annoyed at the overreaction' and 'No matter what her food tastes like, always eat what's on the plate', and I realize these are rules for dealing with one particular person. Obviously Mom. They're tips and tricks for how to act around her. There are pages with a flowchart that map out in fine detail how she reacted to the things Dad said and did.

I knew Dad was always concerned about Mom's mood, but I never imagined he actually made a formal study of it, if that's even what you could call this project.

What a piece of work he was.

I picture him watching to see what her face was doing while he was washing the dishes, or him coming home in the middle of the night as I had just gotten up to go to the bathroom and he got all tense and started to apologize because he must have thought it was Mom and not me, or him stuffing his face with Mom's cooking and raving absurdly about how delicious it was.

I remember thinking all the time that he didn't need to try so hard. I still think that. Then I unfold the crayon drawing again. *Thank you for taking care of us Daddy.*

A few moments pass before I realize that I'm crying. Which is a bit odd, because I'm also smiling. I wasn't feeling like I was going to cry, not in the slightest, but tears keep flowing down my cheeks.

Even though my vision is blurry now I continue reading through the notebooks, now and then bursting into laughter. I just keep thinking how much I want to see him again.

I even catch myself thinking, yeah, it's been too long since we spent any time together, which just shows me that I really haven't fully faced up to the fact that he's gone.

I go back to the paper bag, looking to see if there's anything else worth finding. There's a flyer for a new amusement park called Kids Park. He must have been planning to go at some point.

The last thing I pull out is a small envelope, like one that might contain marriage papers or maybe divorce papers. When I open it up, a key slides out.

*

'Did Dad have a storage unit somewhere?'

Having finished going through his stuff, I bring the garbage bag down to Mom on the first floor and ask her this.

'A storage unit?' Her brow wrinkles.

I could just tell her that I found a key, but I wouldn't want her imagination to run wild and have her start thinking that maybe he was cheating on her after all, maybe it was a key to his lover's apartment.

'Ah, I just thought that it felt like there wasn't that much to go through, and he had a trophy I saw once that wasn't in there so I was wondering where that might be.' It's a pretty clumsy lie. Out of all the things I could have mentioned, why did I go with trophy? I had never once seen a trophy in our house.

'A trophy for what?'

'Um, I can't remember.' For the nervous husband grand prix, probably. 'But I guess he didn't have a storage unit or a separate apartment or anything, huh?'

'An extra apartment? With what money?' But as soon as she says that Mom seems to remember something. 'Oh wait –' She looks like she's staring at the dust motes floating in the light. 'Actually, now that you mention it.'

'Yeah?'

'It was for you, Katsumi.'

'For me?' I wasn't expecting this to have anything to do with me.

'When you said you wanted to live on your own.'

'Ahh.' That I do remember. After I had been in college for a little while I was starting to get tired of the long train ride to school, and more often than not I was coming home late at night, so I started thinking about getting my own place, which I discussed with my parents. I had saved up money from my part-time job and was just about to start getting serious about looking for an apartment when Dad died. After that it didn't seem right to move out and leave Mom on her own.

175

'Your father actually put a lot of thought into it.'

'Into what?'

'Into finding a good place for you.'

'Since when did he know anything about real estate?' When I hear myself say it, I have a vague recollection of saying something similar to Dad, before he died.

KABUTO

'Katsumi, what general area would be good for you to get your own place?' I ask my son as he comes down the stairs, looking sleepy.

'Hrm?'

'You got home late again last night. Weren't you talking about this just the other day? That it takes a long time to get home. And it's true, we are pretty far from your school. You can't really stay out late with your friends.'

'I mean, this way if I don't feel like hanging I have the excuse that I need to catch my last train.'

'I was thinking I could help you look for a spot.'

'What kind of spot?'

'An apartment, or a condo.'

'Since when do you know anything about real estate?'

Katsumi obviously thinks I'm just messing around with him. He's already only half-listening.

But I'm serious enough. Of course, I'd be sad to see my son move out, but if he's still living in the same city then it won't be hard for us to meet up. It would be more upsetting to think that he might stay here living with his parents forever. He has to go out on his own sometime, and now seems like a good opportunity for it.

'Why, though?' My wife had pushed back when I brought it up with her. 'Can't he just keep commuting from here?'

'He could. But he has to move out eventually. Better it be when he's in college than when he gets his first real job. He'll have more time now to get used to it.'

'I wonder.'

It's true that I'm not fully committed to this as the only right move for him. Katsumi should be the one to decide how he wants to live his life. It's more that I want somewhere safe to hide out, somewhere away from our house.

Two days have passed since I faced off against Nanomura at the department store, on night duty with a kitchen knife.

After that episode, I got in touch with the doctor. 'I'm through with surgery,' I told him.

'Why is that?'

'Because that's what I decided.' I had expressed that wish to him countless times before, but never as resolutely as this time.

He was silent for several moments, as usual, and then said in an uncharacteristically grave voice, 'I see.' He didn't add anything about me needing to work just a bit longer if I wanted to retire. I guess it was like they used to say, that you can only ask the Buddha for forgiveness so many times. He must have realized that there was no use in gently explaining to me again why I needed to keep working.

In the past, I was always worried about what might happen to my family, so I went along with what he wanted. But this time was different.

If you want to retire, you need to save up more money. The doctor had said this to me so many times, but only now did I realize that I didn't need to listen to him. We had a business relationship, nothing more. We were equals.

And there were other options than the ones that he laid out.

I saw a story on a morning show about a comedian who wanted to make a break with his management company; the negotiations fell apart, and it blew up into a whole thing. From the standpoint of the management company, it must have hurt – they had taken a no-name performer and spent time and money to help make him famous, and now that the comedian had made it he wanted to go out on his own and leave them behind. But the situation with me and the doctor is different.

I'm not trying to make it on my own or sign on with anyone else. I just want out. And unlike new talent or a new employee, I was earning for the doctor since my very first job. He had been telling me that investments had been made in me, and I accepted that as an explanation. But when I thought about it, I couldn't see what those investments might have been.

'The fire escape is just over there.'

The real estate agent, whose name is so nondescript it might as well just be Mr Realtor, snaps me back to the present.

I look up. We're in the open-air walkway of an apartment building. He's showing me the property. It's a thirty-year-old structure with a tasteful exterior, not great light. The rent is cheap for the area.

I step through the door he's holding open and enter the unit.

'Are you thinking about moving?' Mr Realtor appears to be in his thirties. He looks over the sheet with my details as he asks.

'All depends on finding a good place. Actually, it's for my son. He wants to try living on his own. He's in college.'

I tell him where the school is and he says, 'That's a little far from here.'

'Ahh, hard to get there, you think?'

'Well, not impossible. The world is round, after all.' Mr Realtor seems to think he's making a clever joke, but the world can be perfectly round and you can still head in the completely wrong direction and never get where you're going. I don't quite know how to answer.

The place isn't great but it's not bad, although I suppose it's more bad than great, and while I might be satisfied with the fact that the low price offsets a lot of the negatives, it's hard to picture Katsumi thanking me with a whole lot of enthusiasm when he sees it for the first time.

I recall something my wife once said: 'I'm not looking for special praise, you know. For housework, or for the PTA. But if I do all of that and someone takes it for granted I'll have something to say about it.'

I don't imagine Katsumi just assumes that all parents buy condos for their kids who want to move out, but if he doesn't seem happy about it, I'll be a little sad. But it would also be awkward if he makes a big show of pretending to like it.

'Anything a little closer to where he needs to be?'

'The rent will go up, unfortunately. If your son is living on his own, a studio would probably be fine, I would think?'

'Yeah, true, but there might be some times when I would want to stay over too.'

He looks me up and down quickly and seems about to say something, but stays quiet. I shrug encouragingly, as if gesturing for him to please go ahead. 'That wouldn't annoy your son?' He chuckles.

'Probably would. But I wouldn't be coming by often. Just for emergencies.'

'Emergencies? Does that happen often in your line of work?' He glances at my info on the paper.

'I work in sales at an office supply company.'

'So, for mechanical pencil emergencies?'

'Or erasers.'

He frowns. 'Is it for if you get in a fight with your wife and need somewhere to hide out?'

'Exactly,' I say, but my wife and I generally don't get into big fights. Animals are built for struggle within their group, but when the hierarchy is clear, there is no struggle. I heard that once. The point of struggle is to establish that hierarchy, to vie for authority, to stake out a position. Even leaving out how my wife might feel, in my heart and mind our hierarchy is perfectly clear. So there's no need for us to struggle. When I say emergency, I'm thinking of someone coming for me who wants me out of the picture. I need to be able to get my family somewhere safe. 'There's one other thing.'

'And what's that?'

'It's fine if the rent goes up a bit, but do you have anything that's – hm, how can I put this – anything not well supervised?'

'You'd prefer that over one that *is* well supervised?'

'Or even if there's a good superintendent, a building where the oversight is . . . flexible?'

If some rough characters come anywhere near my wife and son, things will get violent. And if it's a building where the super sticks their nose into everything the tenants do, it'll be hard to do what I need to do.

'Like an older super, who's hard of hearing and kind of out of it.' As I say it I feel sorry for possibly involving some innocent elder, so I add, 'But who's also creepy and unlikeable.'

'I can't say I have anything like that to show you right now, but I can take a look around. And you said that you don't have much more time to look at things today?'

I don't have any more time to look at apartments because the doctor summoned me. It's been a week since I called the doctor and told him I was out. Then yesterday I got a message saying to come in for an exam right away.

You may be dragging your feet, but you're still going, because he called you. If you're ending things with him anyway, just ignore him!

If there's an observer watching my life, no doubt that's what they're shouting right now. Shouting at me that no matter what I do I'll never be able to leave this work behind. But it's easy to shout from the spectator seats what you think is the right thing to do. For the person on the field, it's not so simple. After considerable thought, I'm doing what I think is right.

The moment our negotiations break down, I expect the doctor to move against me and my family. He'll need to demonstrate to all the other professionals he contracts out to that if you try to walk, this is what happens.

I need to make him think that we haven't reached the point of breakdown. That we're still in the middle of negotiations.

'And you have not changed your mind about wanting to discontinue your treatment?' the doctor says, facing me.

'No, I guess not. I don't think it'll be good for either of us if I keep going.'

'For either of us?'

'Shops that keep unenthusiastic employees on staff end up with bad reputations.'

'That does not bother me.'

Even if they're unenthusiastic, when push comes to shove they still get the job done. Which is how it is with me. The doctor knows this. As long as he keeps giving me jobs, he'll profit, like a cormorant fisherman working his birds.

'Well. I'm all done.'

'But to do that you must –'

'No. I don't care. I'm not doing it anymore.'

The doctor doesn't answer right away. This exchange is one we've had so many times, like a couple who keep threatening to divorce one another.

Should I take him out right now?

Part of me thinks I should. The audience in the spectator

seats, assuming they're there watching, they probably think I should too.

It's just the two of us in the exam room. We're sitting facing each other, our knees almost touching. Even without a weapon I can think of more than ten ways to end his life, no exaggeration. I thought the same thing the very first time I came here.

But it's not that simple.

'If anything should happen to me,' he told me during that first meeting. He usually speaks in medical terms, using symptoms and treatments as code, but about this he was brutally clear. 'You will not be able to escape this clinic. The exam room door will lock, the main exit from the office will lock.' Then he explained that the space would flood with poison gas, killing everyone, including his staff and any patients. Basically, if he comes to any harm, he'll take everyone else with him.

Which means that if I want to take him out, I need to get him to leave the clinic. But he almost never does. It's like he's grown roots into the floor. It might be possible to lure him out somehow, but if he ever emerged he'd be on high alert.

'Then if I understand correctly, Mr Miyake, you would like to discontinue your treatments.'

'Like I've been saying for a while.'

'You do understand that if you do this it will result in massive damage to the system, not just to the malignant elements but to benign cell structures as well.'

He's talking about hurting my family. 'Can't you just pinpoint the malignant parts? Medical science is fairly advanced. Maybe you have some groundbreaking new procedure.'

'There is no such procedure.'

'Can I have some time to think it over?'

'Of course. Please think it over very carefully.'

Here we are again, same conversation we've been having for

years. He thinks that by threatening my family he'll be able to keep me in the game forever.

'Once I get my thoughts together I'll be in touch.'

'I have many surgeries I can recommend to you.'

I leave the clinic. Instead of taking the elevator like I always do, I take the stairs, even though they're less convenient. I've just got a bad feeling. The doctor had the same flat expression as always, but he seemed to be avoiding eye contact.

When I exit the building I hail a cab, like I always do, to head back to my office.

The driver says that there's an accident up ahead so he's going to take an alternate route, which is fine with me.

He turns left at the intersection, then makes the next right. At that moment a text message comes in.

It's a woman from work, the office manager. I read it and see that it's a note of a personal nature, which is perplexing. She must have sent it to me by accident. Which would explain it, because we're not particularly close, and she does give the impression of making a fair amount of careless mistakes.

I think maybe you meant to send this to someone else, I write back, but just as I'm about to hit send I notice that the sound of the car engine has changed. We're accelerating at an alarming rate, so much so that I wonder if the driver has lost consciousness. I look in the rearview mirror to check.

He's awake, glaring hard at the road ahead. Accelerating on purpose.

The doctor's face flashes in my mind.

Looks like the driver is planning to crash us into something.

I almost always catch a cab right in front of the doctor's office building. This driver must have been made aware of that.

There's a clear screen separating the front and back seats. I lean way back and thrust my feet forward as hard as I can, breaking through the screen. The driver jerks the wheel. I reach forward and grab him by the neck. No time and really no reason to hold back – I squeeze as hard as I can, trying to snap the bones.

His foot comes off the gas but the car doesn't slow down. Through the windshield I see the buildings lining the street. There's a pedestrian on the sidewalk. A young woman. I strain to reach the wheel from the back seat and manage to yank it once, swerving to avoid her. But I won't be able to avoid smashing into the telephone pole.

I curl up into a ball in the back seat, trying to minimize the damage. Don't want a broken neck. I aim my back toward the driver's seat.

Then comes the collision. I'm thrown against the back of the driver's seat which absorbs enough of the impact. I can hear the airbag deploy. The taxi slams into the pole at an angle and spins in a half-circle, crashing into the nearby wall, the impact jolting my body. I'm tossed to the side against the door like a doll. Pain shoots through my head. I can hear the windshield shatter.

The car comes to a stop. I feel fortunate that I'm able to move, and that I can get the door open. I squeeze out of the car and leave it behind me, wrecked and smoking.

It feels like the vibrations from the crash are still shaking me from the inside. But if that's the extent of it, then I will have gotten off pretty easy.

So the doctor decided to get rid of me. Or maybe this was just a warning?

Maybe he thinks that if an attack like that would do me in then he has no use for me as a professional anyway.

Whatever it was, it's clear that he's not messing around.

People are rushing outside the building, probably looking to see what the noise from the crash was, buzzing like a disturbed hornet's nest. I weave my way through them.

On a nearby side street, someone calls out to me. 'Excuse me, hey, are you alright?' I turn to see the woman who we narrowly missed running over. She looks agitated. Then she thrusts a knife in my direction. My head is throbbing from the crash, but I can still move faster than her.

KATSUMI

'So this is the key? I think we can find out about it. Probably. Not a hundred percent, but probably.' He's wearing a suit and has a cheerful face with what looks like a permanent smile. Considering that I'm a client, his tone and general attitude lean toward the overly familiar, but he seems so upbeat that it doesn't bother me.

I wanted to find out what the key that I discovered in Dad's study unlocks, so I asked a few locksmiths and real estate agents about it. I would lead with, 'There's no way you can find out something like that, is there?' and, as expected, they would answer me that no, there's really no way to find that out. Just as I was on the verge of giving up, this one locksmith said to me, 'Keep this between us – there's a guy who collects records from when keys get made. His data is pretty thorough.'

'Is that something you're allowed to collect?'

He smiled at my apparent shock. 'Of course not.'

So it sounds like this guy keeps an illegal database of keys.

The locksmith who told me about him must have taken pity on me when I explained my reason for wanting to find out about the key.

'You don't strike me as someone who would be up to no good,' he said. I was surprised at how trusting he was, but also grateful.

And that's how I came to meet this fellow, a friendly young

man who looks like someone took a fashion model and turned down the good looks a notch or two so he's more like the rest of us.

'I'm guessing it's for an apartment somewhere.' Thinking back to having talked with Dad ten years ago about wanting my own place, it seems possible that the key opens up some rental unit or condo.

'Could be, yes. I would bet it is. I'll take it and check it against my database. Even if we don't find the exact lock it's for, we might be able to tell where it was made, and you could use that as your starting point.'

'Will you be able to tell right away?'

He stares at me. 'How fast do you think computers can work?'

I suddenly feel bad. I wonder if I've hurt his feelings. 'I don't know, how fast?'

'I don't know either.' His eyes are as calm as still water. He's not mad at all.

'Maybe your father wanted a hideout,' Mayu says as we're eating dinner.

'A hideout?'

'Don't they say that men want to be alone sometimes?'

'The person who said that was probably a man who wanted to be alone.' And I imagine women want to be alone sometimes too.

Sitting next to Mayu is our son, absorbed in the television, his cheeks full of food that he's not chewing. 'Eat your food, buddy,' I say. He chews once, twice, and then his mouth stops moving again. 'But yeah, Dad was always so careful around Mom, it makes sense that he might have wanted a break now and again.'

'Even though your mother is so nice?'

'You know how it can get between spouses.'

From my perspective, Dad was clearly way too timid with Mom. But it's not like she was lording it over him. Actually they got along pretty well.

'What do you remember most about your father?'

'What's this all of a sudden?'

'Just curious. You know I grew up without a dad.'

'Hm. Let's see.'

'What are you smiling about?'

I realize that I *am* smiling, because of the memory that came to mind. 'One morning I woke up and Dad was passed out in the yard, wearing something that looked like he had just gotten back from outer space.'

'Your dad? Did he have a spacesuit?'

'There was this giant hornet's nest in our garden.'

He got up at four, or five, before sunrise anyway, for some reason all fired up and determined to deal with the nest before Mom and I woke up. He went into battle with his spray. Or so I heard later. By the time I was up, it was done. The nest was melted on the ground, I guess because of the liquid pesticide, and there were piles of dead hornets all over. Dad said he felt bad about it, and he really seemed to mean it. He must have been exhausted and overheated from all the layers of skiwear and down jackets that he used for protection because he spent the entire day lying down. And I'm pretty sure I remember Mom giving him a hard time for going so overboard.

Thinking about it now, Dad did all that to protect us, without us even knowing he was doing it.

I notice that Daiki has climbed down from his chair and is standing next to me. I give him a quizzical look and Mayu says, 'I think he's scared,' pointing at the TV.

It's a cartoon, and there's a ghost on the screen with suspenseful music playing.

I lift him up onto my knee and say, 'Don't worry, Daddy's

here.' I'm not just trying to make him feel better, though. I mean it sincerely. When I tell myself this, I feel it deep down.

I'm filled with the desire to protect him from all the frightening things, all the unreasonable things he's bound to experience in life. At the same time, I understand that you can't go through life and avoid everything that's upsetting or tough to deal with.

Always give it your best shot, buddy, I encourage my son silently, and it occurs to me that I'm still trying to give it my best shot. I feel a melancholy smile come on. Dad gave it his best too. I remember my crayon drawing for him. *Thank you for taking care of us Daddy.*

'Do you remember the last thing you talked with your father about?'

'Sorry?'

'What was the last conversation you had before he passed?'

'Aah.' For ten years I had been wondering the same thing. Dad just jumped off a building, no warning, no hint. Was it possible he said or did something that might have given me some inkling of what was coming? 'You know it's funny. I really don't remember. The more I try to remember, the more it feels like, I don't know, like I'm trying to dig something out of the sand but it just keeps sinking deeper.'

'You really don't remember?'

'I guess not.' But the instant I say that, it comes to me. Bubbling up like a spring I had been digging for and digging for, over more than ten years, and suddenly it decides to burst forth at just the lightest touch.

It was morning. I came down from the second floor and Dad was pulling the lid off a plastic cup, pudding or ice cream or something. 'You mind if I have this?' he asked. And then he added vaguely, 'How've you been?'

So I gave a vague answer, 'You know, fine.' And then I said, 'Hey, Mom was gonna eat that.'

He had already dug into the pudding-or-ice-cream, and he grimaced. 'Uh oh.'

'It's not that big of a deal.'

'It *is* a big deal,' he said, clearly concerned. 'I'll buy her another one later.'

Was that our last exchange? 'After ten years I finally remembered.' I tell Mayu about it. 'It was nothing, really, just an ordinary interaction.' I laugh it off, but I'm also genuinely happy that it came back to me.

'If he said he was going to buy her another one, it seems weird that he would have jumped without doing that first,' she says.

There isn't always a logical progression to suicide. Sometimes it comes out of nowhere. I had been telling myself for years that's how it was with Dad, but after what I heard from Tanabe, now I'm not so sure. 'You're right. That is weird.'

'And that was the last thing you ever said to each other?'

'Yeah, it happened that day. I kind of feel like we might have talked more after that, but I can't remember anything else.' Maybe when some more time goes by another memory will sprout up like this one just did. Maybe I'll remember what else we talked about.

Looking down at the top of Daiki's head, I imagine myself sitting on my own father's lap. Not surprisingly, I can't clearly recall it.

'You're getting a call,' Mayu points out, and I look down at my phone. An unfamiliar Tokyo number. I consider just ignoring it, but then I think it might have something to do with the key.

It's not that, but it's in the same neighborhood: it's the doctor I paid a visit to the other day. I'm not thrilled to hear from him. It feels like he's calling to give me some bad test results.

'I am calling about your father.'

'Yes, hello, sorry for showing up unannounced the other day.'

I turn to Mayu and try to gesture that it's the doctor, but the only gesture I can think of for doctor is miming listening to a heartbeat with a stethoscope. She nods, a blank look on her face that doesn't give me much of an indication as to whether or not my gesture made any sense.

'It seems one of my staff remembered something about your father.'

'One of the nurses?'

'He had some dissatisfaction with his job that led him to look for a physician who might help.'

He's speaking obliquely, which I assume has more to do with patient privacy than the fact that this happened a decade ago. 'Something psychiatric?'

'She said he wanted a referral to a specialist.'

'Would it be possible for me to speak with this staff member?'

'Yes.' The doctor's voice is cold. 'And have you discovered anything more about your father?'

'A bit,' I reply. The key. He doesn't say anything else, and suddenly I feel uneasy. 'Just a bit,' I say. 'I wouldn't say it's much of a discovery.'

'But you found something?'

'In Dad's study.' I'm not sure how much I should tell him. I don't even know what it's a key to, so I keep my answer nondescript. Who knows, it could turn out to be a key to his lover's place after all. The chances are slim, but non-zero, and if I just went and told everyone about that I'm sure Dad wouldn't be happy.

The doctor tells me that the clinic doesn't see patients on Wednesday afternoons, so that would be a good time for me to come by.

I check my schedule, tell him I'll come again, and hang up.

When I tell Mayu about the call, she says, 'Your father wasn't happy about his job?' She cocks her head. 'He doesn't strike me as the type, though.'

'You never even met him,' I say with a laugh.

'Yeah, well.' She nods. Then she knits her brow. 'So, hey, what was that gesture you made on the phone, like you were pressing every single button on a vending machine?'

KABUTO

The superintendent says it with a flourish, like it's his catch-phrase: 'If I die, I can't guarantee anything.'

He's old for sure, but he seems solidly built and quick-witted, certainly not like anyone who's going to die any time soon. His face is wrinkled but ruddy.

Mr Realtor delivered as promised. A property that's very close to what I'm looking for.

'I don't get involved with any of the tenants' business,' the super says with a smile. 'I live here, in that back unit on the ground floor, but as long as there's no major disturbances I keep to myself.'

'What if people are wrestling in one of the units?'

'They could be playing football, for all I care. Although there was a guy on the fifth floor who was doing some experimental cooking and something exploded.'

'Oh, I remember that,' Mr Realtor says, almost sounding as if he remembers it fondly. I'm starting to think that he's an odd character as well. 'I wonder if he was actually cooking food.'

'Who knows, maybe he was doing chemistry. Whatever it was, that explosion was loud! The fire alarm was blaring, the fire trucks came with their sirens blaring too, it was a real brouhaha.'

'So the main thing is that you don't want people to be noisy?' I ask.

'I don't want people to be *that* noisy. But in general, like I said, I stay out of it.'

'I guess if someone blows up the room they don't get their security deposit back.'

'Heh. You know, the building was originally all condos. It's getting old now, though, and there aren't many of the original owners still living here. A lot of them rent out their units. I own some units too, though they're all empty. If you've got the money, I would sell one to you.'

'Is there a reason I should buy instead of rent?'

'That way you don't have to give it back!'

'And can I experiment with cooking?'

'As long as you don't blow anything up.'

He gives off the impression of being an old soldier still on active duty. But the unit itself is in decent shape. It was renovated a few years back, and considering when the building was first built it doesn't feel run-down or old-fashioned.

'I don't think my son would have anything to complain about living here.'

'Buying your son a condo? Parents nowadays really spoil their kids.'

'It'll also be a safe haven for me. I can hide out here if I need to.'

'That might annoy your son,' Mr Realtor says.

'Eh, he just has to tell the kid, listen, who do you think bought this place for you,' says the super. 'It's good to have a shelter. There could be nuclear war, or environmental collapse, who knows.'

'You think so?' asks the realtor.

'Every so often God hits the reset button. Like decluttering. Your room fills up with junk, you throw it all out, you start again.

Then things pile up again and it gets out of control again. Same story since the dawn of time.'

'God needs to get better at keeping things organized,' I say, but that one word is now bouncing around my head: *reset*. Washing away all my crimes, erasing everything I've done, wiping the slate clean and starting fresh. It seems like a magic word. At the same time, another part of me sits in stern judgement. *Where do you get off thinking like that? Why should you get to reset when no one else does?*

'Well, what do you say? You want to buy?' The super looks at me.

'What do you think?' asks Mr Realtor.

'I'll sell it to you or I'll rent it to you, whichever.'

'Let's say I buy it today, is it possible I could move in to-morrow?'

The realtor says that it typically takes about a month. Which is what I figured. But happily the super seems more optimistic. 'If you're not dealing with a loan, I can get it ready for you real quick. Like I said, I own a bunch of units, I can handle all the paperwork myself.'

Apparently the superintendent also does real estate. The realtor made the introduction, but the super says he can take care of all the finances and registration himself.

I'll be in touch, I tell him. He smirks and says people who say that don't usually end up getting in touch.

'Kabuto, honey, your manager is being rather emotional.' I'm talking to the owner of a place I stopped by on my way home. A nudie magazine shop called Momo. Everyone calls the owner Momo too. Her body reminds me of a rubber ball, and she's always wearing semi-transparent lingerie. I have no idea how long she's been in business, but back when I first started out everybody told me that if you needed information you went to Momo. And it was true, she did seem to know all the rumors.

'He's not my manager. He's my doctor. And I don't think he can get emotional.'

'That might be what it looks like from the outside, but on the inside it's a different story. Doctors tend to be very proud.'

'That's a stereotype.'

'Sure, maybe. But, you know, if you invest in a player or an employee and then they decide to quit on you, well, you're not gonna be too happy about that.'

'And that's how it is for him, huh?'

'How would you feel if out of nowhere your wife said she wanted to split up?'

'I wouldn't like that one bit.'

Momo laughs heartily. 'Right? When that happens, people lose their cool. No more room for logical negotiations. All they can think about is how to beat the other side, how to make them suffer, and if they're going down they want to bring the other person down with them.'

'I really don't see this doctor getting that worked up.'

'Yeah, maybe not,' Momo concedes. 'But he did move on you with that taxi, right? That is not the action of someone who's being discreet.'

'It's gotten to the point that when my realtor was handing me some papers I was worried he might attack me.'

'Are you really gonna retire?'

'That's the plan.'

'Do you think you'll be able to?'

I regard her carefully. I bet she knows countless professionals – strictly speaking they can be counted, but either way, she must know almost everyone; what they're like when they win, and when they lose. And she's probably seen plenty who have tried to retire. 'You're telling me it's hard to cut ties?'

'No, no, something more important. Think back to all the jobs you've pulled, everything you've done. All bad stuff, I'm sure. Taking people's things, taking people's lives. Do you really think that you can wash away the past, hit reset and just start again?'

This hits me right where it hurts. I almost moan out loud, no exaggeration, but I manage to keep it in.

When I consider how many people I've killed, how many lives I've ruined, I know all too well that there's no wiping it clean. I have no right to do that when everyone else suffered.

'I guess someone who's messed up can't have a change of heart and start over.' Somehow I'm able to get the words out.

'They can, most people. But not you guys. If someone had minus a hundred points, they might be able to make good, but you boys have like minus fifty thousand!'

'Minus fifty thousand.' Enough that there's no point in even keeping track. 'No reset, huh?'

'I mean, he'd get angry.'

I don't ask who.

'Think about how you'd feel if someone came to kill your son for money.'

'Then they'd better be tougher than me. They'd need more minus points than just fifty thousand,' I growl. I know that just imagining it will make me erupt into flaming torrents of rage, so I don't. 'What do you think I should do?'

'How should I know?' Momo laughs again. 'Ask online. Anyway, your manager seems to be heated up, so I would worry about your family first.'

'He knows what I'll do if he touches my family.'

'But if he's upset, there's no telling what *he'll* do.' She must be able to sense my anxiety, and she adds, 'It doesn't hurt to be careful, you know? It could get a whole lot worse than a taxi driver.'

195

'Yeah. Right when I got out of the taxi a pedestrian came at me with a knife.' I had no problem dealing with her, but it's also true that I didn't see it coming. 'Any good ideas at all? I'm not saying I want to reset my crimes. But I am looking for a way to keep the doctor from being able to hurt my family.'

Momo crosses her arms and makes a face like a little girl would make when thinking hard. She's quiet, so I'm quiet, waiting for her answer. Then a text comes in.

'Bad news?' Momo asks. 'Your face got all frightened.'

'It's my wife. She wants me to get some potato starch on the way home. She remembered that she forgot to get it before. When she's in a rush she sometimes forgets things.'

Momo exhales hard, though I can't tell if it's out of mockery or admiration. 'Well – we don't know what your manager's gonna do next, but maybe what you can do is buy yourself some insurance.'

'From where?'

'What if you tell him that if anything happens to you, a letter that exposes him goes out to everyone in the media.'

'That could work.'

'Or you could tell him that if anything happens to your family, you'll spread around some dirt that would ruin him.'

'That is better than doing nothing.'

'Right? This guy is a veteran, but he can't keep going forever.'

'He has been at it for a long time though.' Ever since I first met him when I was around twenty, it's always seemed like the doctor was at the top of the game.

'You know the opening lines of *The Tale of the Heike*, right?'

'The days and months are travelers of eternity?'

'That's *The Narrow Road to the Deep North*. Whatever. The point is, no one can be on top forever. Terahara was the kingpin, and he's gone. Same with Minegishi. The Top 40 list is always changing. The most powerful boss eventually goes out to pasture and turns into a feeble old man.'

'So you're saying if I want to retire, I have to wait for him to retire first?' Also do people still care about the Top 40?

'Don't you want to work?'

'I've had enough violence. I don't want to kill anyone else.'

'I might expect to hear that from some kid who just got into the game, but from you . . .'

'Guess I'm a late bloomer.' As I say this, I try to organize my thoughts. 'Do you have anything on the doctor? Anything that he wouldn't want to get out? Like you said, something that I could use to keep him in check.'

'Nothing comes to mind. But do you really need something?'

'Don't I?'

'The less specific your threat, the more it'll make his imagination work, and the more careful he'll be. Just hint that you've got something really bad. Meanwhile, what if *you* hired someone? Someone to take *him* out?'

'If I need that to happen I can just do it myself.' Then again, I can't hit him while he's in his office, and he barely ever leaves the office. I explain this to Momo.

'You'll just have to lure him out, then. You could be the decoy.'

'How?'

'Who knows? You'll have to figure that part out. But if you do manage to get him out, he'll probably be extra on-guard, so your best bet is to get another pro to move when there's an opening.'

'You really seem to want to make an introduction,' I observe. It's like she's pushing all kinds of wares on me to try to get a finder's fee.

'I'm just trying to help! Besides, if I hook you up with someone, it's not like I get anything out of it.'

'So, got any recommendations for who?'

'Most of the boys I liked are dead and gone, sad to say. Cicada. Lemon and Tangerine.'

'I hope you don't like me.' I say it as a joke. But in the next moment I can see my own death, coming closer.

My own death. That's one way this all ends. Somehow it feels more real than it ever has before.

'I'm going to die,' I find myself saying.

'Whoa, what's that now?'

'Not just me. Everyone dies eventually.'

'Well, yeah, sure.'

'Yeah. I have to die.'

'Seriously, why are you saying that? Hey, how about Asagao? He's good. The Pusher.'

'Does he even exist?'

'Sure he does.'

A professional who pushes people in front of moving cars and trains. Sounds like a method like that would get you caught, but he's supposedly been doing it for a long time. So he must be good. 'That could work.'

I imagine it might be possible to get the doctor outside and trick him into crossing a street.

'I can't set it up for you. You'll have to deal with him yourself,' Momo tells me, and then shares details on how I can get in touch with this Asagao. I never thought I'd be hiring a professional. 'If you really are going to go to war, make sure you cover all your bases. Don't just leave it all to another professional. There might be something you can do too.'

'I know.' In the end, the only one you can really count on is yourself. And if it turns out your own best doesn't cut it, you just have to accept defeat.

'But take care of yourself, honey,' Momo says with a smile. 'You know I like you.'

That's when I realize that none of this is going to work. I

remember what my wife always used to tell Katsumi: *Just do whatever you can do. Beyond that, it's out of your hands.*

And she was right.

KATSUMI

'I found a key in my dad's study,' I tell the doctor, sitting facing me. I feel a little bad for telling him this when I haven't even told Mom yet, but when he asked me there in the exam room, I felt a pressure bearing down, forcing me to answer honestly.

When I asked to hear more about Dad dealing with psychological issues ten years back, the doctor invited me to come by the clinic. Wednesday afternoon's a good time, he had said. His voice was mild enough, but I also picked up on the fact that he wouldn't be willing to meet at any other time. I didn't have a problem with leaving work early to go visit the clinic. But when I showed up and the nurse who Dad had asked for help wasn't there, I was annoyed.

She was the person I came to talk to, and if she wasn't here he could have saved me the trip by letting me know beforehand. I communicated this to him gently, with zero barbs, but maybe I should have put in a barb or two, because he seemed content to just tell me, 'She is not available,' and leave it at that. Then he asked: 'You said you found something about your father?'

That's right, I had mentioned that. And now here I am telling him about the key I found in Dad's study.

'What is it a key to?'

'I have someone looking into it. I think it's an apartment somewhere.'

'An apartment?'

'Here, this is it.' I take out my phone and show him a picture. The actual key is with the guy checking it out for me, but I took a photo just in case I needed it. I'm not sure I should be show-ing it to this doctor, but then he's leaning forward, looking pretty eager.

'Would you mind sending me this photo? It may be that I can help.'

'Help?'

'To find what the key opens.'

That actually makes sense; the more people looking for it the better, I'm about to say, but then: 'I think I'm okay for now.' Why did I stop myself? Maybe because it seemed weird that a doctor would be able to help me locate information on a key. Or maybe I felt like I shouldn't be sharing this stuff outside of a very limited circle.

'I see.' The doctor doesn't seem particularly disappointed.

Back in Saitama, on my way home from our station, someone steals my bag. I'm walking down a narrow street, my largeish bag hanging from my shoulder, when a motor scooter buzzes past me. I dodge to the side but then my whole body gets jerked forward.

They yank my bag off me and I tumble to the ground. The sun's gone down, and though there are a few streetlamps the area is dark and no one is around.

When I get back to my feet I'm feeling more embarrassment than pain, even though I didn't do anything wrong. I take off after the scooter, thinking through what's in my bag.

My phone is in my jacket pocket. My train pass and wallet are in my bag. Is it bad? Not so bad? I'm less upset about losing the cash than I am about having to deal with getting new credit cards and IDs.

I'm not likely to catch up to the scooter on foot, but I run like I haven't run in years.

Run.

I swear I hear a voice and I glance to the side. Dad's right there, running beside me. Of course it's not actually him. But it's like my memory sprang to life, from almost twenty years back; I was ten or eleven, we were in a park, he was helping me with running practice. *Go, Katsumi, pump your arms, you're cooking now.* Was I breathing this hard back then? Was it tougher for me when I had never run a race before than it is now, when I haven't run in so long?

Dad is light on his feet, bounding ahead. Wait for me – I try to keep up – then he disappears around a corner. I have to catch him –

I tear around the corner, pitched forward at full speed when I see the scooter, toppled over on its side. I skid to a stop.

It takes me a few seconds to process. The scooter is on the ground, engine still running, and several feet away is a man with a helmet covering his face. He must have been thrown off the scooter and is now struggling to his feet. I spot my bag on the ground and pounce on it just as the man runs off, helmet still on. He's limping but manages to move fast. I stand there in a daze as a crowd starts to form.

'That's intense. So what happened in the end?' the owner at the cleaner's asks as he refolds the suit I had handed him. 'Did the police come?'

'They did. They asked me a ton of questions.'

'How did the scooter fall?'

'Apparently it slipped on the turn.' I heard that from several witnesses. He took the turn too fast and tipped too far over for the skinny tires. 'The bright spot is that the bike didn't hit anybody when it spun out.'

When I fell over, I scraped up my suit. It didn't tear but there was serious abrasion, so I brought it to the cleaner to ask if they could do anything about it. That's how we ended up talking about the robbery attempt.

'Your wife must be shaken up.'

'She was worried at first but by now it's already just something interesting to talk about,' I say with a laugh.

The owner's face contorts into a frown as he points at the suit. 'I'm not sure we can do much for this. It's damaged pretty badly. But this jacket looks like it might be special to you.'

'Hm?'

'It's fairly old, and these initials are different from yours.' He shows me the monogram on the inside. 'Any particular significance?'

'Ah, yeah, it was my dad's.' I'm impressed that he noticed that detail.

'A hand-me-down?'

'That's right. I'd love to be able to keep wearing it, but I guess you can't wear anything forever.'

'Let me give it a try.' The words lift my spirits a bit. 'It won't be perfect, but we might be able to cover up the damage some.'

'I'm sure it'll be fine.' The truth is that I had been thinking about retiring the suit one of these days. Not only is it a memory of Dad, it's also a pretty fancy brand, and although it fits me well, somehow I'd been feeling like I shouldn't be wearing it all the time. This might end up being the sign I was looking for.

KABUTO

The truly timid husband will greet his wife each morning with an apology for everything that he is going to do wrong throughout the day. I heard a rakugo comedian say that once. I'm not sure if I thought it was funny or tragically identifiable, but this morning when I see my wife and immediately sense emanating from her the cold smolder of discontent, I almost apologize out loud. The only reason I don't is because if I apologize without knowing why she's upset, she might get even more angry and accuse me of giving an automatic apology without really meaning it. It's true that if I had apologized it would have been automatic, but I would have meant it.

We exchange some snippets of banal conversation as I munch my toast. I try to project a light air of contrition in case it actually is my fault.

Before long it comes out: she thinks I've been cheating. When I'm finding it hard to handle the strained atmosphere, I take out my phone to check the weather – wishing that there was a forecast for her mood as well – and she says, 'You didn't put your phone on silent last night.'

Her voice is so chilly that if it blew through a forest it would freeze every living thing within. And then, bit by bit, she comes out with it.

A message came in on my phone last night, and the tone rang. She was annoyed because it disturbed her sleep, and she went to set my phone to silent. When she did, she happened to see the text.

I have no idea what this message is, so I look into my texts and see it there for the first time.

It's from a woman at my office. *Thank you so much for listening*, it says. And, *I had a wonderful night.* Along with heart emoji and cutesy stickers. Sweat starts to stream down my back, more vigorously than any time I'd ever been ambushed in the dark.

This is not good at all.

Of course, I barely know this woman. She's just a coworker, but not even one that I really work with. Once in a while there's something procedural I need to tell her. She has my number in case she needs to get in touch while I'm out on a sales call. But I have no idea what I was supposed to have been listening about, or what kind of a wonderful night we supposedly had.

'She must have sent it to me by accident.' I'm not just

grasping at straws; it actually seems to be the most likely explanation.

Thinking about it, I had gotten that other text from her before, just the other day. I had also seen her chatting with another coworker one night when we were all working late, and the two of them were looking pretty friendly – maybe she meant to send it to him?

My wife just sighs. 'Kind of a lame excuse,' she mutters, and leaves to go hang the laundry.

'I don't have anything against people who move fast. If you have a move, make it, right? Moves are for making!' It's getting colder every day but the super is wearing short sleeves. His arms aren't big, but they're hard and sinewy.

I had previously let him know I was interested in buying and he got the paperwork started, but when I reminded him on the phone I wanted to get into the unit as soon as possible, he said I should come over right then.

The immediate reaction, like a bell ringing out when you strike it, made me wonder if he just had nothing else going on.

I headed to the condo and met him in his office.

The super's room in the corner on the ground floor is surprisingly well-appointed. Leather sofa, large-screen TV, home theater setup. Everything in there has a solid and stately feel.

'When can I start using the unit?'

'If you pay me today, I'd say we can get you in there from tomorrow.'

'That soon?'

'In most places it wouldn't go that fast.' He seems to want me to know that the speed is because he's the one involved. 'Your son wants to move in as soon as he can, eh?'

'Yeah, you know.' I keep my answer vague.

'Oho,' he chuckles, giving me a knowing look. 'Or is it that you've got something you need to hide?'

'What?'

'A while back there was a politician who died, and they found a key for a condo and everyone assumed he was keeping a lover there and rushed over to find out.'

'What did it end up being?'

'The place was full of Gundam action figures.'

'Part of his political agenda?'

I'm not trying to make a joke, especially, but he sounds delighted at that and nods vigorously. 'You can learn a lot about politics from Gundam!'

'Well, anyway, that's not too far off from my situation.'

'So you've got something to stash away that you don't want your family to see?'

'Yeah, well.'

'It's not a dead body, is it?' This startles me for a second, but I can see that he doesn't mean anything by it. Then he adds, 'Not that it would really be a problem.'

'You'd be okay with a body?'

'As long as there are no complaints about the stink, or any weird noises, or insect infestations. Any of that, I'd have a problem, but as long as no one else is bothered, it's no concern of mine. Your private business is your business.'

'I would think that storing corpses goes beyond the level of private business.'

'Maybe,' says the super. I can tell he thinks that body storage is very much within the realm of private business. 'Anything I don't notice is all just your business.'

'I'm not sure that's how it works.'

'Hey, buddy, you're the one who's all hot to start using the unit. I'm taking care of all the paperwork and everything for you.'

'I do appreciate that.' I mean it.

Until just the other day, my plan had been to buy this condo, let my son live there, and use it as a hideout if things ever got dicey.

I decided to shift the plan based on a phone call I got this morning on my way to work.

It was from Momo. The call came in just as I was stepping off the train on my commute. I was surprised at how perfectly she had timed it, but not as surprised as I was by what she told me.

'It's not great news,' she said. 'I think I may have misread the situation.'

'Misread how?'

'Your doctor, he's more of a take-action type than I expected. Or maybe he's more paranoid than I thought. I guess he is a doctor, makes sense he would be into prevention. He's probably the type to take antibiotics before the virus is even going around.'

'Antibiotics don't work on viruses, they're for bacterial infections.'

'I spread our story like I said I would. Kabuto's got dirt on the doctor. If anything happens to Kabuto's family, it'll all come out.'

'Too obviously a lie, huh?'

'The opposite. The doctor's scared. I just made that all up, but it looks like it hit home. Felt too real to him, or maybe he's just too sensitive to the possibility. Whatever it is, he's looking into it now. He wants to know what you know. He's putting out feelers everywhere, hired a bunch of pros to investigate.'

'What happened to "no one stays on top forever"?'

'What goes up must come down, sure. But it doesn't always come down right away. The doctor still has influence. I messed up.'

'So you're calling to tell me to be on guard.'

'Yesterday a different professional was killed along with his whole family.'

I didn't answer right away. The word *family* stabbed into my mind. 'Who?'

'Someone who's the same as you, Kabuto.'

'How?'

'Someone who got work from the doctor but then started saying he wanted out.'

'What happened to his family?'

'They were going into a restaurant when a car crashed into them.'

'And you think the doctor called the hit?'

'Looks like it. Good things come to those who wait, but also sometimes bad things too. I learn something new every day, I guess.'

'Well then.' I could feel all too clearly that there weren't many paths left open to me. 'Looks like the old saying from our industry is alive and well.'

'Which one?'

'Get 'em before they get you.'

Seems like that's how it'll have to go.

After getting off the phone, I called into work and took the day off, then called home and let my wife know I'd be home a little later than usual. She asked what I wanted for dinner, but I didn't have the time or mental space to worry about that. Her voice was a shade darker than usual. I'm sure she was still suspicious about me cheating.

I knew I needed to get things ready as quickly as I could. I had the feeling I should have taken care of all of this much sooner, but I can't be sure that that would have been the right move either.

'So you're not taking out a loan, right?'

'That's right,' I say, and open the bag full of cash to buy the condo. The super looks a bit startled.

'Don't tell me you just came from robbing a bank.'

'I've been working hard and saving up.'

He looks dubious, but says, 'I got no interest in digging into your private affairs anyhow.'

We finish the paperwork and he counts the money.

'I'll get this registered tomorrow and then I can hand over the key,' he says. 'Then it's all yours. How 'bout it, I get things done pretty fast, huh? Know why?'

Because you've got nothing better to do, I think, but I don't say it. 'Because you're that good?'

He laughs. 'Because I got nothing better to do!'

I'm not sure I can call what I'm doing a plan. It's more like the first thing that came to mind. And it feels like it's the only option.

I have to get him before he gets me.

I think back to when I took on the hornets in our garden. They were a threat to my family, and I dealt with them, using what I learned online and the skiwear and helmet I had lying around the house. This time, there isn't anything online I can turn to. Skiwear and a helmet won't help against the doctor.

But it's similar enough in that I'll use whatever means I can to protect my family. I beat the hornets. Maybe I can beat the doctor too. I cling on to the hope.

Getting in touch with Asagao isn't as hard as I thought it would be. In fact, it's easy. I just follow the steps Momo laid out and soon enough I'm speaking on the phone with him. He doesn't ask me anything about myself, or any background on the target either.

All he wants are the basic details he'll need to do the job. Then he tells me how I can go about paying him, says he'll contact me again tomorrow, and hangs up.

It's true that most people in this line of work don't give too much thought to the person they're supposed to kill, or the person who the job is coming from. I never used to give it much thought either. All I needed was a time, and place, and some idea of the risk factors. It was like getting the weather forecast.

But with Asagao it feels different. He just seems completely detached. Lots of people don't even believe that there's an actual human being known as the Pusher who kills people by pushing them in front of cars or trains. They say that it's just a way of making an excuse for someone who had bad luck and died in an accident. A fiction, like the spirits who spirit you away or the *kamaitachi* in a sharp wind. People treat it like it's just a saying – *Poor bastard got killed by the Pusher.*

It felt a little anticlimactic to be having a phone conversation with the fabled Pusher like he was anyone else. But at the same time, just talking to him I could tell that there's something different about him, even though I couldn't say exactly what.

After the call I make my way to a shop in the Fujisawa Kongo-cho neighborhood. To external appearances it's a small fishing gear shop, but in the back it sells guns and explosives. It's been in operation a long time. I'd heard that when the original owner got too old to run it anymore a retired professional took it over from him.

I need to pick up some weaponry and supplies.

'Where are you planning to keep all this? If your family sees it you'll have some explaining to do,' says the bearded shop-keeper as he adds up the bill.

I look at him carefully. I don't say anything, I just take a good look.

He's fit and solid. The rumors that he used to be a pro martial artist could be true. He's loading the guns and bullet-proof vest I picked out into a small suitcase.

'What makes you think I've got a family?' My eyes stay locked on him. I don't want to miss the slightest reaction. I've bought weapons from him a few times before, but I don't remember ever sharing any personal details.

'Don't you? I dunno, I guess you just look like a family man. I mean, everyone's got some kinda family.'

'Yeah, I guess you're right about that.' I don't trust him. The doctor must have gotten to him first. Told him I might be coming around looking to buy some gear. 'Sorry, I changed my mind. I'm not going to need this stuff after all.'

The shopkeeper looks up nervously. 'It's done already, all I have to do is hand it over.' He stands up the suitcase and puts it in front of me.

'I haven't taken it yet. Give me my money back. I don't need the stuff.'

'Hey, what the fuck, man?'

He looks angry but I stare him down. If he says one more thing, gives any hint of aggression, I'm ready to pounce and get my hands around his neck.

He's not dumb. He can see in my eyes that I'm not playing around. He swallows. Then he takes the bills I had just handed over and reluctantly counts them out, then gives them back.

'You tell the doctor.' It's a safe enough bet that he'd get in touch to let him know I came. 'Tell him I want to meet. Tomorrow. If he doesn't come, I'll send everything I've got on him to all the places he doesn't want it to go. Tell him.'

The whole thing feels almost silly to me – I don't know what it is I'm supposed to have on the doctor, or where he wouldn't want it to go, so all I can do is hint – but he nods gravely. Maybe Momo's rumor making the rounds was enough to lay the groundwork, or maybe I did a good enough job selling it.

I take my money and put it back in my wallet. Just as I'm about to exit the shop I turn back around to look at the shopkeeper. He straightens up in alarm. I didn't sense him pulling a gun or anything; I must just be keyed up.

'Guessing you put out a call, huh?'

'W-what?'

I'm sure he has some call button for if someone comes into the shop and starts trouble. On a doorknob, or a pedal on the floor. Somewhere a customer wouldn't see it. It would call the cops, or maybe some tough-guy bodyguard to get rid of any unwanted visitors. Though it doesn't seem likely he'd have someone who could deal with me just waiting around on call, which makes me think that it goes to the cops. Maybe the idea was to have me run into the police on my way out, carrying all the weapons I had bought.

'Does the doctor really think it's a good idea to turn me over to the cops? What if I tell them everything?'

Though as soon as I say it I imagine that it would work to keep me locked down and threaten my family. On top of that, he could easily dispatch a professional to take me out wherever I'm being held. It actually does seem like a good way to neutralize me.

As I step out of the shop, two uniformed officers approach from across the street.

'Excuse me, sir,' one begins, then asks some standard questions, one of which is what I was just doing.

'I was checking out the fishing gear in there but I didn't see anything good,' I lie.

The cops look me up and down, making me wonder whether or not I seem to be the fishing type. 'Mind if we take a look at what you've got on you?'

'No problem.' I take out the contents of my bag and show them what's in my wallet.

I ask them if I can go and to my surprise they don't give me any more trouble.

If they came on a call from the fishing shop then they could assume with eighty or ninety percent certainty that I wasn't an ordinary civilian. The search was no doubt to peg me on weapons possession, but it's possible they had instructions not to take any extreme action if nothing turned up. If they had escalated, I was ready to respond with force, but luckily that didn't happen and I was able to go home.

Still. The net is tightening around me.

KATSUMI

On the wide grassy lawn in the park, Daiki walks around, looking down at his feet. He doesn't quite have a handle on his balance and it looks like he might topple forward at any moment, which makes me keep almost reaching out for him, but Mayu seems to read what's on my mind and says, 'I feel like we shouldn't steady him before he has a chance to fall,' so I hold myself back. 'I don't want him to get hurt. But we can't always be there to watch him.'

She's right – if falling down is part of living, then he needs to get the knack of getting back up. 'I know that, but as far as my feelings go, I always want to be there to protect him.'

Every move Daiki makes, he seems like he's about to tip over.

'One day he'll have to make his way on his own,' Mayu says, sounding like she's trying to convince herself. 'But of course that's a long way off.'

I nod, but I also know that it won't be all that long.

I'm sure Dad felt the same way when I was little.

'You know, you look like your father, Katsumi.'

'You just decided that?'

'You've been talking about him a lot recently, and I wanted to know more about him, so I asked your mother to send me some photos of him. She emailed me a bunch. And I thought, huh, Katsumi really looks like him.'

'You mean like we could be father and son? Ha, no one ever really said that to me before. Most people thought I looked like my mom.'

The phone rings. I feel a flash of annoyance that someone would call on the weekend when I'm relaxing in the park with my family. It's that doctor again. I take the call. He barely gives any greeting, just asks, 'Have you found what the key opens?'

Now this is getting weird. It puts me on my guard. Why is this doctor so interested in my dad? I realize that it was me who first went to go see him, but when I did he acted like he couldn't be expected to remember a patient from years back. Yet now he's calling me on the weekend. Is he that curious about this key?

'No, I haven't found out yet,' I say. 'I feel like I've made you worry about it,' by which I mean, this is not something you need to worry about.

But, like a computer that can't interpret nuance, all he says is, 'I do not mind.'

Mayu looks at me questioningly. Just at that moment, I see Daiki tumble down to the grass. Mayu dashes over to him.

'Sorry, if I find anything out about the key I'll get in touch,' I say, then end the call, ignoring whether or not the doctor had anything else to say. I run over to Daiki also. While he's surprised to be on the ground, he seems to be enjoying himself, and he rolls and wriggles around the grass. Apparently he's more resilient than I had assumed. The need to protect him may have existed in his parents' heads and nowhere else.

The wind picks up, rustling the grass like the fur on an animal's back. I have the momentary sensation that we're standing atop a giant beast. I can almost feel it unfold its legs and stand up. This enormous creature of a sort that I had never seen before is taking care of us. When that thought enters my head, I picture its face as Dad's face.

'What's so funny?' Mayu asks, which makes me realize that I'm laughing.

I tell her that I was imagining a weird fantastical animal, and she cocks her head quizzically.

Later that evening, when I go to the cleaner's to get my suit back, I get another call. I wonder if it's the doctor again but when I answer it I hear an upbeat voice say, 'I found it! It took a little while, but I figured out the building where the key works.'

It's the key specialist.

He sounds excited at his accomplishment, and I get excited too. Even though I'm still in the cleaner's, I exclaim, 'You did it!' He agrees to send me the details by email.

'Some good news?' asks the owner as he emerges from the back room. He folds my freshly cleaned suit and puts it in a bag.

'Well, I'm not actually sure how good it is.' *I'm one step closer to discovering my dad's secret*, I almost say, but I keep it to myself. If he kept it secret, then maybe I shouldn't be going out of my way to uncover it. I even feel guilty about it. But after coming this far, I can't stop myself from going on to the end.

'You know, one of my friends was going through her father's things after he died and she found some high school girl uniforms. It didn't turn out to be anything sketchy or illegal, he just collected them.' Mayu tells me this after we put Daiki to bed and I share with her that I found the condo that Dad's key opens.

'Fashion appreciation?'

'I mean, he might have worn them. Either way, it was a bit of a shock to my friend. And anyway, I was the one who was pushing you to find out more about your father, so maybe it's not fair of me to bring up something like this.'

'I get it.' Who knows what I might find behind that door.

'You need to be prepared. You could be encountering a different version of your father than the one you knew. Your mother didn't know about it either. And maybe there are some things that you're better off not knowing.'

Earlier I had called Mom and worked into the conversation the name of the neighborhood where the condo is, trying to see if there was any connection to Dad. She didn't seem to know anything, though.

'Yeah, I hear you,' I say to Mayu. Although somehow I'm not so very concerned. If it turns out to be some weird sex fetish thing, I'll be surprised but it won't be the end of the world. And if I find a bunch of notebooks full of criticism of Mom, I might even be a little pleased. It'd be nice to know he let off some steam sometimes.

Katsumi, a man who badmouths his wife behind her back is no true wife-worshipper. I can almost hear him say it.

'As long as he didn't murder people and store the bodies in there,' I say, hoping to show Mayu that if I can joke around about it then I'm not all that concerned.

'Maybe your dad just found the key somewhere?' Mayu suggests.

'And then stashed it in his study?'

'Yeah, held on to it for no special reason.'

It could be. 'But I've come this far, I want to see it through.'

I try looking up the condo building online and see that there are units for sale, so I call the listing agent and give him a made-up story that even I think sounds suspicious. But it works, and he gives me the contact info for the building's superintendent.

I could just go straight to the unit, and I do plan to go, but first I want to get any information I can.

I get the super on the phone and he's not at all shy. 'Whaddayou want?' I can't tell if his rough tone is because he's being obnoxious or because he's a rustic type.

It feels like I'll be better off telling him the truth rather than making up some nonsense like I did with the real estate agent, so I explain that I have a key to a unit that I found in my dad's things, who died ten years ago. It seems likely he'll have no idea what I'm talking about, but to my surprise he says, 'Oh, he died, did he? I guess that's why I haven't seen him all this time.'

'You knew my dad?' I ask, a little too eagerly.

'Sure, I sold him one of my units,' he answers. 'And then never saw him again.'

'And that never bothered you?'

'Why would it?'

'What about his mortgage?'

'He paid in cash.'

'Dad bought a condo in a lump sum?'

He had that kind of money? And kept it from Mom?

Where would he have gotten money like that? Maybe that's part of his secret? I can feel my heartbeat getting faster. This could go deeper than I had imagined. His secret hidey-hole might turn out to be a vast cavern. Dark as night, full of pitfalls, the sort of cavern that you don't come back from alive. The possibility dawns on me for the first time.

'Can I have a look at the unit?'

'You've got the key, if you wanna go in, I'm not gonna stop you. It's your dad's place, not mine.'

'Okay then.' If you have a move, make it, right? I might even go today. I can take the afternoon off work.

'Oh, wait,' the super says after a moment. 'No, you can't.'

'I can't?'

'No, I can't let you go in there. That's what he said. I'm not supposed to let anyone in, and especially not his family.'

'Dad said that?'

'I made him a promise.'

'It's a promise from ten years ago, you think maybe it's expired?'

'When it comes to things like this, I'm a man of principles.'

I'm not about to just let the matter drop. I tell him, a little forcefully, that I'll be coming over later this evening.

'He said under no circumstances did he want his family to find out about this. I'm not gonna go against that.'

'I already found out about it.' Now that I know about the condo, I can't un-know it.

I'm fidgety the whole rest of the day at work. Imagining all the different things Dad might have hidden in there gives me a feeling like I'm waiting for the results of a medical exam. Waves of optimism and pessimism take turns crashing over me.

As soon as I finish lunch – which is really only a few nervous bites of bread – I head to the condo.

It takes a few trains to get there. As I'm walking the unfamiliar streets of a neighborhood I've never been to before, I feel like someone's watching me. I look around but there's no one I recognize, and I start to think that I'm feeling Dad watching me from above. *Don't do it.* I picture his face, urgent. *I'm begging you, just leave it alone.*

Don't worry, Dad, even if I find something awful I won't tell Mom.

It's not hard to find the condo building. It stands on an older-looking block, smallish but with a simple exterior that gives it a tidy air. The light is decent, too.

Not a bad place to put up a lover, eh? I feel like I can hear Dad again. If that was the case, would this lover still be living here?

None of this feels real. Even if it wasn't a lover, what if it was someone else close to Dad?

Both of his parents died a long time ago, or at least that's what he said, and neither Mom nor I ever met them. But what if the punchline was that his parents were still alive, here? Then I feel bad for calling that a punchline.

Only, if that were the case, I imagine the super would have run into them at some point.

And I doubt Dad had someone imprisoned in there. Still, the thought of it gives me a chill, and I have a dark premonition. That's when someone speaks to me from behind: 'Is this his condominium building?' I turn around.

I don't recognize him immediately, because he's wearing a jacket and he's out here in the city, whereas before I had only ever seen him in his office, wearing a white lab coat. But it's him. The doctor.

KABUTO

This ends today, I think as I eat my breakfast. I want something sweet to calm my nerves – I look into the fridge and find a pudding cup at the back. I never used to like sweets, but my wife kept making me try, and over time I developed a taste for it. A dramatic change of heart.

She's busy in the laundry room and I don't want to bother her to ask if it's alright for me to eat this pudding, so I just quietly start eating it. That's when Katsumi comes down from upstairs.

He gives me a sleepy good morning, then his eyes fall to my hands. 'I think,' he points, 'Mom was planning to eat that.'

My mouth stops in mid-slurp. But it's too late – I've already thrown out the lid, and I can't put back what I've eaten. 'This is no good. Not the pudding, I mean. The pudding is good.'

'It's not that big of a deal.' Katsumi looks at me with pity in his eyes.

'It *is* a big deal. But it'll be fine if I just buy her another one, right?'

Better to make it look like it never happened than to make a weak excuse. I gulp down the rest of the pudding and start to wash out the plastic cup, trying to eliminate the evidence.

'Here, Dad, give it to me. I'll throw it out in my room.'

'Mm?'

'So that Mom doesn't find out. I'll shove it down to the bottom of my trash can.'

It's a solid idea, and I'm grateful. Overflowing with gratitude, in fact. I hand it over to him with great solemnity: *I'm counting on you.*

'Dad, why are you so afraid of Mom?'

'What? Where's this coming from?' *When have I ever been afraid,* I almost say, but it's so clearly a lie that I leave it out.

'I've been meaning to ask you for a while,' Katsumi says with a gentle laugh. 'Like, if you could live your life over again, I bet you wouldn't marry Mom.'

'That's a hell of a thing to say.' I'm suddenly extremely nervous that she can hear us over the laundry machine.

'I don't know, I just feel like maybe you regret your decision.'

For a moment I'm so confused that I actually don't understand what Katsumi is saying. Then the words start to take on meaning. 'If I could do it over again, I wouldn't change a thing.'

'You would still marry Mom?'

I don't even feel like I need to nod yes. 'And we would still have you. If that didn't happen, I'd be pretty sad.'

'Wow. And then you'd live your life worrying about what she thinks?'

I laugh out loud, naturally, unforced. 'It only looks that way to you.'

'That's the only possible thing it could look like.'

'Maybe.' I don't expect him to understand. 'But there was far more good than bad.'

I realize with a start that I said *was,* past tense. At the same time, I think of all the jobs I've pulled in my capacity as a professional, and I feel like I didn't deserve any of the good things I had.

So where does that leave me?

Before leaving home, it occurs to me I need to do something about the keys to the condo. The keys to the unit I just purchased.

Yesterday the super told me that since I wanted to get into the unit right away, he had no problem handing over the keys. He apparently had new keys ready to go in case a buyer were to show up. After going back and forth on it, I decide to leave the copy of the key in my house. I need a good hiding place, though, or my wife will find it. In that case, there's really only one option: my study, which is just a closet that I call my study. I tuck it into a paper bag that I put in the back of the little room. The bag also has the notebooks full of all the lessons I've learned on how best to communicate with my wife – I certainly don't want her to find those either. I updated them regularly. It doesn't seem right to throw them out. They're basically my life's work. So instead I leave them there in the paper bag at the back of my closet-room. Then I push a large cardboard box in front of the bag, heavy enough that she'll have a hard time moving it.

'What are you doing in there, banging around first thing in the morning?' Her voice floats in from wherever she is in the house, just as I secure the key in its hiding spot. Naturally I apologize and put the rest of the things in the closet back where they were.

After that I bustle out of the house as if I were on my way to work as usual. First I make a few stops to buy the things I'll need for the condo. None of it needs to be fancy, it just needs to do the job. A curtain, a cheap chair. There's no time to wait for delivery. I just take it over myself in a taxi. The rest of the stuff I need I get out of my storage unit. By the time I have everything set up it's past noon.

I lock the door behind me and take the elevator down. In the lobby I encounter the superintendent. He's like a hard old tree still bursting with green leaves, no sign of withering anywhere.

'Hey there, how's it going?'

'I just moved some things in.'

'Things you don't want your family to know about?'

I nod. I've already arranged for the monthly condo fee to be taken out of my bank account – that account is another thing my family doesn't know about. 'I'll appreciate it if you don't worry too much about my unit.' I'm only half joking. The other half is deadly serious.

'It's your place. What would I get from worrying about your place? There's plenty of people living here who I haven't seen for years. Sometimes I wonder if they're not just dead inside their condos!'

'Maybe you should worry just a little bit more.'

'Oh you think so?' He makes a grumpy face. 'You ever managed a building?'

'No.'

'There's only so much you can do. You can't check every little thing, you'd drive yourself crazy. The things that I can see, well, there's plenty enough to deal with. If I start worrying about the things I don't see, forget about it.' It's like he's instructing me in the Way of the Superintendent. I'm not sure exactly what kinds of unseen things he's referring to, but it makes enough sense.

'So if you've got something that you're tryna hide, do it where I can't see it.'

You got it, I tell him, and start to leave, when something occurs to me. 'If my family ever comes around . . .'

'If they figure out your secret?'

'I'm hoping they don't,' I say with a shrug. 'But under no circumstances do I want them to go into that unit.'

'What'll happen if they do?'

I search for the right words. 'It would tear my family apart.' Then I leave.

The place I arranged to meet the doctor is one train stop away from the condo. There's a park in the neighborhood, and near the entrance is a clock tower. I've heard that at night it lights up and people hang around, but during the day the area is quiet and empty. I told the doctor to come to the base of the clock tower.

I assumed that he wouldn't want to leave his office, and in fact he told me bluntly that he doesn't make house calls. But I didn't budge. 'I'm not stupid enough to come to your clinic at this point,' I said. 'It's too dangerous. Am I wrong? The only place I'll meet you is somewhere outside.' I reminded him of the fact that he tried to have me killed in the taxi crash when I last left his place. To put more pressure on him, I said that if he doesn't come to the clock tower, I'll leak everything I have on him. In the end I told him the exact time and location. 'Be there. Or else.' Then I hung up.

'Will he come?' Asagao asked on the phone yesterday, his voice cold.

'Probably.'

'You're hiring me for a job based on probably?'

'I'll pay you in advance. If the doctor doesn't come, you don't need to give it back.'

'Is that so.' He sounded completely indifferent. Again I had the feeling that the Pusher doesn't actually exist. I started to wonder if I wasn't talking to a ghost.

A very strange professional. Maybe I can count on him, and maybe I can't.

On my way to the clock tower, I come across three kids who look like they're in junior high, surrounding a younger kid.

I have too much to do to deal with something like this. I know

I should just walk on by. But instead I shout at them, 'Hey, what do you think you're doing?' Because they outnumber him, and because they're bigger than him. Not fair at all.

The three junior high-schoolers look at me, annoyed.

'This is obviously unfair. There's three of you and only one of him.'

They mutter about who cares if it's not fair, that I should shut up and get lost, but they still look childlike. 'Stay out of it, old man,' one of them says.

'How about if I team up with this elementary-school kid?'

'What?'

'That would make it fair. Actually, our side would probably have a major advantage. So you kids should get some weapons. Do you have any on you?'

The junior high-schoolers look at each other. One of them puts his hand in his pocket.

'You have a knife? If not, I can lend you one. And if you take it, you better come at me with everything you've got. If you kids have weapons, there's no reason for me to hold back.'

I don't have time to waste getting into a fight with kids, but I can't stand it when people think they're tough because they can push around other people who are weaker than themselves.

They end up leaving. The younger kid just stares at me. It's awkward, and I need to go, but I feel like I can't leave without saying something. I fish around in my pockets and find a sucking candy that I picked up at a client visit the other day and I hand it to him. 'Here, have this. It'll make you feel better,' I say. 'Being a kid is hard. Hang in there and do your best.'

I think about Katsumi, when he was a little boy.

'I . . . I don't have any friends,' the kid says in a reedy voice.

'Neither do I,' I tell him. 'But I'm happy. My life is a gift, every day of it.'

The kid looks frightened. I probably said too much. Time to go.

And now I'm standing at the base of the clock tower.

No matter what means of transportation the doctor takes to get here, he'll have to cross the avenue to reach this point, and there's a steady flow of traffic. A perfect place for the Pusher to do his work.

So if the doctor actually makes it here, it'll mean that the Pusher didn't do the job. On the other hand, if I hear from Asagao that it's done, or if there's a sudden commotion on the street and people start shouting about someone getting run over, I'll know that I've won.

I wait to see which one it'll be.

Good fortune or bad fortune, even or odd. But it turns out to be none of the above. It turns out to be an outcome that I never expected. Looks like the crossword wasn't just verticals and horizontals.

A man is walking toward me. I can tell it's not the doctor, so at first I don't pay him much attention. But then I see that he's walking straight for where I'm standing. I feel like maybe I recognize him, and I scan through my memory as he approaches.

Once he gets close enough I know who it is.

Now he's right in front of me, his eyebrows knitted, his face grave.

We last saw each other just the other day, in the department store.

'I'm truly sorry this is how it had to be,' says Nanomura.

That's when I know that my plan isn't going to work out.

KATSUMI & KABUTO

The doctor doesn't give any explanation as to why he's here, or how he knew where I'd be. 'I very much wanted to know more about your father,' is all he says.

Did he follow me? It seems crazy, but there's no way he just randomly happened to be here.

'Don't you have patients to see today?' A useless thing to ask.

Instead of answering, he comes closer. He's holding his right hand out toward me a bit, and I have a moment of surprise as I think he's going to try to listen to my heartbeat right here – that's how confused I am by all of this – but when I look closer, what I thought was a stethoscope turns out to be a gun. Now I'm starting to doubt my own eyes.

Is it a toy gun? There's no way it's real. He presses it into my ribs. 'Let us go to the condo unit now.' Suddenly a chill passes through me and my hair is standing on end.

Is it real?

I don't understand what's happening.

Why is the doctor here? Why does he have a gun?

Everything around me seems to white out, and my head feels like it's floating.

This isn't real.

I'm praying for it not to be real. Which must be why my body is trying to shut off my senses. I can't even feel my feet on the ground.

Things advance without any input from me. I'm like a playing piece in a game, plucked up and moved along to a space further along the board.

The next thing I know we're in the building. I had gotten the unit number from the super on the phone. We take the elevator up, still no feeling of reality to any of this, and then there we are at the top floor.

'Which number is it?' The doctor sounds completely emotionless, and he's behind me, pressing his gun into my back, so I have no idea what his face is doing. I want to turn around and look. 'Walk, please.' His voice prods me forward like a cold steel rod.

We exit the elevator into an open-air walkway that extends left and right. It takes me a moment to figure out which way to go. After seeing how the unit numbers run, I head toward the right.

'We might bump into some residents. What if one of them sees your gun?' The doctor says nothing. 'Why are you so interested in my dad anyway?'

No answer.

Dad. I look up to the sky searchingly. What the hell is going on here?

Standing there facing me, Nanomura slowly blinks a few times. I can sense apology in it. And prayer.

We're on the roof of an office building near the park. Nanomura led us here. We took the elevator up to the top floor then climbed the fire escape to the roof. The area we're in should be locked, but the door was open.

The sky is dazzlingly blue.

It fills me with remorse. The people whose lives I took over the years, they died in cramped rooms, they died in the rain. Many of them never even got a chance to recognize that their lives were over.

None of them had the beautiful setting that I do now. Someone might reasonably accuse me of getting special treatment.

'I didn't think I'd ever see you again,' I say. I'm actually glad to see him. But it could sound to him like I'm bitter.

'I'm sorry.' He still doesn't have any weapons out. Though I imagine he has something on him somewhere.

'It's not your fault, Nanomura-san.'

'Thank you for what you did the other night.'

'What are you talking about?'

'What you put in the coin return of the vending machine.'

'Ah, that.'

'It saved my life.'

226

When he first showed up at the clock tower, Nanomura didn't mince words. 'I have no choice,' he said. 'If I don't, my son . . .'

I could put together the rest. The doctor pushed Nanomura to take me out. Nanomura had been wanting to get out of the business, and he wouldn't be likely to just take the job happily with no questions asked, so the doctor must have threatened Nanomura's son as leverage. He apparently kidnapped the kid and is holding him.

I notice there's a small microphone on Nanomura's collar. The doctor must be listening in, making sure that Nanomura and I don't cook up any schemes to strike back at him.

Now Nanomura has a gun in his hand and he's aiming it at me. He takes a step closer and pats me down. He takes out everything I've got on me, apologizing the whole time.

Including the key to the condo.

'That's—' Before I can say anything else, he tosses it off the roof. From his perspective, there was a definite chance that it was a weapon made to look like a key. I myself had once seen a small bomb disguised as a key. I can't blame him for being careful.

As I watch the arc of the falling key, I can feel my options disappearing one by one.

'Miyake-san, what were you planning?' Nanomura asks. It feels like a post-game analysis after a match of shogi or go.

'I wanted to lure the doctor out. I was going to have him pushed in front of a car.'

I don't know if Nanomura has heard of the Pusher or not. But he shrugs his shoulders with what looks like sympathy. 'Even if he came out, he wouldn't do it alone.' He's right; the doctor is extremely careful and would have had multiple bodyguards. I was betting that the Pusher would have gotten it done anyhow. But at this point my bet is long past mattering.

'No one stays at the top forever. He won't always be able to get bodyguards.' I hope that the doctor's hearing me through the mic. 'One day he'll be all alone, and he'll have to take care of things himself.'

Nanomura gives me a look of pity. 'That won't be for five years or more.'

'Maybe I could try again in five years,' I say with a laugh. 'How about it?'

'I'm sorry, Miyake-san.' The gun extends toward me.

He has nothing to be sorry about. I think about all the awful things I've done.

The words I said to the junior high-schoolers flash through my head. *This is obviously unfair.* The idea that I should live a long, happy life in peace and comfort when I have ended so many other people's lives, that's obviously unfair. All the things I've done have finally come back around.

The doctor follows behind me, but he seems to have less of the mechanical coldness he had when I first met him. He feels somehow older. Maybe it's because in his office he was dressed more like a doctor.

He's saying something quietly, as if to himself. I try to make it out. 'All alone, I'm all alone.' Sadly muttering about having to go outside on his own.

'What are you talking about?' I ask him.

'Face forward and keep moving,' he says.

What's going on with this doctor? It's like he's haunted by something. A delusion? Or something else?

At the end of the passage is Dad's condo. Standing in front of the door now, it suddenly looks enormous.

I think of a warrior's shield, blocking the way.

Is Dad's secret inside?

'Open it, please,' urges the doctor.

I take the key out of my pocket but drop it to the ground. Not on purpose. I thought I was calm enough but my hands and legs are trembling. I hastily bend down to pick it up but fumble it and drop it again.

'Um.' Something occurs to me. 'Do you know anything about how my dad died?'

'No.' The doctor's face is devoid of any expression.

'I don't believe he killed himself.'

The doctor stares hard at me. It's like he's looking inside me. 'Why not?'

'It's not like him.'

There's a ripple in the doctor's face. I can't tell if it's a hint of a smile or a scowl. But it's clear that this man hates my dad. 'How much do you hope to learn about your father?'

'What do you mean by that?'

He doesn't answer.

'So, *do* you know about how he died?' I'm about to ask if Dad had any message for me and Mom, which I realize is what I actually want to know. In the ten years since he passed, I've been looking for anything he might have left behind for us.

'Your father,' the doctor says, his face as blank as a noh mask, 'was afraid.'

'Afraid?'

'Of dying.' He exhales through his nose, and I can tell that it's a gesture of contempt.

'Aah,' I say. Now I realize that I can't believe anything he says. 'Please don't lie to me.'

'Death is frightening. Everything disappears. Your father was no exception.'

'No. You're wrong.' This much I know for certain. 'There was one thing Dad was more afraid of than anything else.'

'What is that?'

'Mom.' I make a show of smiling, but at the same time I feel my eyes welling up.

*

229

I put my hands up and say to Nanomura, 'You don't have to shoot. I'll do it myself. I'll jump. Then it'll be over.'

There's a fence around the edge of the roof, but it's torn in one place, leaving a gap. That's where I can get out over the ledge.

'If I'm dead, this'll be done. It doesn't need to be you who kills me, Nanomura-san.' I'm already walking as I say it. 'To tell you the truth, I feel guilty. The things I've done can't be forgiven. I took away too many people's lives. My single death won't even begin to make up for it.'

'Then it's the same for me.'

'No, you should live your life.' It doesn't make logical sense. But it feels right. 'When you showed up earlier, I knew what I had to do. *Hey*. This all ends here, okay? It's done.' That last part I say to the doctor, listening on the other side of the wire. 'Damn,' I sigh, once more talking to Nanomura. 'My whole plan turned to mochi.'

'And your backup plan?'

'That one's mochi too.'

I pull open the tear in the fence and step out beyond it to the ledge of the building. There's nothing between me and the city below. And in front of me, only the sky. Blue, an ocean, waiting for me.

I marvel at the color.

'Do you—' Nanomura begins, behind me. He doesn't have his weapon on me anymore. Trusting. I almost smile. *What would you do if I tried to make a move*, I want to ask. His trustingness makes me feel like he's a better man than me. 'Do you have anything you'd like to tell your family?'

'My family?'

'Yes. If there's anything, I'll tell them.' His face is earnest.

Good idea. I think to myself for a few moments. 'I'll always be watching over you, and you won't be able to see me, and you might not hear my voice either, but I'll always be there with you, rooting for you.'

'I'll tell them.'

'No, you know what, never mind.' I shake my head. The people I killed never had a chance to leave a message for their families. I didn't like feeling like I had any special privileges. 'You don't need to tell them anything.'

So here's where it ends. It wasn't a bad run. I really mean that. I'm sad that I won't get to see how things turn out for Katsumi, but I always knew we'd never be together forever.

If there's something I'm disappointed about it's that I didn't get to take one last shot at the doctor. That's the one thing that's sticking with me. But I guess it was a fight, and I lost.

I'm not afraid of dying. But what if she's mad at me for dying? That makes me a little frightened.

I jump from the ledge, sending my body into space. My head fills with her face, with Katsumi's face, I float and time seems to stop – and then I start to drop, until I collide with the ground, body and soul tearing apart. But during the fall, scenes with my family play before my eyes, and a warm air spreads through my chest.

As I pick up the key, an old man appears at the far end of the passage. 'You must be the young fella who called before.' He starts toward us.

'Are you the superintendent?'

Looks like he was making his rounds. Next to me, the doctor steps away from the door and smoothly conceals the gun behind his back. He probably wants to avoid any entanglements, but is keeping the gun handy in case the situation doesn't go the way he wants. 'We were planning to inspect the inside of this unit,' the doctor says.

'Sure, sure. It's my policy not to interfere with people's private business. Do your thing.'

'Well then. We shall.' The doctor signals me with his eyes.

I bring the key up to the keyhole. But then the super cuts in: 'Oh wait, that's right – nope, I can't let you go in there.'

'Sorry?'

'Like I said on the phone, I can't let any of his family go into the unit.' The super waves his hand back and forth, like a referee calling for a break in play. 'I made him a promise. And here I was about to break it! Man, I've really been forgetting things.'

The doctor looks at the super dispassionately. 'A promise? The man is dead.'

'Dead or not, a promise is a promise. That's what he said: if anyone from my family goes in, it'll tear the family apart.'

Hearing that confirms it: inside this condo is the secret of a version of Dad we didn't know.

Don't open it. It's like I can hear Dad's voice, deadly serious. Well, if he feels that strongly about it . . . I back away from the door.

The doctor has no intention of stopping though. 'I am not his family. It should not be a problem for me to inspect the unit.' Before the words are even out of his mouth, he plucks the key from my fingertips and inserts it into the keyhole.

For ten years it's been locked, and doesn't seem to want to unlock now. The doctor has to jiggle the key and there are several seconds of rattling. But I don't try to stop him.

Finally the doctor grips the knob and turns, slowly pulling the door open. I feel a surge of hatred toward him for trampling on my father's wishes. There was something Dad wanted to stay secret, and this man is dragging it out into the open.

Stop, I almost shout.

In the next instant there's a sudden rushing sound, like a gust of wind.

It lasts for a single blink of the eye.

I have the sensation that a giant hand has appeared and smacked its palm into the wall of the building, that's how forceful the vibration is – and there's the doctor, picked up off his feet and thrown backwards. His body slams into the railing on the walkway.

I blink several more times.

The doctor's eyes are open, saliva bubbling from his mouth. His lips move faintly, but it's clearly nothing more than the last traces of life escaping. Something is protruding from his chest. I can see that it's an arrow, and I know that it came shooting out of the condo, but I don't understand any of this.

KATSUMI

The super looks shaken up too, but he's steadier than I am. 'What the hell is going on here?' he wonders, ducking down, as if he's wary that another arrow might fly out. Then he gingerly enters the open door. 'Who shot that?'

I tell him it's dangerous and he shouldn't go in, but he doesn't seem to care. Not knowing what else to do, I follow him inside. On the way I steal a glance at the doctor, being afraid to look too directly. He's very clearly dead.

The condo is almost bare. No furniture, just some curtains hanging over the windows. The only other thing is a single chair, at the far end of the hall directly facing the entryway, and on the chair is something that looks like a mix between a bow and a gun.

'Whoa, what is this, a crossbow?' The super steps up beside the weapon and runs his finger over it, as if to confirm it's real.

A crossbow? I know what they are, of course, but I've never

233

seen one in real life before. It looks like one of my son's trans-forming robot toys.

I look back toward the entry. Sure enough, the crossbow is mounted so that it's aimed right at the door. A long cord trails the distance between. 'I guess this is so that when the door opens it would pull the trigger,' the super says. He sounds impressed. 'This is some setup. Did your dad do this?'

I have no idea. Did he? Why would he have? And in any case, would Dad even know how to do anything like this?

My already baffled mind is now even more mixed up. It feels like waves keep crashing inside my head. And it gets even more surreal when someone else enters the condo.

'Is this it? Did I find you?' It's the man who runs the cleaner where I take our clothes.

The pieces aren't adding up. It's like an absurd dream.

Why is he here? Cleaning delivery?

'I –' But no other words will come out.

'The location tracker told me where the building is, but not which floor. I've been searching every floor from the ground up. I finally found you,' says the cleaner.

'Location tracker?' None of this makes any sense.

He scratches his head. 'It's a long story.'

'I'm not sure now's the time for a long story.' As I say it I look back and forth between the crossbow and the doctor out on the walkway floor, though I feel detached, like I'm just staring at the clouds.

The cleaner steps back outside for a moment to get the doc-tor's body and pull it inside the unit. 'Things will get complicated if someone sees this, so we'll keep it in here for now.'

The super makes a dubious face, but then says to me, 'Kid, it's your dad's condo. You do what you want with it.'

The cleaner points at my jacket. 'There's a transmitter in your suit.'

I don't understand what he means. 'In my suit?'

'Yes. There's a transmitter sewn into it that lets me know your location.'

'No there isn't.' I wouldn't buy a suit with a tracker, not even if it was on sale.

'There is. I put it in there the other day when I had your suit. I've put one in other suits of yours before, too.'

I don't quite know how to respond.

Is he allowed to do that? Is that a special service his shop offers? These and other questions occur to me, but none of them seem like they'd be helpful to ask. I just stay silent. Then I start to wonder where this device might be, feel around in the pockets and on the lining, but I don't find anything.

'I apologize for doing that without telling you,' he says. So I'm not crazy, I didn't ask for it after all.

'Why, though? Why would you do that?'

He smiles sheepishly. 'I owe your father a lot. So does my son.'

'Wha–?' He owes Dad? And what does that have to do with putting a tracker in my suit?

'Your father died in order to protect me and my son.'

'He died to . . . ? Hang on a second. I don't understand any of this.' Utter confusion. It feels like something of critical importance has just been casually tossed to me. I know I have to catch it, but I have no idea how.

'I thought that the least I could do was protect his son.'

'Protect me?' Stop, stop – I wave my hands frantically. I need him to rewind and start from the beginning. 'So you put a tracker in my suit jacket. Have you been watching everything I do?'

'No, no, nothing like that.' The area around the cleaner's eyes shows a slight flush. 'I knew that nothing good would come if this doctor got anywhere near you, so I was on alert. I would have preferred to take more direct action, but the doctor would have been on guard against me, so I couldn't make a move.'

'Make a move? Suspected you? What exactly do you mean?'

'I got word that the doctor left his office today, which almost never happens, so I figured something was happening. That's why I checked on your location and followed you here. Only, as I mentioned before, I didn't know what floor you were on, so I had to check every floor.'

'And . . . what about this?' I point at the crossbow. The booby trap feels harder to process than the tracking device. And I'm also wondering why the cleaner doesn't seem more concerned that the doctor is dead. Maybe I should ask him that instead.

'This,' the cleaner begins, staring at the weapon. 'This I didn't know about.'

'What is it, though?'

'Something your father put in place, I imagine.' He lowers his voice to a barely audible murmur. 'The backup plan. Not mochi after all.' At least that's what I think I hear him say. Mochi?

'And what was Dad –' What was he hoping to do with this? He set up a crossbow trap – is that something that a normal person would think to do?

'Taking one final shot,' says the cleaner. In that moment something comes back to me from years ago. A conversation I had with Dad. The ax of the *toro*. When a praying mantis faces down a much larger creature and holds up its little blades, ready to fight. Didn't the saying mean to fight a losing battle? But sometimes the mantis gets in one good chop – was it me who said that? Or Dad?

The super pipes up. 'So that means this trap has been sitting here waiting for ten years?'

'So it seems.'

'Well, now, that's really something,' the super exclaims, again running his fingers along the crossbow. 'It didn't jostle or budge this entire time. What if we had to come into the unit for renovations, did he think about that?'

'I can't imagine he expected it to be here for ten years or longer,' says the cleaner.

'But what – what does all of this –' I sink down to the floor. It feels like all the strength in my legs has leaked away, and I'm worried that if I try to stay standing I'll fall over.

After a few moments the cleaner comes over to me with a look of concern. 'Please, let me take care of this.'

'Take care of it?' I repeat.

The super chimes in, his brow furrowed, 'Yeah, what exactly do you mean by take care of it?'

'All of this.'

'All?'

'I'll make it as if this body were never here. I'll make it so that none of this ever happened. So what I need from you –'

'– We never saw anything, right?' The super is much quicker to process this than I am.

'Exactly.'

The super folds his arms and stands there quietly for a few moments. Eventually he shrugs. 'Fine with me. Whatever goes on inside the unit, that's the tenant's private business, and I try not to stick my nose in.'

And he's okay with that? This very clearly exceeds the bounds of private business. How can he just turn a blind eye? How could anyone?

Paying no mind to my consternation, the cleaner says, 'Thank you.' I have no idea why he would be thanking us, but I nod back to him. Don't worry about any of this, just leave it to me, he assures us.

The super seems satisfied. 'Life sure is interesting. I think I'll keep on living.' With that, he leaves, looking almost upbeat, as if everything has been solved.

Hello, someone died here, in your building! How can you be so nonchalant?

Then a thought occurs to me – maybe it's crazy, but – if the super had said he was planning to call the police, it doesn't feel like the cleaner would just meekly go along with it. He might have tried a more forceful approach. When he said please leave it to me, there was a subtle menace behind it. He wasn't making a request. It was a threat. I bet the super picked up on that. And if that's what it was, then I have no choice but to accept his plan too.

Now that it's just the two of us, he says, almost haltingly, 'For so long I was doing dirty work.'

'Sorry?'

'I wanted to do something where I could make things clean and beautiful.'

'I don't understand.'

'That's why I opened a cleaning shop. And because I was worried about you, I opened it near where you live.'

'I'm sorry, I'm not following any of this. Can you – what is this all about?'

The cleaner's eyes soften. Smile lines show on his face. 'You and your father.'

Me and Dad?

I try to figure out what he means, looking at him searchingly, and his face rumples into an even deeper smile, like his cheeks are fruits he wants to squeeze all the juice from, and in fact tears start flowing from his eyes, which only makes me more confused.

'You and your father, together, you defeated him.'

'Defeated who?' The doctor? But why were we even fighting him?

Now he's fully crying. He nods solemnly. 'You and your father teamed up to defeat him.'

'What –' I feel bad that I can't join in with his emotional moment, but I feel hemmed in by question marks, bound tightly

238

enough that I can't move an inch. 'What *was* my dad?' Finally, the key question.

His eyes shine with tears. 'Your father?'

'What was he?'

'He was your father. That's all.'

'I don't . . .'

'Just a regular, good father. Isn't that right?'

KATSUMI

On my way back home I still feel like I'm wandering through a dream. I float through the train station and back to my own condo in such a daze that it's amazing I don't stumble into traffic.

'Please forget all of this,' the cleaner had said, his words now echoing in my head. 'You can just put it all out of your mind.'

'You want me to forget?'

'Not your father – you must never forget your father,' he said with a smile. 'But you're better off not holding on to what happened here today.'

Dad's secret condo, the dead doctor, the crossbow rigged to fire when someone opened the door, the tracking device in my suit – it was all so out of the ordinary that there was no way I could forget it – and yet – maybe because I didn't want to accept any of these astounding revelations, the closer I got to my home, the more the sensation of having experienced all of this seemed to evaporate, leaving behind something hazy and indistinct.

The only other thing the cleaner and I talked about was Dad's condo. Dad had bought it, but I had no idea how the monthly fees were being paid. When I said that, the cleaner told me he'd look into it. I don't know what he was planning to do, exactly, but assuming Dad had an account, a secret account, and there's still any money in there, I asked the cleaner to donate it all somewhere.

'Did my dad kill himself?' Only at the very end did I remember to ask the thing I wanted to know most.

'No, he didn't.'

I wasn't expecting such a straightforward answer. I almost didn't know what to do with it.

When I asked why he died, the cleaner was vague, saying only that Dad got wrapped up in some dangerous stuff. 'But Miyake-san did not choose to die,' he assured me.

When we parted ways, the cleaner wished me farewell, and I got the strong feeling that the cleaning shop wouldn't be in business anymore. I pictured going to drop off my clothes and finding a notice on the door saying that they had closed.

As I unlock my door and pull it open, I half-expect an arrow from a crossbow to come hurtling at me. Of course, that doesn't happen. If the arrow was a symbol of bad fortune that destroys lives, then what flies at me now is the polar opposite, a beam of light that enriches my life, namely, my son Daiki, galloping toward me and throwing his arms around me, shrieking joyfully that Daddy's home.

'Grandma's here too!'

'Oh yeah?'

Mom is in the living room. There seems to be some significance to her showing up on the same day that I stumbled into something dangerous and unexpected from Dad's past. Just as I'm wondering why she decided to come over, Mayu comes in from the kitchen. 'I wanted to hear some stories about your father,' she explains.

'Texting about it takes too long,' Mom says. 'I thought it would be easier to come over and talk to Mayu about it.'

Seems like a lot of trouble to go to when they could have just kept texting, I think, but the thought must show on my face because Mom says, 'What's with that look? Your face is all rigid.'

I picture Dad. 'My face isn't rigid. I'm probably just tense from work and my cheeks are a little tight.' I can see him squirming and trying to explain himself.

'Well, it's just one more time that your father put me out.' Holding Daiki on her lap, she turns to Mayu. 'Really, that man caused me such trouble.'

I dart a look at Dad's photo. He caused her trouble? Not the other way around?

Her version doesn't match mine as she shares several episodes, laughing at Dad's blunders and mishaps.

'But you know,' I say, after Mom finishes one of her stories, and as I say it I feel a strong sense of duty, as if Dad's there behind me saying *Fight for me, counselor.* 'Dad was also pretty great. He was always trying to make Mom happy.'

'Who? Your dad? Trying to make me happy? When?' Mom's eyes are wide and she's clearly taken aback, which makes me feel nervous too.

'When? I mean, always.'

Mom bursts out laughing. 'No way. He was always just hanging around, taking it easy.'

Mayu nods politely and says wow, really, and I feel like I need to raise my hand. Objection! Plaintiff is falsifying testimony to fit their agenda!

Overruled, says a voice that seems to come from Dad's photo, and I just have to laugh. I'm trying to argue your case here, man.

'But how did you two meet?' asks Mayu.

'How *did* we meet? It was so long ago.' Mom cocks her head.

'You didn't really forget something important like that, did you?'

'It was a long time ago!' Mom repeats. 'I think maybe one of my friends introduced us.' *Right?* she asks her absent husband. *Yes indeed,* I can imagine him saying.

KABUTO

It's raining. I go out the back exit of the building and pick my way around the puddles as I hurry back to the main street. Somehow it seems that when I'm on a job it's raining more often than not. Sometimes I wonder if I'm haunted by a powerful rain spirit.

I check my watch. Almost exactly on time. Good. There's pain in my left arm. My sleeve is torn and the skin underneath is bleeding.

He's fearsome, the doctor had warned me, and though I wouldn't exactly say this guy was fearsome, he had a fighting style I'm not used to and some kind of blade I've never seen before, so it wasn't easy. I should be grateful that I got out of it with only a little injury like this.

I step into a puddle and the water splashes up.

I've always been slogging through the dark. No one to take care of me growing up, just walking the backstreets of life, looking down at the ground. I can't get a proper job, maybe because I didn't really go to school or maybe because I've got a hard look in my eyes, and any time I think I've found a job that might be legit it always ends up with someone's face streaked in tears and blood.

Only muddy roads that are tough to walk, and when I look to the left or right everyone else seems to have a nice, paved path.

Sometimes I wonder if it'll always be like this, and when I have those thoughts I immediately snuff them out. Of course it'll always be like this.

I step out on the broad avenue and quickly duck into a shopping arcade. I don't have an umbrella so I'm glad for the covering over the street, but I feel like it might as well be raining on me anyway. Here I am walking on solid ground, but it just feels like my feet are sinking in.

I hustle along when a hand pops out in front of me.

'Here you go,' someone says. The hand is holding out a flyer.

Looking up, I see a girl, early twenties, must be about my age. I have no interest in the flyer but then there it is in my hand.

I say nothing and start to walk past but she says 'Hey, you're bleeding,' and points at my arm.

'I am? It's okay.'

'If you're bleeding, I don't think you're okay.'

Is that . . . true?

'You look like you're upset about something. Did something happen?'

I'm on guard, thinking that she knows about the job I just did. But it doesn't seem like it. 'Nothing really.'

'But you do look like you're upset.'

'Do I?'

'What if you try thinking of something happy? I bet you'd look great if you smiled.'

Her familiar attitude puts me on the defensive. 'I can't think of anything happy,' I answer. 'Happiness has got nothing to do with me. My life . . .' . . . isn't worth anything.

'Really?' Her voice is kind. Natural. 'You don't seem like a bad person to me.'

This almost makes me laugh. You could put me in a display case with a sign challenging passersby to find a man as bad as this. I'm well aware of the weight of my crimes. 'Reading people –' is not your strong suit, I'm about to say, but she points at the flyer in my hand.

'You can use that and get a discount!'

I look at it. *Kids Park Grand Opening*, it says. Looks like some kind of amusement park. You get a discount if you go with your kids. Now I really do laugh. 'I don't have a family.'

'Oh no?' The tone of her voice, I can't tell if she sounds interested or not. 'But . . .'

'But what?'

'You seem like you'd make a good dad.'

I don't know what to say to that. It's like I'm being asked to consider something that I've never even imagined. After a moment, I exhale, warmer than any other breath I've ever had.

See, it's much nicer when you smile, says this girl to me. All I can do is stare at her.

Read on for an extract from

THREE
ASSASSINS

Kotaro Isaka

Translated by Sam Malissa

SUZUKI

LOOKING OUT AT THE CITY, Suzuki thinks about insects. It's night but the scene is ablaze with gaudy neon and streetlamps. People everywhere. Like a writhing mass of luridly colored insects. It unsettles him, and he thinks back to what his college professor once said: 'Most animals don't live on top of each other in such great numbers. In some ways, humans are less like mammals and closer to insects.' His professor had seemed pleased with the conclusion. 'Like ants, or locusts.'

'I've seen photos of penguins living in groups all bunched together,' Suzuki had responded, gently needling. 'Are penguins like insects too?'

His professor flushed. 'Penguins have nothing to do with it.' He sounded endearingly childlike, and Suzuki had felt that he wanted to be the same way as he got older. He still remembers it.

Then a memory of his wife flashes through his mind. His wife died two years ago. She used to laugh at the story about his professor. 'You're supposed to just answer, "You're absolutely right, professor," and then everything works out,' she used to say.

It was certainly true that she loved it anytime he had agreed with her and said, 'You're absolutely right, honey.'

'What are you waiting for? Get him in the car.'

Hiyoko's urging startles him. Suzuki shakes his head to ward off the memories, then pushes the young guy in front of him. The guy tumbles into the back seat of the sedan. He's tall, blond hair. Unconscious. He has a black leather jacket on over a black shirt, with a pattern of little insects. The unsavory pattern matches the guy's general unsavory vibe. Also in the back seat, on the other side, is a girl. Suzuki had forced her into the car as well. Long black hair, yellow coat, in her early twenties. Her eyes are closed and her mouth slightly open as she sleeps sprawled on the seat.

Suzuki tucks the guy's legs into the car and closes the door.

'Get in,' says Hiyoko. Suzuki gets in on the passenger side.

The car is parked just outside the northernmost entrance to the Fujisawa Kongocho subway station. In front of them is a big intersection with a busy pedestrian crossing.

It's ten thirty at night in the middle of the week, but this close to Shinjuku things are busier after dark than they are in the daytime, and the area is thronged with people. Half of them are drunk.

'Wasn't that easy?' Hiyoko sounds totally relaxed. Her white skin has a luster like porcelain, seeming to float in the dark car interior. Her chestnut hair is cut short, coming just to the top of her ears. Something about her expression is cold, maybe because of her single eyelids. The red of her lipstick shines brightly. Her white shirt is open down to the middle of her chest and her skirt doesn't quite reach her knees. She's apparently in her late twenties, same as Suzuki, but she often shows the craftiness of someone far older. She looks like a party girl, but he can tell she's sharp, with the benefit of a proper education. She's wearing black high heels, and has one foot on the brake. *It's amazing she can drive in those,* he thinks.

'It wasn't easy or hard, I mean, all I did was get them in the car.' Suzuki frowns. 'I just carried these two unconscious people and put them in the back seat.' *I take no further responsibility,* he wanted to say.

'If this sort of thing rattles you, you won't get very far. Your trial period is almost over, so you better get used to jobs like this. Although I bet you never imagined you'd be kidnapping people, huh?'

'Of course not.' Though the truth is that Suzuki isn't all that surprised. He never thought his employer was a legitimate company. 'Fräulein means "maiden" in German, doesn't it?'

'Very good. Apparently, Terahara named the company himself.'

When she says that name his body tenses. 'The father?' That is, the CEO. 'Obviously. His idiot son could never come up with a company name.' Suzuki has a momentary vision of his dead wife and his emotions boil. He clenches his stomach and feigns calm. The idiot son, Terahara's son – anytime Suzuki thinks of him he can barely contain himself. 'I just never thought that a company with a name that means "maiden" would actually prey on young women,' he somehow manages to say.

'It does seem strange.'

Hiyoko may be the same age as Suzuki but she's been with the company for a long time, and has the according rank. In the month since Suzuki joined as a contractor, he's been reporting to her.

As for what he's been doing in that month, it was all standing in shopping arcades, hailing passing women.

He stood in the busy spots, calling out to women walking by. They would say no, they would ignore him, they would swear at him, but he still kept trying. Almost all of the women just walked away. It had nothing to do with his delivery, effort, technique or skill. They scowled at him, they looked at him warily, they avoided him, but still he kept calling out to every woman who walked by.

But there was usually one woman each day, maybe one in a thousand, who showed interest. He would take her to a cafe and give her a pitch for makeup products and diet drinks. He had a basic script: 'You won't see the effects right away, but after about a month you'll see dramatic changes.' He would improvise, saying whatever felt most appropriate, then show her the pamphlets. They were printed in color, full of graphs and figures, but not a single thing written in them was true.

The gullible girls would sign an agreement right then and there. The more suspicious ones would leave saying they'd think about it. If he could sense that there was still a chance, he would follow them. After that, another group would take over, far more persistent, starting their illegal solicitation. They would force their way into the woman's home and refuse to leave, keep constant surveillance on her, until she finally gave in and signed the agreement. Or so Suzuki understood. But that part of the arrangement was still all hearsay to him.

'Well, you've been with us for a month. Shall we take you to the next level?' Hiyoko had said this to him an hour earlier.

'The next level?'

'I can't imagine you planned to spend the rest of your life soliciting women on the street.'

'Well, I mean,' he answered vaguely, 'the rest of my life is a long time.'

'Today's job is different. When you get someone into a cafe, I'll be coming with you.'

'It's not that easy to get someone to listen,' he said with a pained smile, thinking of the last month.

But for better or for worse, inside of thirty minutes Suzuki had found two people willing to hear him out. The guy and girl who are currently passed out in the back of the car.

First the girl showed interest. 'Hey, don't you think if I lost a little weight I could do modeling?' she asked the guy casually. He answered encouragingly, 'Sure, babe, you could definitely be a model, for sure. You could be, like, a supermodel.'

Suzuki called Hiyoko, took the couple to a cafe, and started introducing products as he normally would. Whether it was because they were young and stupid or just gullible, the young man and woman seemed almost comically willing to go along with what Suzuki and Hiyoko were pitching. Their eyes lit up at the barest of compliments, and they nodded enthusiastically at all the bogus data from the pamphlets.

Their complete lack of skepticism was enough to make Suzuki feel concerned for their futures. He had a surge of memories of his students from when he was still a teacher. The first place his mind went, for some reason, was to one poorly behaved kid. He remembered the boy saying, 'See, Mr Suzuki, I can do good too.' He was always acting out, and the other students didn't like him much, but one time he surprised everybody by catching a purse-snatcher in a shopping district. 'I can do good too,' he had said to Suzuki, smiling with both pride and embarrassment. Then he said, 'Don't give up on me, teach,' looking like a much younger boy.

Come to think of it ... The guy in front of him flipping through the pamphlet, face pockmarked from acne scars, somehow reminded him of that student. He knew he had never met this person before, but the resemblance was striking.

Then he noticed that Hiyoko had gone to the counter to order refills of coffee. He took another look and saw that she was doing something with her hands over the cups, then realized: she was drugging the coffee.

Before long the guy's and girl's eyes glazed over and their

heads started sagging. The girl said, 'They call me Yellow, and he's Black. Just nicknames, you know? That's why I'm wearing a yellow coat, and he's dressed in black.' Then she mumbled, 'Hey, I'm like, sleepy.' And she nodded off. Next to her, the guy said, 'Yeah, but my hair's blond, and yours is black,' slurring nonsensically. 'Why is that . . .' Then he passed out too.

'Well then,' said Hiyoko. 'Let's get them to the car.'

'Depending on how we use them, these two dummies could make us some decent money,' she says, sounding bored.

Would you do this to my students? Suzuki has to tell himself not to ask it out loud. 'Are we . . . just staying here?'

'Normally we'd be leaving now.' Her voice sharpens. 'But tonight's different.'

A sense of foreboding runs up his spine. 'Different, how?'

'I need to test you.'

'What are you testing?' Suzuki's voice quavers a bit.

'We don't trust you.'

'You don't trust me?' He swallows. 'Why not?'

'If you're asking what's fishy about you, well, there's plenty. You were really determined to join our company. And you seem like a pretty straitlaced guy. What was it you did before?'

'Teacher,' Suzuki answers. He doesn't see any reason to hide it. 'I worked at a middle school. I taught math.'

'Yeah. You *seem* like you taught math. That's why we didn't trust you from the get-go. You're clearly wrong for this. A middle-school math teacher going out of their way to get involved with a company like ours. I mean, we scam young people – does that seem like work a teacher would ever do?'

'It doesn't matter what most teachers would do, here I am doing it.'

'I'm telling you it would never happen.'

She's right. Of course it would never happen. 'You may not be affected, but there's a recession on, and it's tough trying to find work. So when I heard about this company called Fräulein that was looking for contract workers, I applied.'

'Bullshit.'

'It's true.' It was bullshit. Suzuki hadn't found out about Fräulein randomly. He had been searching for them. He realizes that his breathing is becoming rough, and his chest is starting to rise and fall. *This isn't casual conversation. It's an interrogation.*

He looks out the window. Young people are gathered in front of a fountain outside a hotel. It's only the beginning of November but there are already Christmas decorations on the trees lining the sidewalks and the signs hanging from the buildings. The clamor of car horns and young voices laughing seems to fill the air, mixing with the curtain of cigarette smoke.

'I'm sure you knew we weren't a strictly above-board company, but do you know exactly how dirty we are?'

'I don't quite know how to answer that,' he says with a forced grin, shaking his head. 'Now, this is just what I imagine . . .'

'Your imagination is fine. Go ahead.'

'Well, I've thought that maybe the things I'm selling aren't health products, but something else. Something habit forming, something that's, uh, how might you put it . . . ?'

'Illegal?'

'Right. That.'

Over the past month, he had met several of the women using the Fräulein brand products. All of them were jittery, with bloodshot eyes. Most of them had begged him with unsettling urgency to send more. Their skin was chapped and their throats painfully dry. It would be far easier to believe that they were on drugs than on a health regimen.

'Correct.' Hiyoko's color doesn't change even a shade.

Like she's testing me. Suzuki grimaces. 'But is it actually effective to solicit people on the street like we do? It's fishing with a rod instead of a net, I mean, it feels like the ratio of effort to profit is all off.'

'Don't you worry. We have much more ambitious scams too.'

'Ambitious, how?'

'Like sometimes we'll hold a beauty seminar at a venue and invite lots of girls. Like a big sales event, and we sell plenty of products.'

'People fall for that?'

'The majority of the women are plants. If fifty come, forty of them are with us, and they get the buying rush started.'

'So then others join in?' He had heard about schemes like that targeting seniors.

'Do you know about the Performers?'

'Performers? Like a theater troupe?'

'Not quite. The Performers work in our industry.'

He's starting to get a sense of what she means by 'our industry': people in the business of illegal, illicit activities. The more that's revealed to him the more improbable it all seems. Apparently in the world of professional criminals everyone has eccentric aliases.

'There's a group called the Performers – I don't know how many of them there actually are, but they have all kinds of actors. You can hire them to play basically any part. Do you remember a while back when a Foreign Ministry official was killed in a bowling alley in Yokohama?'

'Um, I missed that story.'

'All the people at the bowling alley were members of the Performers. They were all in on it. But nobody ever found out.'

'And so?'

'We hire them too, to come to our sales events. That's how we get our plants.'

'So people in our industry help each other out.'

'Well, now there's some friction.'

'Friction?'

'What got paid, what didn't get paid, it turns into trouble.'

'I see.' Suzuki isn't all that interested.

'Then there's the organ business.'

'Sorry, what?'

'Hearts,' Hiyoko says like she's listing off products, 'kidneys.' She pushes the climate control button and cranks the temperature dial.

'Ah. That kind of organ.' Suzuki does his best to look calm. *Yes, internal organs, of course I knew that, naturally.*

'Do you know how many people in Japan are waiting for organ transplants? Plenty. Which means there's plenty of business. We really rake it in with that.'

'I could be mistaken about this, but I'm pretty sure it's not legal in Japan to buy and sell internal organs.'

'That's my understanding as well.'

'Which means you can't have a company that operates that way.'

'That isn't a problem.'

'Why not?'

Hiyoko shifts to an indulgent tone, as if she's explaining the way the world works to a naive student. 'Say, for example, a little while ago, a certain bank went out of business.'

'A certain bank.'

'But it ended up getting rescued by an infusion of trillions of yen.'

'And?'

'Or take another example – an employment insurance scheme, which all company employees paid into. Did you know that several hundred billion yen of that was used for unnecessary building projects?'

'I might have heard about that on the news.'

'Buildings no one needed that cost hundreds of billions and never recouped the expenditure. Sounds strange, right? And then they say that the employment insurance fund doesn't have enough to cover what's needed. Doesn't that make you angry?'

'Yes it does.'

'But the person responsible for that needless spending goes unpunished. They could throw away hundreds of billions of yen, trillions in taxes, and not get in any trouble. Not only that, they still get a nice fat bonus when they retire. Footloose and fancy-free. It's crazy. And you know why it happens that way?'

'Because the Japanese citizenry is so kind and forgiving?'

'Because the people at the top have a shared understanding.' Hiyoko raises her index finger. 'Life has nothing to do with right and wrong. The people with the power make the rules. So if they're on your side, you have nothing to worry about. That's how it is with Terahara. He and the politicians have a give-and-take. They work together like they're in a three-legged race, basically inseparable. If a politician says that someone is in the way, Terahara takes care of it. In exchange, the politicians never go after Terahara.'

'I've never met Mr Terahara.'

Hiyoko adjusts the angle of the rearview mirror and touches her eyelashes. Then fixes Suzuki with a sidelong gaze. 'But your business is with his idiot son.'

Suzuki shudders, as if an arrow has been shot straight into his core. 'I have business with Mr Terahara's son?' His voice is flat, and he's barely able to get the words out.

'And this takes us back to the beginning of our conversation.' She makes a little circle with her finger. 'We don't trust you.' She sounds like she's enjoying herself. 'I meant to ask, but forgot – are you married?'

He clearly has a ring on his left ring-finger. 'No,' he answers. 'I'm not. I was.'

'But you still wear a ring?'

'I gained weight and I can't get it off.'

Another lie. If anything, his ring is loose. He's lost weight since he was married. It always feels like his ring might slip off just from walking around.

Don't lose your ring, his wife would say with great gravity, when she was still alive. *It's the symbol of our connection. Whenever you look at it, I want you to think of me.* If he lost it, she'd be furious, even now that she's dead.

'Shall I guess?' Hiyoko's eyes glitter.

'This isn't a quiz.'

'I'm guessing that your wife died because of Terahara's idiot son.'

How does she – He struggles to keep himself still. His eyes want to dart around. His throat wants to swallow hard. His brow wants to tremble. His ears want to turn bright red. His panic wants to burst out of every pore. At the same time, he pictures his wife, crushed between the SUV and the telephone pole. He clenches his stomach, tries to block the memory out.

'Why would Mr Terahara's son kill my wife?'

'Killing for no good reason is just part of the idiot son doing his idiot thing.' Hiyoko's face says that she expects Suzuki to know this. 'That moron causes all kinds of trouble. He's always stealing cars in the middle of the night and going on joyrides. Getting drunk, running people down. He does it all the time.'

'That's terrible.' Suzuki tries to keep any emotion out of his voice. 'It's just terrible.'

'Isn't it though? Hard to forgive and forget. So, how did your wife die?'

'Why would you assume that she's dead?'

He's picturing his wife's mangled body again. He thought the memory had faded away, but now it roars back, all too vivid. He sees her: soaked in blood, face crushed in, shoulders shattered and askew. Suzuki had stood there, rooted to the spot, while next to him the middle-aged forensics cop got up from examining the ground and muttered, *They didn't even try to brake – looks like they actually sped up.*

'Wasn't she hit by a car?' Bullseye. That's exactly what happened.

'Don't make assumptions.'

'As far as I recall, two years ago the idiot son ran over a woman whose family name was Suzuki.'

That was also right on the nail. 'That can't be true.'

'Oh, it's true all right. The idiot son is always bragging about his adventures. No matter what he does, he never faces any consequences. And do you know why?'

'No idea.'

'Because everyone loves him so much.' Hiyoko raises her eyebrows. 'His father, the politicians.'

'Like with what you were saying about taxes and employment insurance.'

'Exactly. And I'm sure you're aware that he never got into any trouble after killing your wife. Because you looked into it. And you found out that he works for his father's company. You found out about Fräulein. So you joined us as a contract worker.' Hiyoko reels off the facts, like she's reciting a report from memory. 'Isn't that right?'

'Why would I do all of that?'

'Because you want revenge.' She says it like it's obvious. 'You're waiting for a chance to get back at the idiot son. So you've stuck it out for a month. Am I wrong?'

She was not wrong. 'These are baseless accusations.'

'And that,' she continues, raising the corners of her red lips, 'is why you are currently under suspicion.' Over her shoulder, the garish lights from signs blink off and on.

Suzuki swallows hard.

'Which is why yesterday I got special orders.'

'Orders?'

'I'm supposed to find out if you're just working for us or if

258

you're out for vengeance. We have plenty of use for dumb employees, not so much smart guys with vendettas.'

Suzuki says nothing, only smiles vaguely.

'Oh, and by the way, you're not the first one.'

'Sorry?'

'There have been others like you who have a bone to pick with Terahara and his idiot son and joined the company looking for revenge. We're used to dealing with this sort of thing. So we let them work for a month and keep an eye on them. And if something still feels off, then we test them.' Hiyoko shrugs. 'Like we're doing with you today.'

'You're wrong about me.' As he says this Suzuki feels a deep hopelessness wash over him.

The fact that others have tried this before makes his vision go dark. Working for a shady company like Fräulein, spending a month selling young women what he was sure were drugs, it was all so he could avenge his wife. He told himself that the women he was scamming should have known better, trying to smother his guilt, to push aside his fear and sense of decency, to focus only on his plan.

But now he's finding out that his mission is a rerun, a rerun of a rerun, and it's like the bottom drops out from under him. He feels scattered, powerless, lost in darkness.

'So now it's time to test you. To find out whether you're actually interested in working for us.'

'I'm sure I can live up to your expectations.' But as he says it Suzuki is aware that his voice sounds tiny.

'In that case,' Hiyoko says, jabbing her thumb at the back seat, 'why don't you kill those two back there? Just some guy, some girl, nothing to do with you.'

Nervously Suzuki turns his head to look between the front seats at the back. 'Why me?'

'To clear up any suspicions, obviously.'

'Doing this won't prove anything.'

'What does proof matter? The way we operate is very straight-forward. Potentialities, evidence – we don't care about any of that. We just have some simple rules and rituals. So it's like this: if you kill the two of them, right here, right now, you'll be a full member of the team.'

'A full member?'

'We'll get rid of the contract part of your contract employee title.'

'But why do I have to do *this*?'

The car is off, and it's quiet. Suzuki can feel vibrations, but he realizes that it's the thrumming of his own heart. With each breath his whole body seems to rise and fall, and the expansion and contraction transmits through the seat and shakes the whole car. He exhales, then inhales, the smell of the leather seats filling his nose.

In a daze, he turns back to the front and looks out the wind-shield. The green of the pedestrian signal at the intersection starts to blink. It looks like it's in slow motion. It feels like it might never turn red.

How long is it going to keep flashing?

'All you have to do is shoot those two back there and we'll be good. Shoot them and kill them. That's your only option.' Her voice brings him back to reality.

'But what's killing them going to achieve?'

'Who knows. If they've got good organs we might cut those out and sell them. The girl might end up as a decoration.'

'A . . . decoration?'

'Sure, if we cut off her arms and legs.'

He can't tell if she's joking.

'Well? Are you going to do it? The gun is right here, sir, at your disposal.' Hiyoko's overly polite word choice is mocking, as she produces the dull-colored instrument from under her seat. Then she aims it at Suzuki's chest. 'And if you try to run away, I'll shoot you.'

Suzuki freezes. The blunt reality of a gun pointed at him takes away his ability to move. It's like someone is staring at him from deep within the black hole of the barrel, fixing him in place. Hiyoko's finger is on the trigger. *All she has to do is bend her finger, apply just the barest pressure, and a bullet will rip into my chest.* The realization of just how easy it would be drains his blood.

'You're going to use this gun to shoot our friends in the back seat.'

'What if,' he begins, afraid to even move his lips, 'you give me the gun and I aim it at you instead? What would you do then? Purely a hypothetical question.'

Hiyoko is unfazed. If anything her look is pitying. 'I'm not going to give you the gun just yet. Another company member is on the way. Once they're here I'll give you the gun. Then you won't be able to do anything rash.'

'Who's coming?'

Casually, as if it's nothing at all, she says, 'The idiot son. He'll be here soon.'

Suzuki's whole body clenches and his mind goes blank.

Hiyoko switches the gun to her left hand, and with her right she points toward the windshield. Then she taps it once, seeming to affix her finger to the glass. 'He'll come from right over there, across that intersection.'

'Terahara?' There's a crash inside Suzuki's head, like everything he had in there has collapsed. 'Terahara is coming here?'

'Not Mr Terahara. His son. You two haven't officially met yet, have you? Well, you will now. How lucky for you! The idiot son who killed your wife will be here shortly.'

Hiyoko says Terahara's son's name, but Suzuki doesn't process it. He'd rather not acknowledge the man as a flesh-and-blood human being.

'Why is he coming here?'

'I told you, to get a look at you and see what you do. When we test people like this he always comes to watch.'

'Nice hobby.'

'Oh, you didn't know that particular detail?'

He's at a loss for words. Somehow he manages to look out the windshield. The pedestrian crossing of the big eight-way intersection looms like it's right on top of them. There's a crowd of people waiting for the signal to change. They look like they're gathered on the shore, looking out over the boundless expanse of the sea.

The density of the crowd once again calls to mind what his professor had said. *He was right, it's like a swarm of insects.*

'Oh, there he is. The idiot son,' Hiyoko says cheerfully, pointing. Suzuki jolts upright and cranes his neck forward to look. Slightly off to the right, at the diagonal crosswalk, is a man in a black coat. He appears to be in his mid-twenties, but his long coat and suit give him an expensive air. He grimaces as he pulls at his cigarette.

Hiyoko grabs the door handle. 'I don't think the idiot has noticed us.' As soon as the words are out of her mouth, she's out of the car, gun still in hand. With her other hand she waves to Terahara's son.

Suzuki also gets out. Terahara's son is just a few meters away.

He recalls what his wife always used to say: *Guess you just have to do it.* No matter the situation, she would clap Suzuki on the shoulder and say that. If you come across a door, you have to open it. If you open it, you have to step through. If you meet a person, you have to talk to them, and if someone puts a meal on the table, you have to give it a try. *When you have a chance, you should always take it.* She was always saying that, so light and bright. It also meant that when she was online she would say, *I just have to click on it*, and she did click on everything, so her computer was always riddled with viruses.

Suzuki gets a good look at Terahara's son. There's a brash aura that seems to clear the way around him. His shoulders are broad and his spine is straight. He's tall, and even handsome, like a Kabuki actor who plays romantic leads. Without realizing it, Suzuki is leaning forward. Now he's got Terahara's son in his sights, he's locked on. His vision seems to be zooming in, giving him a clear view of the man's face.

He sees the thick, rich eyebrows, the flat nostrils on the snub nose. The lips that hold his cigarette. Then the cigarette is done, the butt tossed on the ground, bouncing once off the pavement. He sees the left heel that crushes the cigarette butt with a fastidious twist. In Suzuki's mind the crushed cigarette doubles as his wife. Underneath the black leather coat that is both expensive and tasteless, he sees a red necktie.

Suzuki pictures what will happen next. The light will turn green, and Terahara's son will cross. He'll come right up to Suzuki. As soon as Suzuki gets the gun from Hiyoko, he'll turn it on Terahara's son. It may not work, it may have been doomed from the start, but that's his only choice. *If I have the chance, I have to take it. I just have to do it. Like you always used to say.*

'Wait, what?' It's Hiyoko. The moment the traffic light turns yellow.

Terahara's son steps out into the street. The pedestrian signal is still red, but he seems like he's starting to cross, one step, another.

Then a car slams into him. A black minivan moving at full speed.

Suzuki fixes on the moment of impact, like he's trying to capture it with his eyes. The world around him falls silent. It's like his hearing has shut off so that his vision can sharpen.

The bumper collides with Terahara's son's right thigh, which twists inward, breaking. His legs lift off the ground and his body is swept up onto the hood of the car, sliding him toward the windshield on his right side. He crashes against the glass, his face grinding into the wipers.

Then his body rebounds off the car, tossed onto the street where he lands hard on his left side, then rolls, his left arm wrenching under him. Something small flies off and hits the ground – Suzuki sees that it's a button popping off his suit. The button spins away in an arc.

The body tumbles into a depression in the asphalt, rotating with the head as the fulcrum, the neck bent at an unnatural angle.

The minivan keeps barreling forward after sending the body flying, now running over Terahara's son as he lies on the ground.

The right tire rolls over the right leg, ripping the pants, flattening the thigh. The whole car bumps up onto the chest. Ribs break, organs are crushed. The minivan skids a few more meters before finally coming to a stop.

The spinning button slows, then falls flat.

It's like when the symphony ends, everyone in the hall takes a breath, and silence fills the space for a moment – then explodes into applause. Except instead of applause, people start screaming.

Sound returns to Suzuki. A flood of car horns, shouting, the din of confused voices, like a river bursting its dam.

He's shaken up, but he still keeps staring. He saw someone. Amid the chaos across the intersection, a man was there, a man who turned around to walk away.

'What just happened?' Hiyoko says, her mouth hanging open. 'He – he got –'

'He got run over.' Suzuki can feel his heart hammering like an alarm.

'But did you see what I saw?' She sounds uncertain.

264

'Huh?'

'You saw it, didn't you? There was – *somebody* – somebody shady-looking leaving the scene.' Now she's talking quickly, almost breathless. 'You must have seen it. Someone was there. And it looked like the idiot was *pushed*.'

'I –' Suzuki isn't sure how he should answer. But then: '– saw it.' The words are already out. 'I saw it.'

Hiyoko falls silent. She peers at Suzuki's face, then looks down at her feet. She clicks her tongue. Then she looks back across the street. Her eyes say that she's made up her mind. 'Go after him.'

'Go . . . after?'

'You saw a man, right?'

'I –' Suzuki is still trying to wrap his head around what happened.

'Don't get the wrong idea. You're not off the hook yet. But we can't let whoever pushed Terahara's son into the street get away.' It appears to have been a highly unpleasant decision for her. 'And don't think about trying to escape yourself.' Then she brightens up, as if she's had a great idea. 'Actually, if you try to run, I'll kill those two in the car.'

'How does that –'

'Get after him! Go!'

The chaotic turn of events is destabilizing, almost hallucinatory, but before he realizes what he's doing Suzuki is on the move.

'Go get him!' Hiyoko shouts almost hysterically. 'Find the guy who pushed him!'

He runs like a racehorse under the lash. As he runs he looks back over his shoulder. His eyes fall on Hiyoko's black high heels. *She'd never be able to chase anyone in those – I guess she didn't think she'd have to.*

penguin.co.uk/vintage